# PLAY

# LIST

# SEBASTIAN FITZEK

# PLAY

# LIST

**TRANSLATED BY**

**JAMIE BULLOCH**

HEAD
ZEUS

*An Aries Book*

First published in Germany in 2021 by Droemer Knaur

First published in the UK in 2024 by Head of Zeus,
part of Bloomsbury Publishing Plc

9 7 5 3 1 2 4 6 8

A catalogue record for this book is available from the British Library.

ISBN (PB): 9781804542422
ISBN (E): 9781804542392

Cover design: Simon Michele | Head of Zeus

Printed and bound in Great Britain by
CPI Group (UK) Ltd, Croydon CR0 4YY

FSC
www.fsc.org

MIX
Paper | Supporting
responsible forestry
FSC® C171272

Head of Zeus
First Floor East
5–8 Hardwick Street
London EC1R 4RG

WWW.HEADOFZEUS.COM

# P L A Y
# L I S T

When a teenage girl went missing, the only
trace she left behind was her music playlist.

All the songs on Feline's playlist mentioned in the book really exist; they were composed specially for this thriller. These artists' music and lyrics were inspired by the story, and in turn had a considerable influence on the plot.

*For Ben (keyboard), Jörg (bass) and Jacques (guitar),*
*who many, many years ago dreamed the dream with me.*
*Unfortunately, reality caught up.*
*We ought to meet up again soon. Band practice?*

# 1

At exactly 18:42 – three weeks, two days and nine hours after his daughter had disappeared without trace on her way to school – the doorbell rang twice, and Thomas Jagow learned that there are no limits to human fear. Fate couldn't care less that you've already reached breaking point.

'Hello?' he said into the emptiness of the deserted front garden.

They'd been living in Nikolassee for three years, a neighbourhood far beyond their means, albeit in a modest bungalow that was just about big enough for a family of three. The grey, flat-roofed building, which stood rather timidly among the elegant villas, was on the edge of the Rehwiese park. Buyers with money would have flattened the bungalow and put up in its place a luxurious new build more in keeping with the surrounding properties. At the beginning, when Thomas hoped he'd be promoted to headmaster of the Grunewald private school where he taught geography and physics, they'd had a similar dream. But the job went to someone else and his earnings had stagnated ever since.

His wife, Emilia, was a nurse, and their combined income was just sufficient for the essentials once the mortgage and bills had been covered. Their daughter, Feline, now fifteen, represented their greatest outgoing. What she cost them in clothes, shoes and sports gear alone had doubled from year to year. Until it dropped to zero overnight.

*When she was abducted*, Thomas thought. He still clung to the idea that at some point he'd get a call demanding ransom money, even though he knew how improbable this was. The Jagows didn't have anything to take – no inheritance, no savings – as a brief glance at the outside of their house made perfectly clear.

'*You can tell people's true wealth by their garden*,' his mother liked to say, and if she was right then the Jagows were indeed impoverished; unlike their neighbours they couldn't afford landscape designers to transform their garden into a work of art and maintain it. Whereas the hedges of the Heussners opposite looked as if they'd been cut by a 3D printer, the Jagows' lawn and path were strewn with autumn leaves all the way up to the front door that Thomas had just opened.

Because of the leaves Thomas almost missed the brick on the doormat, only noticing it when he took a step out into the drizzle – suicide weather, typical of October in Berlin – and stubbed his toe on the red, book-sized obstacle.

Surprised, Thomas bent down and saw a note affixed to the brick. The Sellotape didn't stick properly to the porous surface; the next gust of wind would have blown the note away and Thomas may never have read its contents. The handwriting suggested it had been scrawled by a girl:

*I'm back, Dad.*

# 2

Kneeling beside the brick, Thomas stiffened. His fingers trembled and his body went red-hot, as if he'd stepped in front of a fire rather than outside.

*What does this mean?*

Without getting to his feet he looked around: not a soul in sight. It must have been one of the neighbours' kids playing knock down ginger. Someone who'd been regaled with the grisly details of Feline's abduction, first in the conventional media, then via the social networks.

As Thomas picked off the note with an unsteady hand, the brick wobbled. He turned it over and found a second message, more mysterious than the first.

It was in the form of a tiny key, which reminded him of the one for Emilia's suitcase. This too was stuck to the brick just with a small piece of Sellotape, and almost fell into Thomas's hand when he lifted the brick.

*What's going on?*

Still on his knees, Thomas turned to the front door, which the wind had blown wide open, and wondered whether to call Emilia. His wife had just taken her evening dose of Valium, which would, as so often, be followed by a pill, probably around midnight. With luck she might get a few minutes' sleep around two in the morning before her anxiety over Feline woke her again, releasing her into another day of terrible uncertainty.

For now Thomas decided to investigate the matter himself. He was convinced he'd find some giggling children on the other side of the garden gate, who'd scarper the moment he confronted them.

The garden path was on a slight incline. Tall, evergreen hedges blocked his view of the pavement. Normally the weathered wooden gate was closed, but now its hinges squealed as it was buffeted by the wind. Thomas's joints creaked as he stood up and saw the arrows.

Three of them, about ten centimetres long, one almost fully covered by leaves now, had been drawn in red chalk and were pointing towards the gate.

*A signpost?*

Now that his initial excitement had subsided, the cold and wet ate through Thomas's thin clothing as he followed the arrows. He would have happily kept wearing the same chinos and long-sleeved polo shirt he'd had on the day Feline disappeared – Thomas found it a real struggle to pay attention to his appearance at a time when this had lost all meaning for him – but he couldn't allow himself to look scruffy or let his dark, curly hair get untamed. Not when the public was scrutinising him through the lens that the media held out to their sensation-hungry readers and viewers. If he let himself go, it would create a bad impression. But the same would be true if he pranced around like a fashion model advertising dark suits. And so, when he went out, he always chose an outfit that was as simple as possible but smart: blue shirt, black jeans.

Every day.

Since Feline was kidnapped.

If she had been kidnapped.

*Fingers crossed.*

Thomas opened the garden gate and stepped onto the deserted pavement. He was wearing the slippers he'd put on when the bell rang out of the blue. The wet seeped through his soles and his socks soaked it up like a sponge. He felt feverish, as if he'd already caught a cold, but it was probably the surreal situation he had literally stumbled into. He almost slipped on fallen chestnut burrs.

The cobbled street was so wide that cars could have comfortably parked on both sides, but the few homeowners here had come to an agreement that they'd leave their cars on one side only – the one facing the Jagows' bungalow. Even without this unofficial arrangement Thomas would have noticed the panel van parked a couple of metres away on the 'wrong' side, contravening neighbourhood etiquette.

The van was grey or white, impossible to tell for sure because it was so dirty. Like their garden gate, the van's left rear barn door was ajar.

Only slightly open, but as noticeable as the fact that the van didn't have a number plate.

'Hello?' Thomas called out again, pointlessly; the person who – for whatever reason – had made the effort to orchestrate this stunt was hardly going to jump out from behind a tree.

Thomas stepped over to the van and walked around it.

Then he peered into the driver's cab: nobody behind the wheel. On the spur of the moment he decided to open the barn door, shielding his face with his left elbow in case somebody leaped out and attacked him.

But he wasn't assaulted by fists or weapons. Thomas was struck by a single word that threw him off balance as if the ground had opened up beneath his feet: 'Dad?'

# 3

Thomas couldn't believe it; he worried he was hallucinating.

But it really was his daughter's voice. And the figure cowering in the darkness in the right-hand corner of the van reminded him of Feline too. Slim, average height for her age, shoulder-length hair that fell into her face.

'Feline?'

'Dad?'

*Oh God.*

'Feline, is that you?'

For a while they were so excited they talked at cross purposes. And even though Thomas was in no doubt that it *was* his daughter, he couldn't believe it. He felt as if he were in a state of delirium.

*Please don't let me snap out of this. Please let me hug Feline*, he thought as he climbed into the vehicle.

There was no light; the van was parked equidistant between two street lamps and only a vestige of the dim glow made its way inside the load area, which reeked of dust, tools and fear.

Thomas knocked his knee as he got in, but the pain was nothing compared to the happiness he felt when he embraced his daughter.

The fifteen-year-old, who despite her fear and distress still smelled like his daughter. Still felt like his child, even through the thick shirt she was wearing. The contours of her body were more and more like the voice he'd been missing for so long and which deep down he'd thought he might never hear again: Feline!

'Dad, please undo me.'

Holding his beloved daughter tightly in his arms, breathing in time with her, so caught in this moment, it took him a while to understand what she was trying to tell him.

'Undo?'

Only now did he realise why she wasn't hugging him with both arms. Her right hand was shackled, the arm pointing upwards. He heard a metallic rattling when she moved it.

Handcuffs.

She must be chained to a metal strut on the underside of the roof. Feline was hanging from a small but immovable tube.

*Handcuffs?*

All of a sudden Thomas realised what the key he'd found beneath the brick was for. He'd put it in the little fob pocket which almost every pair of jeans had for purely aesthetic reasons. And indeed the key appeared to fit, as he discovered when, after what seemed like an eternity, his numbed fingers fished it out and thrust it in the lock of the handcuffs.

'Hurry up, Dad! Please! I'm really scared!'

'Everything's going to be fine, sweetie. Everything's going to be fine.'

Just as he was about to turn the key, the melancholic tune started up. Thomas felt as if his heart would burst through his chest and in shock he dropped the key.

'Oh no, I'm sorry,' he stammered. His words were drowned out by Feline's sobbing and the music that Thomas realised was a ringtone only when he picked up the flashing mobile from the floor of the van.

'*After all this time, it hurts so bad that we mean nothin' no more,*' sang the brittle and profoundly sad voice.

On the screen of the smartphone he saw a message:

**YOU'D BETTER ANSWER, THOMAS!**

*What's going on?*

Thomas wondered whether to ignore it. He wanted to find the key on the load bed, free Feline and take her back to the place where they'd once been happy.

Of course everything inside him was screaming to dismiss the call and the heart-wrenching music, save for a lone inner voice that pointed out the obvious: *No one who's gone to so much trouble arranging the brick, note, key and chalk arrows is going to let you get away that easily!*

**YOU'D BETTER ANSWER, THOMAS!**

That's why he paid heed to the suggestion. And in doing so made the greatest mistake of his life when he answered the call just after the singer finished with: '*Live in peace!*'

'Hello?'

The voice on the other end of the line didn't say much. A few words that left him unable to breathe. Then unable to think. By the end, his soul was poisoned.

'Dad?' Feline said, still shackled to the tube.

He gazed at her, grateful that in the gloom of the van he couldn't look her in the eye.

'I'm sorry,' Thomas whispered, putting the mobile back down on the floor.

'What do you mean?' Feline said. Her voice was cracking; it sounded as if it were coming from an ancient cassette recording.

It wasn't only Thomas's heart that was in tatters, his mind was too, and yet there was nothing he could do.

'I'm really sorry, sweetie.'

She put her free hand out to him, but he knew he mustn't touch her, or it would all be over. He'd waver; he wouldn't be strong enough. And superhuman strength was what he needed now.

'WHAT ARE YOU SORRY ABOUT???' she howled with every ounce of her energy, like someone condemned to death.

*And that's exactly what she is*, Thomas thought. He turned away and got back out of the van.

'What are you doing? Dad? Please don't! Don't leave me alone!'

The tears were streaming from Thomas's eyes, heavier than the raindrops now pelting the roof of the van. 'I love you, my angel,' he said, closing the door. No sooner had it clicked shut than the engine started up, stealing away the thing he loved and leaving him with nothing but pain.

*'DON'T LEAVE ME HERE!!!'*

Thomas staggered, forgetting to breathe, then hyperventilated as he clung to a tree for support. The scramble back up to his bungalow was more exhausting than a marathon.

Fortunately the rain had turned heavier and so at least he didn't have to explain the tears to his wife, who met him in the hallway, alarm writ large on her face.

'What on earth were you doing out there?' Emilia asked, eyeing him suspiciously. She stared at his dripping hair, wet trousers and sodden slippers. 'What's going on?'

'Nothing,' Thomas said, avoiding her gaze in shame. As he closed the door it felt as if he were shutting out all the happiness in his life forever.

'Just a delivery man,' he said flatly. 'Got the wrong house.'

*You'd better make that call*
*'Cause no one's gonna come looking for you.*
*Or say goodbye to your life*
*Now that it's through.*

**MAJAN – 'Junkie'**

# 4

## ALEXANDER ZORBACH

*Three days later*

The cuts in the skin of the thirteen-year-old girl had been made by someone with experience. The encrusted blood was fresh, not even two days old. Just like the fist-sized bruise and the hole that the stubbed-out cigarette had left on her thigh.

'Now do you see what kind of fucking pervert we're dealing with here?' Klaus Althof said. His lower lip was quivering with hatred and yet he was trying to whisper, which was totally unnecessary because his daughter, Antonia, was in her room and well out of earshot. 'I bet the madman enjoyed it. Just look at *that*!'

The father's invitation was unnecessary. I couldn't help but stare at the horrendous photographs documenting Antonia's injuries and feel very depressed.

By now I believed that all the evils of mankind were down to the fact that we lacked the answer. The answer to the question: 'Why am I alive?' And by that I wasn't referring to the general meaning of life that philosophers and scientists had been discussing since we became sentient beings. I'd have been satisfied by an answer that related to me alone: '*I, Alexander Zorbach, thirty-nine years old, one metre eighty-five and ninety-two kilos – why am I on this earth?*'

Did my life serve an overarching purpose? Or was my existence some insignificant whim of the universe? Did it make any sense that as a policeman I tried to save other people's lives until I had to shoot dead a madwoman who was about to throw a baby she'd abducted from hospital off a motorway bridge?

Would there at some point be a higher authority praising me for my work as an investigative journalist after my time in the police force, and for having saved a child from the clutches of a serial killer who is still at large today? Or would I, at the end of my life, be scoffed at by that higher being, who sets out the rules of our existence, because in my endeavour to save strangers I destroyed my own family and killed an innocent man by accident? One thing was certain: had I taken greater care, my wife would still be alive today and my son, Julian, now thirteen, wouldn't be torn from his sleep all the time by nightmares.

'Are you saying that your daughter was abused this weekend?' I asked, still holding the Polaroids.

'That's right,' said Christine Höpfner, the neighbour of the distraught father. I had a great deal of respect for Christine. Over the past few years in which she'd been my defence lawyer, we may not have become friends exactly, but we had developed a relationship of trust that went beyond the purely professional. Precisely what happens when you spend hour after hour with a person in whose legal hands your destiny lies.

'*Could you do me a favour?*' Christine recently asked me. '*It's to do with a good friend of mine.*' Seeing as she'd done so much for me, I had no choice but to take her neighbour's problem on board. And so I'd agreed to this meeting.

We were sitting facing each other at an antique-looking and no doubt wickedly expensive farmhouse table in the dining room, after I'd been allowed to have a brief chat alone with Antonia in her bedroom.

Whereas Christine Höpfner was careful not to make a show of the prosperity she'd achieved as a result of her first-rate legal work, her neighbour, with his chunky designer watch and shirt sporting a flashy logo, wasn't so restrained.

'How long has your ex-wife had this new boyfriend?' I asked Althof.

'About six months.'

'Do you share custody?'

'I'm the primary carer. Antonia only stays with Astrid every second weekend.'

I nodded. 'And has your daughter often come back with injuries like this?'

Klaus gave me a surly look. 'I don't check her body for irregularities every time, Herr Zorbach. I only found out because Antonia's best friend pointed it out to me. Fenya stayed the night here and saw the injuries. But yes, Antonia's behaviour has always been strange after her weekends away. Since Norman's been on the scene at least. And last weekend my ex had to go off for a training session, so Antonia spent a long time on her own with her mum's new boyfriend.'

'I see.'

I put the Polaroids face down on the table, having seen enough. 'Who took the pictures?'

'Sarah, my fiancée. She and Antonia are close. Basically she and Astrid got on well too. I wouldn't say they became mates after the break-up two years ago, but they'd meet up from time to time. It was pretty good for a patchwork family. Until that biker hooligan turned up.'

'Norman?' I said, repeating the name he'd just uttered.

'He works in a shop selling motorbike accessories and he rides one of those souped-up bikes.' Althof made it plain that he found it most unseemly for his wife to be involved with such common types.

'We'd like you to shadow Norman. Anyone capable of that has got more skeletons in the cupboard.'

I exchanged glances with Christine, who gave me a signal that I should continue listening to her neighbour for the time being.

'I don't want him getting off with a suspended sentence for bodily harm,' Klaus said angrily. 'I want you to uncover something that'll see him put away.'

'I see,' I said again. I peered outside through the large windows. The park opposite allowed an uninterrupted view. Just for once the sun was shining, only sporadically veiled by cloud. In the past, the sight of such a baby-blue sky would have let me forget my worries for a moment. Today it seemed as if my body wouldn't be able to cope if my dark soul weren't in harmony with nature's gloom.

Antonia's father turned the Polaroids over again, spreading them out like memory cards. 'Have you ever seen anything more disgusting?'

I looked at Christine. My lawyer knew, of course, what was on the tip of my tongue. By way of an answer, the following monologue shot through my head:

'Have I ever seen anything as bad as that? Well, let me think for a moment, Herr Althof. There was this case a couple of years back. At the time I was working as a crime reporter for a national newspaper. One day a physiotherapist came to me and said she'd just treated Germany's most-wanted serial killer. Maybe you've heard of the "Eye Collector", as he's known, who abducted children, then gave the parents forty-five hours and seven minutes to find their kids before killing them and ripping out their right eye. The woman in question was called Alina Gregoriev and nobody would believe her at first because she's blind. But what she said did in fact put us on the trail of the killer, who was holding eleven-year-old Tobias Traunstein captive. We managed to free the boy before the Eye Collector could drown him painfully in a lift shaft in Köpenick. Unfortunately the psychopath killed my ex-wife, kidnapped my son, Julian, and then gave me an ultimatum to find my boy before he murdered him too.'

Obviously I didn't say any of this. Besides, Christine Höpfner knew the story only too well, having defended me in the cases I faced as a result of my hunt for the Eye Collector.

So my reply was this: 'To answer your question, Herr Althof, on my hunt for a serial killer I saw drowned children with one eye ripped out. I saw people imprisoned in dark cellars, wrapped in clingfilm and kept alive by ventilators so they didn't die of the suppurating open wounds they were rotting with. I held my murdered ex-wife in my arms and abducted an innocent man from the operating theatre, thus causing him to die, because I wanted him to take me to my son. So my answer is, yes, regrettably I have had to witness things as bad as that, and on multiple occasions. So often, in fact, that it broke me.'

I gazed at Althof's eyes, wide open in shock. I could see he was wondering whether he was talking to a traumatised madman or a seasoned expert. If he'd asked his neighbour, she would have probably said both were true.

'So... er... are you going to help us?' he asked after a minute of all of us staring at each other.

How I could let him know the truth as gently as possible? Without him breaking down under the weight of it?

Concluding that there wasn't an easier way, I asked bluntly, 'Is your daughter left-handed?'

'Yes,' her father said, baffled.

'Then I'm not going to take on your case.'

# 5

Even though I could have done with the cash. And it would have been money for old rope. The fee would have enabled me to make my houseboat riverworthy again. Anchored in a creek not visible from the water, and only accessible via a narrow path through the Grunewald, it had been my fixed abode for the past few years. Three months ago, however, a forester had discovered and reported my illegal mooring, thus forcing me to sell my favourite place on earth.

'Are you out of your mind?' Althof asked in shock. 'What bloody difference does it make what hand my daughter plays tennis or holds a pen with?'

'Well...' I began, turning the Polaroids around so they were the right way up for Antonia's father and my lawyer, 'all the injuries are on the right-hand side of her body.'

'And?'

'The cuts,' I continued, pointing at one of the pictures, 'aren't deep and they're very even. Also, there aren't any on the inner parts of the body.'

'Where are they, then?' Christine Höpfner asked, a touch

too calmly. As an expert in criminal law she knew exactly what I was getting at.

'Those places where it hurts less.'

'What are you implying?' the father asked.

I looked Althof in the eye. 'That in all probability Norman has nothing to do with your daughter's wounds.'

'What the hell makes you think that?'

I cocked my head, cracking my vertebrae, but it didn't ease any of the tension. 'Well, I know it's been a few years since I did a course in forensic medicine, but long, parallel cuts in places that are easy to reach... I've also seen your daughter's wrists and there aren't any signs she was held or tried to defend herself. To me it looks like a classic case of self-inflicted injuries.'

Althof flew off the handle. 'Are you suggesting that Antonia—'

'Not just suggesting.'

'But...' He was gasping for air like a fish out of water. 'Why would she do anything like that?'

I shrugged. Young people who self-harmed suffered from serious psychological problems. It might be an attempt to relieve some emotional stress or to punish herself. Was Antonia a victim of bullying at school? Had her parents' separation sparked a trauma? I didn't know her well enough for a diagnosis, nor was my expertise sufficient to plumb the depths of her teenage soul. So I said to her father, 'I don't know what's causing her to do it, but that's precisely what you need to find out. And for that, Antonia doesn't need a lawyer or a private detective. She needs therapy.'

He leaped up from his chair. 'Who the hell do you think you are, you miserable little private eye? You think you can come into my house and make such outrageous claims about my—'

Althof didn't say any more, not because Christine gently put her hand on his, but because – like all of us – he heard the voice.

'Please, Dad.'

We all turned to the door in sync. Antonia had appeared from nowhere, as if a projector had been switched on and her image beamed to the far side of the room. I had no idea how long she'd been listening to us, but it was no doubt long enough. Although she was weeping, we could clearly make out her words.

'He's right.'

We all winced when she slammed the door shut. Then she ran down the hallway, presumably back to her room.

# 6

'Why did you want me to come? You must have known yourself.'

Christine Höpfner had accompanied me downstairs to the entrance of the building. We were standing in the driveway, which had just been cleared with a leaf blower, as one would expect at a smart, newly renovated period apartment block in this area.

'Of course I knew you wouldn't take the case on. If only for lack of time. But the self-harming?' She wiggled her hand; it looked as if she were trying to imitate an aeroplane in turbulence. 'I suspected it, yes. But I didn't ask you here because of my neighbour.'

'Why then?'

'Because of Antonia. I've spent a lot of time with you, Herr Zorbach. I've watched you, studied you properly. And I know the effect you have on witnesses, judges and the public prosecutor. I've understood why you were such an outstanding policeman and journalist.'

'My employers took a different view,' I said. It was meant

to sound funny, but unfortunately came across as a touch self-pitying.

The lawyer let go of my hand, but her eyes continued to grip me tightly. 'You're honest. Genuine. You never beat around the bush and you give off an aura of trustworthiness. I'd hoped you'd have the same effect on Antonia.'

Her plan had come to fruition. Before my conversation with Althof I'd chatted briefly to Antonia, albeit nothing more than deliberate small talk. Not a word about abuse, injuries, her father or Norman. Instead I'd let her advise me whether I should send my son a follower request on Instagram or whether that was embarrassing.

Christine's gaze softened. In it was something I'd seen time and again over the past few weeks and which was at odds with her professional aloofness in public: melancholy.

'In three days,' she said quietly. A chestnut leaf sailed past us, falling to the ground as slowly as a bubble.

'In three days,' I echoed.

My mobile rang, and I took the opportunity to say goodbye and return to my houseboat – while it still belonged to me.

*Three days.*

Then I'd have to begin my two-and-a-half-year sentence. Because of Frank Lahmann. A young man I'd mentored when he worked for me as a trainee at the newspaper. And who I'd then tortured to death.

'Hello?'

As I took the call from the unknown number I fished the key for my old Volvo out of the inside pocket of my parka.

'Herr Zorbach?'

'Yes?'

'The journalist?'

'I used to be. Why are you calling?'

'My name is Emilia Jagow.'

I guessed the woman wasn't older than forty, although the pain in her voice made it hard to tell. It seemed as if this pain were ploughing deep furrows in her vocal cords, which reinforced my hunch of who I was talking to.

'*The* Emilia Jagow?' I said, getting into my Volvo.

The case of fifteen-year-old Feline, who had left her house as usual a few weeks back, but had never made it to school, disappearing without trace, had naturally caught my attention. Feline's story – the media frenzy ensured you couldn't miss it – reminded me of those cases in my past that I never, ever wanted to have anything to do with again.

Which is why my neck tensed painfully when Emilia Jagow confirmed her identity to me and said, 'I'm desperate, Herr Zorbach. I urgently need your help.'

# 7

## FELINE

'You're back,' said the woman who called herself Tabea and who Feline wished would only exist in her nightmares.

But Tabea was still here: the pale, petite, black-haired woman with a fringe she wore like a helmet, making her look like a Playmobil figure. It was the second time Feline had woken up from sedation in this prison next to her fellow inmate, who was as mad as an *'iguana on crack'*, to use one of Olaf's favourite sayings. Olaf, her best friend, who couldn't help her any more, even if he'd wanted to.

Feline had only a sketchy recollection of the first time – waking up the day she was abducted. The figure had been lying in wait for her at Nikolassee station, on the small woodland path she used as a cut-through when she cycled. The bearded man wearing a cap pulled down over his face said her scarf had fallen out of her basket, so Feline stopped to check. And thereby sealed her fate. She heard a noise, the cracking of a twig beneath a heavy boot. Before she could turn around she felt the hand over her mouth, smelled the acrid scent, then everything went black.

When she came to, like Tabea she was in a scratchy nightie that tied at the back. As Feline would discover, there was no change of clothes down here. Her abductor (or was it several?) had at least remembered toiletries such as toothbrushes, toothpaste, shampoo, shower gel and tampons. And – thank God – a curtain which screened off the chemical toilet.

Feline had felt sick when she realised the hopelessness of her situation. Carried off to a prison she was forced to share with a weird, if not completely deranged, stranger by an unknown man who'd undressed her while she was unconscious.

And now it had happened a second time.

Once again her bizarre fellow hostage was sitting beside her. And once again Tabea's hand on her brow felt like a dead fish. Feline asked her to stop stroking her head and Tabea, who must be twenty years older, sulked as she teetered down from the bunk like a small child.

Feline sat up, looked around, and what she saw intensified the nausea fermenting inside her.

*You sent me back to hell, Dad. And nothing's changed.*

What made it unbearable here wasn't the lack of windows, but that the place had everything else, such as the grey rug or the multifunctional coffee table whose height could be adjusted for eating. The bunk beds stood as close to the oval wall as possible. On top there was space for two people. Below were built-in bookshelves and cupboards, as well as an extra fold-down bed for 'guests', as the madwoman she was locked up with had told her in all seriousness.

*I've woken up from a bad dream into a nightmare*, Feline thought at the time, only to realise that the bony person in the stained nightie with fingernails chewed so badly that they bled wasn't a figment of her imagination. Tabea was as real as the microwave in the galley kitchen and the rounded concrete walls of the 'tank'.

*Tank.*

That's what Feline called the prison, because unlike the cells, dungeons or hovels she knew from horror films, her prison had a lid rather than a door. A hatch in the middle of the ceiling, similar to how she imagined the entrance to a submarine. It was around three metres above her head, unreachable without a ladder, even from the bunk. Were she somehow able to brush the curved metal lock with her fingertips, it would be futile anyway because the hatch opened from above. This had only happened once before.

Without warning, a hole had suddenly appeared and a rope ladder dropped from the lid of the tank. With a message on the lowest rung: *We're going on a trip, Feline. Put a bag over your head, you'll find one in the cupboard. Then climb up to me.*

Which is what she did, climbed the ladder blind until a pair of strong arms grabbed Feline and hauled her out of the tank. Then the madman, who wouldn't say what he had in store for her, gave her an injection. Another one. When she came to, she was sitting in the back of a van, chained to the roof, and then spent what seemed like an eternity imagining all the horror scenarios now awaiting her. Feline had anticipated everything. Torture, pain, even death. But not that the door would open and she'd see her father.

Who'd sent her back to damnation.

Feline's eyes welled with tears when she thought about how close she'd come to freedom.

*Why, Daddy, why?*

She'd been given another injection. And now she was back in this tank, where she'd been stuck for days or weeks now in a state of utter hopelessness, trying not to lose her mind.

There were no clocks, and the absence of a window meant you couldn't see the change from day to night. Just a chain of lights dangling between the bed and the galley kitchen – the only source of light here in the tank – which (as now) was switched off for a number of hours at a time, presumably to simulate night and day. Then Feline had to sit in the dark with this complete lunatic, who now and then would scratch her neck and forearms. Each time Feline saw it happen her skin started to itch too.

*Am I going to start losing my mind as well, and harm myself like Tabea?*

Feline closed her eyes and fell into a short, restive sleep that wasn't sufficient to restore her strength after repeated sedations. She was woken by the vibrations that shook the tank at regular intervals. And that appeared to activate something else that Feline had only discovered by chance one day. Something that might mean the difference between life and death if she used it correctly.

Feline sat up and listened intently in the darkness.

*Is Tabea asleep?*

She focused on the regular breathing noises that were occasionally interrupted by a snore from her 'flatmate'. Feline felt gently for the secret she'd hidden beneath the mattress at the head of her bunk.

Among the books, pens and paper, her kidnapper had failed to spot the watch in the inside pocket of her school rucksack she'd found in the cupboard beside her clothes. Maybe he'd deliberately left it for her?

*Why bother taking something away from a hostage when you're going to rob her of her life soon anyway?*

Feline covered her head with the duvet so Tabea didn't notice when she pushed the button that illuminated the watch's display. She didn't trust her fellow hostage, who clearly suffered from Stockholm syndrome, calling her abductor 'my boyfriend'. Here inside the tank, Tabea seemed to be getting stranger by the day. The scratching became more intense and she wouldn't stop singing the praises of their jailer, who she wanted to marry and for whom she'd even be prepared to die.

Maybe Tabea was just a highly gifted actress? Perhaps the kidnapper had put her here to keep a close eye on Feline?

*If so, she mustn't find out that I've got a—*

'What the hell…?'

Feline gave a cry.

The duvet had been jerked off her head and the Playmobil face was hovering above her.

Tabea angrily snatched the watch out of her hand. 'What are you hiding from me, you little shit?'

# 8

## ZORBACH

I had trouble getting the stove going. The birch wood was too damp, and by the time I finally succeeded, the cabin was full of smoke. I opened a porthole and apologised to my visitor, who had already passed the first intelligence test by listening carefully and finding her way to my houseboat this afternoon. I'd never received visitors here in the past. The houseboat was my refuge, my secret retreat. So inconvenient to get to that I used to hope I'd be able to shake off the demons which pursued me in my day-to-day life on the muddy path through the undergrowth to the shore. I'd long given up this hope. Finding the way to my 'oasis' used to be even trickier. I'd always taken care that nobody saw me when I turned off Nikolskoer Weg into the woods shortly before Potsdam. At first I was so paranoid that I would unscrew my number plates before squeezing my battered Volvo through the brambles until it was far enough from the road that it couldn't be seen even in good weather. But then Alina Gregoriev discovered my hideaway. She came and told me about her experiences with a patient

32

she'd treated, who she suspected of being Germany's most-wanted criminal. Since that day my houseboat had never been a refuge again.

'Are you putting your stuff in storage?' Emilia asked me. We were sitting opposite each other on two of the packed removal boxes scattered throughout the boat. From her seat she had a view through the window of the weeping willows, which formed a natural carport above the creek, invisible from the river.

'I think I'm going to throw it all away,' I said, taking a sip from my enamel mug. Instant coffee with whitener. I could understand why Feline's mother didn't want any, but I wasn't set up for discerning visitors and I rather liked the dishwater. 'I can't afford a garage. I'm going to prison.'

'I know,' Emilia said, which didn't surprise me. Even though my sentence hadn't made great waves in the press, it hadn't been hushed up altogether. The trial lasted two years and Christine Höpfner had pulled out all the stops. She'd argued convincingly that there were mitigating circumstances: I'd acted out of necessity. For a moment even I believed in my innocence and thus agreed to the appeal we lodged against the first verdict. In retrospect this was a mistake but at least it gave me another respite, which I used to spend more time with my son, Julian.

Ultimately there was no doubt as to my guilt. I'd thought that the critically injured Frank Lahmann on the operating table in Martin Luther Hospital was the Eye Collector I was hunting. And I'd had every reason to believe this because my mentee had confessed to it on the phone to me. What I didn't know was that he'd been coerced into making the confession by the real killer, who'd held a gun to his head while he talked. *Mike 'Scholle' Scholokowsky.*

And because I also believed that Frank had abducted my son, I didn't want to run the risk of him dying during surgery before he told me where Julian was. So I forced my way into the operating theatre and made the anaesthetist bring Frank out of his sedation. Which cost my trainee his life – and me my freedom. Rather than being found guilty of murder, which the public prosecutor was calling for, I was 'only' convicted of assault resulting in death, in recognition of my tormented emotional state. But Christine Höpfner wasn't able to wangle me less than four years, of which I'd definitely have to serve two and a half. I wasn't angry at her about this. On the contrary, I was eternally grateful to Christine merely for the fact that I didn't have to spend the time until I was sentenced on remand. As far as I was concerned, the verdict was correct. Even though Frank might have died on the operating table anyway – this couldn't be ruled out – I'd undoubtedly robbed him of a chance of survival, and intentionally so.

'When do you begin your sentence?'

'The day after tomorrow.'

'Oh,' she said, sounding surprised. 'So soon?' She must have overlooked this detail in the press. 'I hoped you'd have a bit more time. As things stand I don't think you'll be able to help me.' She made to get up.

'First, why don't you say what's brought you here?' I asked. 'You didn't want to tell me over the phone.'

Emilia gave a faint nod and sat back down. Her eyes wandered to the flickering wood burner. Together with the oil lamp that I'd hung from a hook on the low ceiling, it gave the cabin an almost romantic atmosphere, at odds with the reason for her visit. I suspected Emilia was happy about the dim lighting. The reddish-yellow glow acted like a soft-focus lens that went some way to smoothing out her worry lines. She looked tired, like someone sensing she's coming down with a cold and is desperate to go to bed, but can't because there's a particularly burdensome task she can't put off. I couldn't tell, however, if her blue eyes really were gleaming feverishly, if she was crying, or if it was just the drizzle that had settled in again outside. Her dark hair was wet too. Her shoulder-length ponytail shone like a rope dipped in oil.

'I don't know where to begin,' she muttered, looking at her shoes. She was wearing ankle boots encrusted in mud from the woodland path, which looked far too small for her long legs. I was certain that before her daughter was kidnapped, the majority of men would have labelled her as beautiful, attractive, even jaw-dropping maybe. But grief had drained her of all magnetism; her skin was blotchy and her facial features set around a high forehead and prominent cheekbones, which would have once been striking, now looked as limp as the handshake she'd given me when she arrived.

'I presume it's about Feline,' I said, giving her a prompt. Emilia nodded.

'Have you got problems with the police investigation?'

'I've got problems with my husband.'

I paused and held my mug in front of my face without taking another sip. 'In what respect?'

She looked up at me. I felt intuitively that she'd been waiting for this moment. She'd been agonising over whether to trust me and had now reached the point of no return.

'It was just under a week ago. I was having a rest in our bedroom. We live in Nikolassee.'

I was familiar with this from all the police interrogations I'd done as well as the interviews I'd conducted later as a journalist. People anxious about what they were going to confide to a stranger tended to babble. They filled their sentences with snippets of trivial information to put off the revelation of the terrible truth weighing down on them so heavily.

'Anyway, I heard the doorbell go, which annoyed me, as I'd actually managed to fall asleep and now wouldn't be getting any rest over the coming hours despite the Valium. We weren't expecting anyone – who was going to be paying us a visit? I mean, our neighbours avoid us and most of our friends have cut themselves off, as if the loss of a child were an infectious disease. I don't blame them, frankly. Besides, the handful of people who can cope with the oppressive silence in our bungalow don't turn up unannounced.'

'So the doorbell rang...' I said, trying to get her back on track.

'My husband, Thomas, he opened the front door and went outside, which really surprised me.'

'Why?'

'The rain was as persistent as it is today. And Thomas was only in his slippers and a pair of light trousers. But he stayed out in the foul weather for ages.'

'Who was it who rang the bell?'

'That's precisely why I'm here. My husband says it was a delivery man who'd got the wrong house.'

'And you doubt him?'

'I was watching Thomas from the bedroom. At least a

minute after the bell rang he went to the garden gate and stepped out onto the pavement.'

'Why?'

'That's what I was wondering too. From where I was standing I didn't have a perfect view, but I did see a van opposite.'

'That tallies with the story about the delivery man,' I interjected.

'You think that's why he marched outside in felt slippers? No!' she protested. 'In any case, it wasn't a DHL, UPS, Hermes or any other firm's van for that matter, but a dirty vehicle without any company logo.'

'Many delivery men and women use their own cars these days,' I pointed out. The poor buggers work as 'independent contractors'. I'd recently watched a documentary painting this practice as a devious form of exploitation and evasion of employer obligations.

Emilia nodded. 'I know, but still there's something not quite right.'

'What in particular makes you think this?'

She seemed to be mulling over her answer. Hesitating, probably, because she'd got to the crux of her account.

'When I saw Thomas trudging over to the delivery van I went to the front door. The view from there was more restricted and it was raining more heavily. Like a veil. But through it I saw my husband get out of the vehicle.'

I screwed up my eyes as if something had just flown into them. 'He got *out* of the van?'

'I think so, yes.'

'Didn't you question him about it?'

'I did, but he said I was mistaken.'

'Did you see him get in?'

'No. And, to be honest, my eyes might have been playing tricks on me. I mean, I had taken Valium just before.'

'Have you mentioned this to the police?' I asked.

She forced a desperate smile. 'And totally destroy my husband's life? You've been a policeman and crime reporter. Surely you know who the suspicion usually falls on first in cases like this.'

I nodded. In over eighty per cent of murders – and sadly the Feline Jagow case must now be classed as one of these – the killer was a close relative.

'We've been harassed on social media since her disappearance became known. People even find it suspicious that Feline goes to the same school where Thomas teaches.' Now Emilia's voice sounded throatier. 'When the news about the missing mobile seeped out he was on the social media hitlist for days.'

'What missing mobile?'

'My husband lost his phone shortly before Feline's kidnapping. The police focused on this for a while but it proved to be a dead end. Unfortunately the information leaked out and people have been spreading the most scurrilous rumours ever since. What do you think would happen if I now expressed the slightest doubt about my husband in public?'

*Easy prey.* His life would be over. Even if in retrospect he could prove his innocence.

I didn't have to say this to her; Emilia's question had been a rhetorical one.

'Sure, but you wouldn't be here if deep down you weren't certain your husband had lied to you, would you?'

She shook her head.

'Okay, let's assume you *did* see him get out of the van. Can you think of an explanation for that?'

She shrugged. 'Not a good one.'

I nodded. That's how our minds work, sadly. There might well be a very simple reason for Emilia's husband's behaviour. Perhaps he helped the delivery man with a heavy package, forgetting to put his shoes on in his hurry? Afterwards he felt embarrassed and preferred to deny the whole thing rather than be nagged about him catching his death of cold. When a brain doesn't know the whole truth it makes things up to fill the gaps, and these are often negative. It's how conspiracy theories emerge. If we don't know how someone has made their fortune, we assume they've been involved in dodgy dealings. If we don't understand the spread of a new disease, we think there's a programme to control the population behind it. And if we see someone very close to us climbing out of a van in the pouring rain, we think they're deceiving or betraying us, or even worse.

'Basically it's no more than a gut feeling,' Emilia said softly. 'I think he lied to me and I don't know why.'

'Did he behave strangely afterwards too?'

'Yes, he's changed. Obviously he's not the same man he was before Feline disappeared, in that respect all of us have changed. But that evening he removed all the photographs of her from our shelves. And he's refused to talk about her ever since. I get the feeling he's given up on her now altogether.'

'And that's why you think his lie about the delivery man – if it was a lie – has got something to do with your daughter?'

She wiped away a tear that had run from the corner of her eye. 'Right now I link everything to Feline.'

I sighed because I understood her despair. I felt the same when Julian was abducted.

'I'm going to be honest with you. You fear that your husband is concealing a dreadful secret from you. The only thing you can do to combat your doubts is to commit a breach of trust of your own. You have to spy on him.'

Emilia blinked; she looked shocked.

'You want to know if he's keeping something from you. You're only going to find that out if he's kept under surveillance. But even then no detective will ever be able to completely dispel your doubts.'

This was the reason why many of the private detectives I knew wouldn't work for clients who wanted their partners shadowed. Either way they were unhappy with the result of the investigation. If it was concluded that their partner was faithful, nagging doubts remained that this might only be true for the period they were under observation. If there was proof of cheating, the detective was accused of wrecking the relationship.

'This kind of surveillance doesn't come cheap. And, like I said, I can't take the job on. It might take weeks and I'm...'

... *on the verge of going in the nick*.

Emilia nodded impassively; she'd zoned out somewhere in between *spying*, *doubts* and *doesn't come cheap*. Because I felt sorry for her I said, 'I can recommend someone reputable who does excellent work. I know him from my time in the police.'

Now she nodded hectically like someone so desperate they're prepared to accept any offer just so long as they get some sort of help. 'That's very kind. I don't have a clue about these things and I don't want to be saddled with a charlatan or rip-off merchant.'

I took my mobile from my coat pocket. 'Just out of journalistic interest, may I ask how you came by me?' I said as I searched for the investigator's number in my contacts.

Emilia cleared her throat and when I looked up I sensed she felt uncomfortable again. Once more she groped for the truth and said evasively, 'Via Feline, actually. Years ago our daughter had a riding accident and she's had trouble with the vertebrae in her neck ever since. Last year she was meant to have an operation but just beforehand a complementary therapist, who specialises in spinal problems, started work at Friedberg hospital, where I'm a nurse. My new colleague advised against the operation and offered to treat Feline instead. I don't believe in esoteric or alternative therapies, but what can I say? After the third session Feline's pain had drastically reduced and the misalignment is almost completely corrected. Just through manual therapy.'

'And this colleague of yours suggested me?' Emilia's words had suddenly made me feel uneasy. Like a stranger in my own home.

'Not directly,' she replied. 'I tried on a couple of occasions to turn the conversation to you, Herr Zorbach, but she was very cagey. I did, however, read something in the newspaper about your shared past. That you'd once saved a child from the clutches of a kidnapper.'

The bad feeling grew inside me like a malignant tumour.

'Are we talking about…?'

She nodded, letting the cat out of the bag with its razor-sharp claws.

'Alina Gregoriev.'

The blind physiotherapist to whom I was connected by the best and worst in life.

Death and love. Torture and affection.

On our hunt for the Eye Collector we were able to spend only a few hours together that weren't filled with torment and pain. But these hours were sufficient to ensure that I still longed for her as if she were a missing part of my body.

*Alina.*

The woman I'd tried in vain to contact over the past few months. She kept her distance from me for good reason: she didn't want to die.

# 9

## PRIVATE PRACTICE OF DR REJ, BLEIBTREUSTRASSE, CHARLOTTENBURG

*Two days later*

He loved the moment when the bonnet of his Mercedes angled downwards and he shot like a torpedo down the serpentine track of the underground car park. It was like a rollercoaster ride with the added thrill of possibly damaging the paintwork to the tune of several thousand euros. Or ruining the absurdly expensive sporty wheel rims that the ambitious garage manager on Salzufer had conned him into buying.

'*It's so you, Dr Rej.*' Sure, like a 320-horsepower missile was part of a Berlin psychiatrist's standard equipment.

And yet he had every reason to hurry. He'd been dealing with a compulsory hospitalisation and now he was just going to make it in time for his last patient of the day.

How awkward if she were already waiting outside his door.

'No, I don't do couples therapy,' he told the anxious caller over the speakerphone. He would never subject himself to the whingeing of quarrelling married couples, not even if the husband offered an hourly fee of five hundred euros.

'I specialise in severe post-traumatic stress disorders,' he went on, noting in his head that marriage could sometimes trigger these. Dr Rej knew all about this, his own wife having left him out of the blue one day.

'Are you still there?'

Rej couldn't hear him any more. This was the disadvantage of a parking spot below ground. Signal boosters had supposedly been installed in this new building, but there was no sign of them down here. When he got out of the car and headed towards the lifts, he still couldn't make out what the caller was saying.

'If you can hear me, I'm sorry I can't help you further. On my website you'll find recommendations of very able colleagues who I'm sure will be able to offer support. I wish you all the best and hope you have a good weekend.'

He hung up, ducking his head as he entered the lift, as tall people typically do when going into a room. It should take the lift a matter of seconds to convey him from the underground car park to the penthouse of this luxurious new build, from which he and his patients had a dreamy view over the sights of City West.

It happened a mere three seconds after he pressed the brass button labelled 'PRIVATE PRACTICE OF DR SAMUEL REJ' and the steel doors closed. The lights went out and the lift stayed where it was.

*A blackout?*

This had never happened before.

Rej whipped out his mobile, which still had no reception, but at least he could use the torch function.

He tried to stay calm and pressed the alarm button on the touchpad.

It started ringing but nobody answered.

*For fuck's sake. I pay forty euros per square metre a month without bills and now I'm just trapped here in the dark.*

In anger he kicked the lift door, shouted, cursed and slammed his fist against the panelling. Well aware that this was pointless.

He didn't have any colleagues who'd be wondering where he'd got to. It was past 6 p.m. and those in the offices below his would have gone home by now. Besides, the lift was still underground and so he could scream and hit the walls as loud as he liked.

Nobody would hear him.

Not even the blind woman with bat-like hearing.

*Alina Gregoriev.*

The only patient he was still expecting to see today.

# 10

## ALINA GREGORIEV

'Christ, what's wrong with your lift?' Alina felt borne by a wave of anger that flushed her into the psychiatrist's practice.

No sooner had he opened the door than she hurried past Dr Rej, grumbling her head off. Not because she'd had to ring the bell three times; she wasn't that petty. No, there was a different, much more serious reason for her wrath. And it preyed so badly on her mind that for the first time in her life she had to resort to psychiatric help.

'Have you got a different aftershave on today? Whatever. Yes, yes, I know what you're thinking, doctor. The specs. But I can't manage without them. And wait, before you say "*not yet*", just let me get one thing straight: I might want to reverse all this. I mean, how long ago was the operation? Five weeks? And I still haven't got beyond the stage of a baby yet.'

Alina had been to see Dr Rej four times already in two weeks, and by now she'd memorised the layout of his practice. The reason she was talking so much was not just a reflection of her despair, she was also using the sound reverberation to orient herself.

'The doctors clap each other on the shoulder and say, *"You're making great progress, Frau Gregoriev"*,' Alina sneered, adopting a tone of exaggerated enthusiasm when she cited the surgeon who'd operated on her in the private eye clinic in Hanover. '*"How marvellous that you've reacted so well to the stem cells from the donor cornea that we injected around your irises. You can already make out shadows and movement – this doesn't always happen so quickly after a transplant, Frau Gregoriev. And certainly not in someone who was blinded so young in life."* But do you know what, doctor? I don't care if other patients have more problems than me. I was blind for almost three decades. But before my operation I was able to tell a man from a bag of rubbish. And now? Now I inhabit a world that only consists of blots, puzzling patterns and blurs. I confuse balls with cubes, for God's sake. Quite apart from the fact that I sit at a café and wonder who's shuffling past me: a long-haired bloke, a bald girl? Fuck, I may have my sight back but there's bugger all I can do with it because you see with your brain, not your eyes. Mine has been wrongly programmed over the past few decades and is no longer capable of thinking spatially. I don't know whether I'm standing by a line on the floor or a step.'

Alina knew that her voice sounded slightly hollower in the hallway, and that the noise the soles of her Dr Martens made on the parquet floor became duller as soon as she went beyond the coat rack. Two paces beyond this you turned left through the double doors into the large therapy room, two thirds of which was covered by an old Persian carpet. The large glass coffee table and water carafes on it afforded her voice a faint echo. As soon as Alina's sonar-like hearing detected this change in frequency she knew it would be three more short steps before she could confidently drop onto the sofa and put two of the three cushions behind her back, which she now did. Moaning all the while:

'Promised me the earth, they did, if I put myself forward for this brand-new operation! *"You'll be able to see again. You'll discover a whole new world after more than twenty years!"* What actually happened was that I turned into a dumb wreck of a woman, eaten up by self-pity, stumbling my way through a hallucinogenic sea of colours and outlines the moment I take these specs off, which is why I certainly won't be getting rid of them in a hurry.'

Taking hold of the chunky frames with both hands, she tugged at them like a swimmer trying to empty water from their goggles. 'With these dark glasses I'm almost as intact as I used to be. Apart from the fact that I lost my talent as a result of the operation.'

Alina paused for breath for the first time and, as usual, her doctor didn't say anything. *If there's anyone who's perfected the art of listening, it's Dr Rej.* Not for the first time she wondered whether talking to the wall would have the same effect. It would be cheaper at any rate. Rej's hourly rate was more than four times what Alina charged her physiotherapy patients.

'I know you're going to think this ridiculous, but I'll tell you all the same. In the past I was able to look into the souls of my patients. I touched them and observed the world with my inner, seeing eye. Unfortunately this only worked when I felt pain. I had to hurt myself beforehand.'

Her anger welled up once more, opening another dangerous crack in the protective wall of reason that any healthy person has around them.

Alina leaped to her feet and followed the ludicrous impulse to numb her anger with pain. Bending down, she rolled up the right leg of her ripped jeans as far as her knee and swung her leg back as if about to kick an imaginary football. Then she crunched her bare shin against the edge of the chrome-reinforced glass table. To stop herself from screaming, she bit her hand, though this didn't make the searing, burning pain any more bearable.

'Don't get up,' she ordered the psychiatrist as she groaned and hobbled across the Persian carpet to where her therapist was sitting. 'Oooh. Shit. I feel like I've got an axe sticking into me. When I used to touch someone in this state, something totally inexplicable would happen.'

Alina felt for Rej's shoulders and squeezed. Before the operation, this would have been the moment when the visions appeared – she'd never found a better word to describe it. From one second to the next she'd have an almost out-of-body experience, which in her exasperation she hadn't described to the psychiatrist properly. For the pain didn't only activate her inner eye, it was as if she were suddenly seeing the world through the eyes of the person she was touching. *But right now...*

'*Nothing*,' was on her tongue, but she couldn't say it. Her throat had become an arid desert, her tongue a sheet of sandpaper. For even if it wasn't the same as before her operation, what she felt now wasn't *nothing*. Nor was it a vision, but a shockingly real sensation, albeit one her rational mind couldn't find an explanation for.

'Who are you?' she asked the man whose hands she was now feeling, and who certainly wasn't Dr Rej. She was as certain of this as of the fact that she was now completely at his mercy.

# 11

## ZORBACH

'*You?*'

Alina recoiled so violently that she stumbled and I was worried she'd collapse onto the coffee table. But before I could get to her she recovered and yelled at me.

'WHAT ARE YOU DOING HERE?'

'Let me explain.'

'I'm going to call the police.' She took a mobile from her trouser pocket. Still the old one she could activate with her voice.

'Don't do that,' I begged her. 'I just want to talk.'

'But I don't want to talk to you. You must be out of your mind. Hold on…' She paused. 'Aren't you supposed to be in prison?'

'Day after tomorrow.'

'It'll be sooner than that now.'

If I didn't know better I'd have thought she was staring at me through her opaque glasses. The monstrous things couldn't hide the fact that she'd barely changed in the last couple of years.

In truth Alina, now thirty, looked even younger and prettier than I remembered, which might have been down to her fiery-red hair. It seemed like she was still choosing a new wig every day, one that corresponded to her current mood. Today she'd plumped for the insubordinate Pippi Longstocking specimen.

The red of her plaited wig matched the gloss on her full lips that were quivering with anger.

'Where's Dr Rej?'

'Stuck in the lift.'

'Did you…?' She shook her head and raised her hand defensively. 'Actually, I don't give a fuck how you managed to cut the power. You've clearly gone mad.'

'Please, I just want to talk.'

'And so you break in to my psychiatrist's?'

Which wasn't particularly difficult because for a new build they'd scrimped massively on the security doors. My old lock-picking set had proved perfectly adequate for both the fuse box in the cellar and the front door. Rej's office didn't have a functioning alarm system either, although there probably wasn't much to nick in a psychiatric practice. I imagined it would be a different story at the property auction firm one floor below.

'This is breaking and entering, unlawful detention…' She paused in her enumeration of my crimes. 'Hold on, how did you find me here?'

I asked Alina whether we might leave the building (according to the regulations, a technician had to turn up within thirty minutes of the alarm being activated in the lift) but, frothing with rage, she refused to budge an inch. So we stayed put.

'A colleague of mine gave me your new address. I rang the bell and waited half the night for you, but you didn't come home. So I rummaged around in your mailbox and came across the bill from your psychiatrist. Your appointments with him are on Wednesdays and Fridays, always at the same time. I hoped you'd stick to the pattern.'

Rej's bill had been a stroke of luck among all the advertising flyers. The decrepit, rusted mailbox in the grimy hallway of the Berlin apartment block was literally bursting at the seams with flyers and mailshots. I'd simply pulled open the flap that was hanging on its hinges, without any serious hope that I might find a clue to Alina's whereabouts. Because who writes to a blind person? But bills are, of course, sent out automatically.

'My mailbox?' She gave a pained laugh. 'Okay, then let's add stalking and interfering with the mail or whatever it's called. Anyway, I'm going to call the cops.'

I wondered whether I could dare move forwards and touch her, but decided to play safe. 'Please listen to me! I tried to contact you through John.'

Her best friend had told me in no uncertain terms, however, that Alina wanted nothing to do with me. She regarded me, in her words, as a *'magnet for pain'*. Each time our paths had crossed she'd taken a step closer to death, she said. Given what we'd gone through together, I couldn't deny that. So I left her in peace for a while, lost contact. When I tried to get in touch again before embarking on my prison sentence I couldn't find her among all the addresses I had. Only John answered the phone; he was at an airport in Los Angeles.

'He told me you'd flown back to the US with him.'

Alina groaned. 'And when you realised John had lied, didn't it occur to you that there might be a good reason why I never wanted to be in touch with you again?'

'It's not about me, but the life of a young girl who's disappeared.'

'Are you taking the piss?' Alina said, pulling up her sweatshirt. Her belly button was cut in two by a jagged ten-centimetre scar. 'Look at the souvenir our acquaintance left me with last time we freed a young girl. And that's only the one you can see.' She wiped her nose with her elbow like a little child with a face full of snot.

*Or like a woman in tears.*

'I can understand your anger, Alina,' I said as sensitively as possible. 'But please don't blame me for what someone else did to you.'

*Or us.*

She nodded and even softened her tone slightly, though she still sounded irate. 'I don't. I just don't want to get caught up in your mess ever again, Alex. Both of us...' She seemed to be searching for the right words. When she'd found them, she started the sentence again, now pointing at her eyes hidden behind the glasses. 'Before I met you I might have had a disability but at least I had a fulfilling life.'

'I know.'

Alina was what journalists liked to call an 'extreme blind person'. The daughter of a building contractor, she'd grown up in California, where, at the age of three, she'd filled a litre jar in the shed with water. Stupidly there was calcium carbide in it. Although she lost her sight as a result of the explosion, this didn't stop her from demanding, at the age of eight, to help the other pupils cross the road. Alina simply refused to accept that she was different from her sighted friends.

At seventeen she was apprehended by the police because she'd taken her drunken friends home. *By car!* In the middle of the night with the windows wound down she'd driven across the small town, relying on her sonar-like hearing. She won third place in a windsurfing competition out of two hundred sighted people; she backpacked around Asia, during which she learned shiatsu techniques and later trained as a physiotherapist.

People who didn't properly know her found it strange that Alina should set so much store by her appearance, but she did for the same reason she rejected using a stick. She wanted to be seen as a person, not someone with a disability. She wouldn't allow anything in life to be made any easier or more difficult just because she'd had an accident when she was a child. For this reason she wore striking clothes that accentuated her figure (like the skin-tight claret velvet trousers she had on now), she put on make-up and had tattoos.

'But then we met and all of a sudden my life consisted of nothing but anxiety, terror and violence.'

I nodded and had to remind myself that she couldn't see. At least while she was wearing those glasses. I'd only just learned that she'd had an operation, which moved me as intensely as that familiar scent of hers, which I hadn't smelled in so long. Even though she was dissatisfied with the result of her eye operation, I found the idea that she could see anything at all – that at some point she might be able to form an image of me – both exciting and troubling.

'I just don't want to get caught in your downward spiral. Never again.'

'Okay, I get that,' I said truthfully. 'Just hear me out for a minute, answer one or two questions, and then I'll disappear from your life again, okay? For Christ's sake, they're going to lock me up. There's no risk to you.'

She turned away from me. 'Don't you lie to me! The missing girl, whoever she might be, is just an excuse. It's not about her, is it? It's about you.'

'You're wrong,' I countered feebly, for Alina had touched a nerve. Ashamed as I was to admit it, to a degree Feline was indeed just the means to an end. An excuse for me to resort to extreme measures, to get back in contact with Alina. At the very least I'd wanted to see her one last time before going to prison. And yet I did care about the girl. I always cared about children.

'Her name is Feline,' I said. 'A former patient of yours from Friedberg hospital.'

She turned back to me and for a moment I again thought she was staring at me through those glasses.

'Feline Jagow.'

'That's her.'

'Was she abducted?' Alina sounded like I'd felt when she told me about her eye operation. Overwhelmed. Struggling to find words.

'Haven't you heard about the case?' I asked in astonishment; the sensationalist reporting had been full-on. Alina kept up to date via a news app that read the latest reports aloud, or at least that's what she'd done in the past. 'Haven't the police questioned you?'

She shook her head. 'I've been in rehab,' Alina replied. She looked shocked.

'Because of the operation?'

Again she raised her hand. Two silver bracelets clunked together. 'Please, I don't want to talk about it.'

The news had floored her. She sat back down on the sofa, shaking her head slowly. 'How long's she been missing?'

'Three weeks ago Feline left the house at 7:15, as she did every morning, and cycled to Nikolassee station. From there it's a five-minute train ride to Grunewald, where she would get back on her bike and head for school. But that day she never arrived. In all likelihood she never got on the train because they found her bike in Nikolassee, in an underpass near the station. Since then there's been no sign of life, no witnesses, no ransom demand.'

Alina nervously touched her lips.

'How well do you remember her?'

'Very well, because she was so unusual. Smart, fun-loving. The conversations we had during her therapy sessions were really animated. She told me she wanted to be a musician, but it was going to be hard because her father was so strict and old-fashioned. She wasn't allowed to have a mobile phone or computer – apart from for schoolwork – not even a radio for her to pick up inspiration from contemporary pop music. I felt sorry for her.'

Alina gave a dry cough and I poured her a glass of water from a carafe that the psychiatrist had thoughtfully placed beside a box of tissues.

'Unlike all her friends she couldn't stream her favourite songs or at least hear them on the radio. It made me so sad that at the end of her treatment I gave her my MP3 player.'

'MP3 player?'

'Yes. It was a freebie. Actually it's quite cool because it looks like a watch and you wear it on your wrist. It has very few features, and not even all of these function any more because the cheap touchscreen is badly scratched. But Feline was able to listen to music if she could connect it to a wireless network. There wasn't one at home. And because her father must never find out she had one of these demonic devices, the "watch" was a brilliant disguise.'

My jaw dropped. Euphoric and anxious in equal measure, I said, 'Do you realise what you've just told me?'

# 12

## FELINE

*We've had our ups and downs...*

Loud and shrill. But that didn't seem to bother Tabea. She sat on the bottom bunk, singing Beth Ditto's 'I Need You' at the top of her voice.

*... We've had our runarounds...*

Ever since Tabea had discovered the watch, she'd wanted to spend all day listening to the songs that Feline had carefully downloaded to her MP3 player these past few days. It was a miracle she'd managed it at all. In many respects.

The first and perhaps greatest miracle was that on she day she was abducted she'd put the MP3 player and headphones in her rucksack. She even had the charging lead, which luckily could be plugged into the multiple socket in the galley kitchen.

*... Who cares what others think
Cause you're my everything...*

The walls of the tank vibrated again.

'Hey, Tabea.'

Her fellow hostage reluctantly looked up at Feline.

'I need my watch.'

Tabea morosely shook her helmet haircut like a stubborn child refusing to hand over a toy.

'Please!'

Feline climbed down from the bunk.

*I must make use of the interval.*

The brief period between vibrations.

These came with great regularity, having just announced their arrival again with the gentle jangling of the spoons in an enamel mug in the sink. A clattering like that of a distant jackhammer, which made the concrete walls oscillate. Feline had learned that these occurred in two waves. One that built up slowly, pausing for about half a minute when it reached its climax, then ebbed until it had faded into the distance after another thirty seconds. Feline recalled the noise back home when a large lorry drove down the cobbled road outside their bungalow, stopped to unload something, then roared off again.

Sometimes when the vibrations awoke her at night she wondered whether she might be close to home.

*Am I in a secret bunker, perhaps, that Dad's built for me in the hill our house is on?*

She remembered that occasion when she'd fiddled with the watch in desperation. Pressing the On button beneath the duvet, even though it was pointless. But what else could she do?

Then she froze.

The watch had found a network.

*Free Wi-Fi Berlin.*

The droning faded. And the signal became weaker until it disappeared again altogether.

Whatever was producing the muffled, menacing vibrations, it had a wireless network in tow!

Feline was so excited that she failed to realise at first what this discovery could mean for her survival. Only later did it occur to her that she might have found her ticket to freedom. To begin with she just thought how lucky it was that she'd mistrusted Tabea from day one, her concern being that Tabea might take the MP3 player away from her or even break it in one of her crazed moods. The behaviour of her fellow hostage was ever more disturbing; now she often scratched herself until she drew blood, while her aggression and unruliness had reached new levels. Feline suspected that she was somehow in cahoots with the kidnapper – she did, after all, call him her 'boyfriend' when going into raptures about him. When Tabea discovered Feline had been hiding the watch from her, she was so furious that Feline thought she'd attack her then grass her up to her 'boyfriend'. But Tabea merely put the earphones in and started listening to the playlist.

Over and over again. Like now.

Some people thought of music as medicine. Tabea was clear proof of this thesis. The songs soothed her at a stroke. She scratched herself less and seemed more relaxed, almost even-tempered. So long as she was listening to the playlist, at any rate.

*... give me 85 minutes of your love...*

'Please, Tabea, I need my watch,' Feline tried again, then heard a crunching noise. She stiffened, her legs turned to jelly, her throat hurt when she swallowed, and when she looked up at the lid she felt numbed, even though she hadn't been given an injection. But it couldn't be long now. Feline heard the bolt slide above her head and pressed her hand to her chest, where her heart was beating faster and faster. The tank's hatch opened.

'Hello?' Tabea called out excitedly beside her, waving in eager anticipation of seeing her 'boyfriend'. At least Tabea had put the watch and earphones in the pocket of her nightie before the kidnapper appeared in the gap above.

'What do you want?' Feline shouted at the dark hole where she could make out a shadow, but not a recognisable face. Instead of an answer the rope ladder was lowered again.

*Please, no. Not again.*

Tears came to Feline's eyes. She sobbed out loud, which unexpectedly seemed to elicit a reaction from the madman above them. For the first time since their encounter in Nikolassee he said something. Unfortunately, what he said crushed Feline's belief that she might get out of this nightmare alive: 'Your mother's hired a private detective to look for you,' the man said. Calmly. He almost sounded like a voiceover for a commercial. 'And she's made a big mistake.'

'My mother?' Feline said.

'Yes. And now I'm afraid you're going to have to pay for her error!'

# 13

## ZORBACH

'You live *here?*' I asked, once I'd convinced Alina that Feline's life might depend on a visit to her apartment.

'Don't bother making a note of the address,' she said. 'You're going to stay a couple of minutes max and you'll never be coming back. Is that clear?'

The place Alina had taken me to was sandwiched between two 1960s buildings that had been decently renovated but were fairly plain.

When we left the practice I'd followed Alina a mere few hundred metres down Kurfürstendamm, into one of Berlin's hippest neighbourhoods.

On the corner of Pariser Strasse and Ludwigkirchplatz, the sandstone-coloured new build with its gently curved façade was reminiscent of Gaudí's inimitable architecture in Barcelona. Like the building overall, the door itself was a work of art. Crafted from fine wood and stained white, it refracted the few rays of the gloomy autumn light, making them appear summery.

'I thought you lived in Moabit.'

That's where I'd nicked her post.

'Yes, there too.' Alina, who on our way here had made it quite plain that she didn't want a private chat with me, touched a sensor beneath the bells, which were only labelled with numbers rather than names, as so often when the owners of such luxury apartments wished to remain anonymous. The electrically operated door sprang open with a faint buzz and I felt as if I were entering a church.

The floor of the lobby that led to the lifts was laid with brightly polished marble, while a chandelier a good ten metres above our heads lit up several paintings on either side of the entrance hall. The lift arrived without a button being pressed. Nor did I spot Alina selecting a floor number when we got in, yet the brassbound doors closed and we soared upwards to the penthouse floor, as at Dr Rej's.

'Did you win the lottery?' I asked, and saw her smile for the first time.

'Sort of.' The lift doors opened again and I stepped into the living room of an apartment straight from the cover of *Vogue Living*.

Though I'd marvelled at the practice in Bleibtreustrasse, this place redefined the word 'luxury', downgrading the psychiatrist's rooms to the category of social housing. The massive green wall in the hallway alone, lined with real plants, must have cost a bomb. And in front of it, opposite me, stood a sporty-looking man around fifty-five, who also looked like an item of furniture. With his neatly parted, greying hair, a casually buttoned three-hundred-euro linen shirt paired with designer jeans that complemented the concrete colour of the floor, he smiled at us in his snow-white trainers and patted the head of Alina's guide dog. The fact she hadn't needed his assistance on the way to see her doctor showed how well she knew the area. She must have been living here for some time.

'Hey, TomTom,' I said to the retriever, who wagged his tail as if he recognised me. He'd gone slightly grey around the nose, which made the dog look more dignified than me. I'd rarely felt so out of place in my faded jeans and worn-out boots still filthy from the woods by my houseboat. By contrast, the man opposite me oozed the sort of confidence that came from living in an apartment that was larger and more expensive than many a villa in the city.

'Alex, this is Nils,' Alina said as she dropped her handbag on the floor in the hall beside a white globe, presumably meant to be a work of art. Then she said something which, in other circumstances, would have made me hate this Nils before I'd even shaken his hand: 'My fiancé.'

# 14

*Nils.*

I hated myself instead.

His existence made it crystal clear that I'd been deluding myself all these years. The countless days and nights when I'd thought of Alina, absolutely pining for her, presuming that she was the weaker of us two. An ex-girlfriend battered by fate, who without my help was having a tougher time of it than me and who, should I ever summon the courage to step into her life again, would very soon realise that I was the support she needed. (At the time these thoughts filled my head, I was still hoping I'd get off with a suspended sentence.)

Such hubris!

In truth I was the one whose life had stood still while Alina had moved on. I'd got tangled up in the tentacles of my dark past whereas she had shaken off the shackles and embarked on a future that was manifestly more promising and agreeable than mine.

'Alexander Zorbach?' Nils asked, as he shook my hand.

Not so limply that I'd think him a weakling, nor so firmly to brand him as self-important. 'I've heard a lot about you.'

TomTom pricked up his ears as if keen not to miss a word of our conversation.

'I hope you don't believe everything you've been told,' I said, trying a touch of humour and failing miserably, for the simple reason that Nils wasn't just more elegant, better looking and richer than me, but also more charming.

'I believe everything Alina tells me,' he said with an affectionate smile. I wish I could say it sounded slimy, but he was being honest and genuine. Like the kiss they gave each other before Alina freed herself from their intense embrace.

'Alex needs help in an investigation.' With the confidence of a visually impaired individual who can call up the layout in their mind and trust their flatmate not to move items of furniture, turning them into bone-crunching obstacles, Alina navigated her way across the living room, past the open-plan kitchen and into a study. I hurriedly followed her.

'The MP3 player wasn't an Apple Watch but some unbranded product made in China,' she said, having sat down at the glass table and switched on her computer. Alina and Nils obviously shared this working space, because opposite her was an identical table with another PC.

'I can't imagine I went to the bother of registering it,' she said.

'Let's try all the same,' I urged her.

She felt for the pimple on the numeric pad of her keyboard. Every computer, public telephone or cashpoint machine has a raised dot on the number five button so that blind people can find their way around the numeric pad. Alina used to have a keyboard with a braille display, but she didn't seem to need that any more. The password for her computer must only be made up of numbers, and she hammered it in more quickly that I'd have been able to tap my PIN into a cashpoint.

While the computer started up I continued to look around. In the study too the interior designer had pulled off the feat of not making the wickedly expensive furnishings look showy.

In vain I searched for certificates and diplomas on the wall or shelves that might tell me what Nils did for a living. Maybe he didn't have a job and had inherited money instead? The hope of finding some sort of blemish on his character evaporated when I discovered the bound periodicals on the bookshelf.

'Systems for controlling hybrid trains,' I muttered. Too loudly, as it turned out, for Alina remarked, not without pride, 'Nils is an engineer. His firm holds patents for technology that's used in almost every high-speed train on the planet.'

'Wow!' I said to Alina, who was opening some software that would read her the contents of websites. She removed her wig and put a headset on her shaven head.

'Hmm, at a party I bet it doesn't sound as sexy as "I'm an investigative journalist",' Nils said from the door, holding up his coffee cup to me. Clearly he knew who I was. 'I've taken the liberty of making you a coffee from the machine. Black, I assume?'

'Don't get pally with him,' Alina growled from the desk. Then she whispered something that sounded like 'Shit!'

'What?'

From the red blotches on her face I could tell she was

buzzing. The programme must have informed her that the MP3 player she'd given Feline was indeed registered. Even better, one glance at the large monitor in the centre of the desk revealed something quite unbelievable.

'How's that possible?' Alina muttered, shaking her bald head. She took off the headset, then turned to Nils and me.

'What do you mean, darling?' her fiancé asked. He couldn't know that Alina had unearthed a miracle. Feline had disappeared near on a month ago. If she'd been abducted, the kidnapper or kidnappers must have frisked her and taken away all her personal belongings. Even if she'd been allowed to keep the cheap watch, there was no way it would have any battery left after all this time. I'd been hoping that the tracking software might at least give us the girl's last location before she went missing, but I'd expected this would be her parents' house. Despite this I'd begged Alina to go home and check on her computer if she'd activated the MP3 player's Find function. But not only had Alina registered the device for GPS location, it was still active!

There was no other explanation for the flashing flag on Google Maps. In a place that certainly wasn't where Feline lived.

'Maybe we've just found her,' Alina said, both excited and unable to believe what she'd found.

Feline.

Or her body.

*Under the world*
*I'm full of doubt.*
*It's silent, dark and cold*
*Where's the way out?*

**Johannes Oerding – 'Under the World'**

*You're trapped in your skin*
*Your walls have bricked you in.*
*In your maze you know the way about*
*Every path winds in but none leads out.*

**LOTTE – 'Maze'**

# 15

## ZORBACH

Death doesn't only stalk ugly places.

On the contrary, I now believe that suffering and torment like the discrepancy. Often when I'm driving down an avenue in one of Berlin's smartest districts, where well-tended gardens are laid out in front of grand villas or architects' extravagant properties, I can't escape the feeling that nothing but pain and despair lurk behind façades of wealth and happiness. Sometimes I've wanted to stop and ring at some door just to make sure that the discreetly lit, luxury new build isn't harbouring a devil keeping someone hostage, torturing women or abusing children. I've never dared go through with it, but it would be a pointless undertaking anyway, for why should Death show his face just because I've knocked at his door? Today, however, fate had led me to an idyllic spot in Havelland, Brandenburg, where my theory was confirmed without any need for action on my part.

*It's so beautiful here.*

I felt I could be gazing out at a bay in the Adriatic or

Mediterranean, though it was merely the silver shimmer of the Schwielowsee in the clear starry night.

'*Where the hell are you?*'

While I snuck across the meadow I heard Philipp Stoya's voice in the earbuds that were connected to my mobile, and I stopped briefly to glance at the screen.

'According to the positioning system, just under fifty metres from the location of Feline's "watch" with its integrated MP3 player,' I answered the policeman.

'For Christ's sake, have you taken leave of your senses? What did I tell you?'

'Whatever you do, don't go alone,' I said, repeating Soya's words that I'd obviously ignored. For years I'd had a love–hate relationship with the chief inspector investigating the Feline Jagow case. When we were colleagues there was a mutual respect, but we'd never gone out for a beer after work. Later, during my time as a crime reporter, we both benefited from information we were able to pass each other. Today we steered clear of each other because neither of us wished to be reminded of how badly we'd failed in our hunt for the Eye Collector, the notorious serial killer who was still on the loose.

'I'm just going to have a quick look around,' I said, trying in vain to reassure Stoya. About ten minutes ago I'd sent him a screenshot of Feline's possible location. Early enough to request help if my hunch was right. But too late for Stoya to make me abort my solo effort.

'Get away from there at once, you nutter! You've no idea where you are.'

'*Oh, I think I do.*'

According to my mobile I was in the grounds of a

hotel called Ambrosia-Resort. A little research had set my alarm bells ringing, because no rooms were available at the Ambrosia-Resort on any of the booking portals or on the hotel's website. And not just for the coming weeks and months. For the next two years it was impossible to reserve anything there.

'Zorbach, you bastard, you're going to leave the grounds right now. You're trespassing and I can't help you. The Berlin Police has no authority there.'

'We haven't got time for nitpicking,' I countered. The music streaming service Feline had used to listen to her songs with Alina's watch showed when a playlist had last been modified. According to this, Feline's song selection had been updated only yesterday, which might well be the first sign of life of her in weeks. If this was a cry for help we couldn't ignore it just because of some silly squabbles over jurisdiction. So I asked Stoya, 'What are you going to do if I refuse to go home? Lock me up?' I was the only one who laughed at my joke. Maybe my last as a free man. 'I'll get back in touch when I've found Feline,' I said, hanging up.

My wet trouser legs chafed my calves as I tried moving out of the beams of light cast by the lanterns in the park. I'd had to struggle my way through the reeds along a narrow, boggy path by the shore. The main entrance was better secured than many prisons, with hedges several metres high and even taller railing fences. Another indication that this wasn't a hotel here, quite apart from the fact that I couldn't see guests or staff anywhere. Not even on the terrace of the main building facing the lake, which from this distance looked magnificent. The bungalows dotted along the shore, on the other hand, appeared dated. Simple, flat-roofed barracks which had only been patched up post-reunification, if at all.

According to Google, the Ambrosia-Resort was on the grounds of a former centre for physical culture that in East Germany had become a weekend and holiday retreat for those loyal to the regime. After reunification, the property was bought by an American holding company.

*Ten metres to go.*

The GPS signal I was following on my mobile could only be coming from a single bungalow, the one furthest from the main building and closest to the eastern side of the lake. It was dark and looked deserted.

The bungalows were connected by narrow gravel paths which I had to avoid if I wanted to make no noise. And so my route took me across a meadow covered in leaves, which was so wet that I was worried I might lose my shoes if I sank into it.

Having got to the bungalow, I walked around it once and discovered in the wall facing the lake a small window with a candle flickering behind it.

I crouched directly beneath the window. My head was so close to the wooden wall that I could hear the people inside. There were at least two of them talking in hushed tones – so softly that I couldn't make out a single word. The noises of the night around me were louder than those from the building. The rustle of the wind in the reeds, a heron flapping its wings. A car accelerating on the main road. And of course my own breathing.

I was just wondering whether I might risk standing up to take a peek through the window when I heard footsteps. Followed by a creaking sound. Someone left the bungalow.

Closed the door behind them. And stepped onto the gravel path.

I crept around the corner and tried to take a look.

Female, slim, about fifty years old, I noted.

When she was far enough away that I could no longer hear her footsteps on the gravel path I went back. And looked through the window.

*Good God.*

The images that played before my eyes changed as in a film on fast forward.

The streaks on the glass.

The flickering of a candle.

A bed. White with bars, like in a hospital.

On it…

Feline?

Shit, I couldn't tell in the dark, even though my face was pressed up to the window and the person on the bed was looking at me.

All I could see were those eyes.

Dull, vacant. *Dead?*

Judging by the build it could have been a young girl.

*What the hell have they done to her?*

The sight of her – the little I was able to make out – was so shocking that all the colour drained from my face, making me feel as if I'd become transparent.

The mobile buzzed in my hand and in my attempt to switch off the flashing screen I took Stoya's call by mistake.

'You've got to make yourself scarce right now!' he cried.

'I'm going inside,' I countered in a whisper.

To the girl with the dead eyes. And the mouth which at that moment appeared to open for a silent scream.

'No you are *not*!' Stoya yelled.

'Send in your men.'

'Leave this instant!'

'No way,' I hissed, hanging up while he continued to protest.

Nothing was going to stop me from helping the poor, suffering girl in this bungalow.

Or so I thought.

For about a second.

I made it to the small step that led up to the wooden front door. Felt the cold of the handle.

Pressed it down carefully.

Then the blow to the side of my head hit me so hard that I passed out, the noise of a skull splintering in my ears.

# 16

## ALINA

She did it between Möckernbrücke and Gleisdreieck. For the first time today. For the third time this week.

She opened her eyes.

And once again, no sooner had she parted her lids just a crack than the nails pierced her pupils and drove right into the wasps' nest behind her eyes. Millions of light insects swarmed from it, livid at the disturbance that had snatched them from the darkness. They dashed against the newly transplanted retina from behind, stung the inside of the pupils and ensured that it took every ounce of Alina's self-control to avoid screaming out loud in the underground.

*Fuck, that hurts!*

She was desperate to put her protective glasses back on and smother the explosion of colour inside her head. But she forced herself to put up a while longer with her eyes that had narrowed to slits. At least until the flood of tears had run dry and the pain had subsided to a bearable level.

'This is predominantly a psychosomatic reaction,'

Professor Broder had told her when he'd removed the bandages after the operation at the private eye clinic in Hanover. 'Understandably you're afraid of the world that for so many years you've only heard, smelled and felt but not seen.'

Well, for a hallucination brought on by fear, the pain felt remarkably real. Alina was grateful for the opaque spectacles she was given when discharged. *As a precaution, until your brain has got used to the optical impressions.*

The nurse had assured her she soon wouldn't need them. *But in my case 'soon' has been going on for weeks.*

The underground train arrived at a station and Alina felt TomTom tense up between her legs. The dog knew when she wasn't feeling well. His sixth sense was more pronounced than her first.

Weirdly she found it easier to take the glasses off in public than in front of the mirror at home. She'd always perceived herself as sensual and charismatic. Maybe not beautiful in the classical sense but, rather, starkly attractive.

*Whereas in reality?*

In her newly operated eyes she saw herself as a strangely two-dimensional being with a round head and two big cavities beneath her brow.

*I look like a monster* was her first thought when Nils finally persuaded her to take a peek in the mirror. Now too, as the train pulled away and the darkness of the tunnel loomed, she was worried about glimpsing her face as a reflection. She wondered whether the impressions around her – the curiously spotted cushions, the harsh lights above her head or this pungent scent that someone had been wearing nearby – would be more bearable with music.

Alina fished her smartphone from the inside pocket of her parka.

'Open Spotify,' she ordered Siri. This was an indisputable advantage of the degenerate digital world. If people could fiddle with their smartphones incessantly, even during family dinners, it was also possible to talk to your mobile in the underground without anyone batting an eyelid.

'Play Alina's "Eyelids" playlist.'

*Eyelids*. This was the kitschy name she'd given to the list of her favourite songs one night when she was consumed by self-pity and fuzzy-headed after a few joints. It was in the hospital, just before her final parting from Zorbach, with whom she'd never had a serious relationship and yet who'd wounded her heart more deeply than all those men before him. That she now felt a stab of melancholy when Siri said, *Okay, Alina, I'll play your 'Eyelids' playlist on Spotify for you*, was down to Zorbach's sudden reappearance in her life.

*His invasion of my private sphere yesterday.*

Normally Majan's haunting cry at the start of 'Junkie' would have shaken her awake, but the almost hypnotic beat of the rap plunged Alina even deeper into a depressive mood. Also because the first few lines of the lyrics made her think of Feline's likely hopeless situation.

> *Hold on tight, cos I'm coming.*
> *No, I'm never getting outta here.*

The idea that the MP3 player she used to listen to her playlist on was interwoven with the fate of a missing girl was preying on her mind.

*My God, Feline. What the hell's happened to you?*

Zorbach hadn't got in touch again, and because there was no update in the news about the missing persons case, she had to assume that the location of the watch had led to nothing. Alina clicked inquisitively through the playlist that Feline had changed. Once she'd played an extract of all the songs she felt a profound unease. She listened to all the tracks again.

1 Junkie
MAJAN

2 Evermore
Namika

3 Maze
LOTTE

4 Erlking
Kool Savas

5 Under
Justin Jesso

6 Rose
Rea Garvey

7 Silver Lining
Tom Walker

8 Live in Peace
JORIS

9 Alone in a Crowded Room
Charlotte Jane

10 Million Tweets
Silbermond

11 85 Minutes of Your Love
Alle Farben, Hanne Mjøen

12 Under the World
Johannes Oerding

13 I Need You
Beth Ditto

14 Open Eyes
Tim Bendzko

15 Para Paradise
VIZE, R4GE, Emie

After this she felt even tenser.

Something wasn't right with this playlist.

For one, there were so few songs. When she'd first put together the selection for Feline there'd been more than two hundred.

*And now only fifteen?*

Alina felt the fine hairs on her arm stand bolt upright beneath the sleeves of her blouse. She didn't get to fathom the reason for this reaction, however, because all her senses were suddenly distracted by something far more urgent.

TomTom started growling just as they were entering another station, a man who'd sat beside her placed a hand on her knee, and she felt as if she were in a dense forest after a summer storm. Which was because of the strong aftershave her menacingly intrusive neighbour was wearing. Then he thrust a hand into her lap. Where she'd put her mobile.

And snatched it so violently that the headphones were yanked off her ears.

'Oi!' she shouted, louder than TomTom's barking.

The pressure on her knee had gone and the shadow which had just been sitting beside her hurried away.

'Oi! Arsehole!' Alina called out to the man, even though she couldn't be sure of his gender. She'd guessed it because of the scent.

Now Alina leaped up too. 'Stop!' She elbowed her way past passengers getting off the train, with TomTom at her side. Blinded by streaks of light and misled by shadowy outlines, she alighted. After weighing it up briefly, she decided to take the risk that she might fall, and rushed headlong down the platform of Wittenbergplatz underground station in pursuit of the thief.

For a second she considered letting TomTom off the lead, but one, he was a guide dog rather than a hunting hound, and two, she needed him to help her find her way. She determined the direction, he avoided the obstacles. Together they were a team. A team that didn't get very far.

Only as far as a drinks machine, which was roughly in the middle of the platform and behind which the thief had disappeared with her iPhone. In her attempt to catch him up she'd crashed into a metal bin and let go of TomTom's lead in shock. The next thing she heard was him howling, followed by cry of outrage from an elderly lady: 'Oh God!' Now she heard voices from all sides. Passengers shouting over each other.

'Jesus, did you see that?'

'Animal abuser!'

'Help, someone needs to get help!'

Amid the confusion of voices and shadows, Alina totally lost her orientation and turned around in circles.

'TomTom!' she cried, then felt a hand on her shoulder. She flinched.

'Is that your dog on the tracks?' someone asked.

On the tracks?

*No, please no!*

Slowly she made sense of the uproar around her, piecing together the visual fragments, voices and sounds into a horrifying reality.

*TomTom!*

The thief must have kicked him off the platform.

And onto the tracks.

'He can't get back up on his own,' someone said. Her guide dog must still be stuck.

'It's too high!'

'Is she blind?'

'TomTom!' Alina screamed, now teetering on the edge of the platform. She dropped to her knees but was held back by several hands.

She heard TomTom leap up to the platform edge one last time: his lead clanked against something metal; his paws slid down from the concrete.

Then she could hear someone breathing right by her ear.

A man who smelled of an expensive aftershave.

*Cardamom, pepper and rosewood.*

He whispered something into her ear, but she couldn't make it out. Nor could she fathom why her mobile phone was suddenly back in her hand.

Then she heard TomTom bark hysterically.

People shouting behind her.

A train pulling into the station.

# 17

## STOYA

'I hope you appreciate my cooperation, Chief Inspector Stoya. Officially I have no obligation to get involved in this matter.'

Stoya nodded.

The first word that came into the policeman's head when he saw Dr Susan Lieberstett was 'severe'. Severe bun, angular features, an austerely slim body. They were standing in the Ambrosia-Resort visitors' car park.

'Everything I tell you is confidential,' said the grey-haired woman of around fifty, who'd introduced herself as the hotel manager. In her white coat and closed Birkenstock sandals, however, she looked more like a consultant who cared for patients rather than guests.

'Could we perhaps continue our conversation in the lobby?' Stoya said, eyeing the main building.

It was drizzling and the wind was whipping up the leaves at their feet. Dark clouds obscured the view of the grounds.

Ever since he'd lost a lot of weight he'd become more sensitive to the weather. Bladder cancer, *so devious and treacherous!*

'Did you not listen to what I said on the phone?' Lieberstett said haughtily. 'This is a place of rest. Outsiders like yourself need to keep your distance from our relaxation rooms. I only agreed to our meeting to hear your apology for yesterday's trespass.'

'To set things straight,' Stoya protested as calmly as possible, 'the unlawful entry into your so-called hotel wasn't authorised or arranged by us.'

'What do you mean "so-called"?' Lieberstett asked caustically, even though it was obvious that this set-up wasn't a hotel fully booked for the foreseeable future. Because it was lacking two elements essential for a hotel: guests and staff. The only employee Stoya had set eyes on was the porter at the gate who hadn't left his hut and had operated the barrier from behind a window.

'We *are* a hotel,' Lieberstett insisted. 'Just not a hotel in the conventional sense. We see ourselves as a sanctuary for victims of extreme violence.'

'A women's refuge?'

Lieberstett made a dismissive gesture. 'We don't differentiate between the sexes. Our patients include both men and women.'

'Okay, so you're more of a rehab clinic?'

'A privately funded sanatorium, if we're going to be precise. And a sanctuary. Here our guests are safe from their tormentors.'

Stoya nodded. If the Ambrosia really was a refuge, it wasn't a bad idea to disguise it as a luxury hotel to prevent abusers from finding the place. And it would explain the elaborate security and high fences.

'Is this the only resort you operate?'

'In the US, yes.'

'In the US?' Stoya said. 'According to my satnav we're in Havelland district, not North America.'

Lieberstett smacked her lips impatiently. 'Let's not play games, Inspector. You know damn well who I am.'

Stoya nodded and recalled the notes he'd made while studying Lieberstett's file back at the police station:

*Susan Lieberstett, daughter of German immigrants, born in Washington where she grew up, studied human medicine at Harvard, but then pursued a diplomatic career like her father. Worked until two years ago at the embassy on Pariser Platz, responsible for coordinating emergency medical responses. Currently on leave for reasons unknown.*

Even though she was taking a break from her work at the US embassy, Lieberstett was still in possession of a diplomatic passport, which prevented the German authorities from interfering in her affairs. Although it was a myth that the premises of an embassy or – like here – the private residence of a diplomat was extraterritorial land that didn't belong to Germany, state jurisdiction here was so limited it effectively amounted to immunity. It would take forever to get hold of a search warrant for this place.

'Did you purchase this lakeside site through an investment firm of yours?' Stoya asked.

'Is that unlawful?'

'No, but it is unlawful to hide an abducted girl.'

'Who says we're doing that?'

'The witness who your security men beat up so badly he was hospitalised.'

Lieberstett shook her head sullenly. 'Not my security men. That was me.'

Stoya's eyebrows twitched briefly. It was rare that someone he questioned freely admitted to an act of violence. But nor was it often that he spoke to a diplomat who believed themselves to be immune from prosecution.

'Well, just before you knocked him out, the man thought he'd discovered a person who'd been missing for weeks, in one of your bungalows.'

'And?'

'And?' Stoya was getting increasingly irate, but still able to control his temper. 'Frau Lieberstett, we have good reason to believe that this girl is Feline Jagow. Her parents are desperate for some sign of life. Would you please let me see her?'

Lieberstett shook her head. It sounded as if there were real regret in her voice. 'I'm afraid that's not possible.'

'What are you afraid of?'

'Nothing. We've nothing to hide here.'

'Then let me see the girl.'

'No.'

Another dirty cloud made it gloomier in the car park, and Stoya's face darkened too. 'You're abusing your immunity to commit or cover up a crime.'

'I'm not.'

'Look, we've picked up the signal from an MP3 player

belonging to the missing girl. It's coming from one of your bungalows.'

Lieberstett gave no discernible reaction. Without the slightest hesitancy she said firmly, 'Hmm, I don't know where you got this information from, Herr Stoya. Because it's wrong. Yesterday our security cameras filmed the intruder on his way from the shore of the lake to bungalow twelve.'

She took a map from the inner pocket of her coat, unfolded it and showed it to Stoya. He saw the shore and the huts that were marked as rectangles on the map. Beside the one furthest to the east someone had made a mark with a biro that looked like crosshairs.

This must be the bungalow where Zorbach had looked through the window. And saw the girl. With the dying eyes...

'Is this where you assume the abducted child is?'

Stoya nodded.

'Good, that's settled then,' Lieberstett said, putting the map back in her pocket. She made to go.

'What do you mean, settled?' a baffled Stoya called out behind her.

She turned back to him. 'It means your man is lying and I can't help you.' Lieberstett sighed. 'Bungalow twelve has been empty for months. It's uninhabitable due to water damage.'

'Could I see it?'

'I'm afraid not. We tore it down an hour ago.'

# 18

## ALINA

'Zorbach?' she panted. He'd tried three times in the last twenty minutes. Only now could she summon the strength to take his call.

'Sorry not to have called earlier. But yesterday I was attacked and had to go to hospital.'

'Oh.' Alina couldn't say more than this for the time being. She was still in shock from the events at Wittenbergplatz underground station. Right now she was walking home down Kurfürstendamm towards Uhlandstrasse, the driving rain lashing her face almost horizontally.

'Did you find Feline?' Alina forced herself to ask, even though she wanted to hang up. Not because she wasn't keenly interested. Nor because she was still worried that contact with Zorbach was poisoning her mind. But because she was on the verge of a nervous breakdown, and didn't want to collapse here and now on Kurfürstendamm in the pouring rain.

'No idea,' Zorbach answered cryptically. 'And if so, I can't be sure she's still alive.'

'I don't understand. Did you find her or didn't you?'

This question was the trigger for a lengthy monologue, by the end of which Alina had made it one block further to Fasanenstrasse. Now she knew all about Zorbach's night-time excursion to the Ambrosia-Resort by Schwielowsee, his discovery of a girl who was clearly suffering in a hut by the lake, and his concussion.

'Stoya is there at the moment, speaking to the woman who's allegedly the hotel manager,' he said, concluding his remarks. 'A diplomat, apparently. The entire property is sovereign territory, it seems, which it why it's going to take a while to get a search warrant.'

'What a pain in the arse,' Alina said.

Six words too many.

She'd tried to sound as normal as possible, but at the end of her sentence her voice had cracked.

'Alina?' Zorbach said, alarmed. The concussion hadn't made him lose his intuition. 'What happened?'

'Nothing.'

'Don't lie to me.'

She sniffed and wiped the rain from the glasses she couldn't see through anyway. 'I was attacked too,' she said. 'TomTom...'

Her throat constricted. For fuck's sake, no. Alina didn't want to cry now. Didn't want her hands to tremble so badly. She had trouble keeping the phone to her ear as she walked. She was used to being strong – a woman who, although blind, had found her way in the world better than many sighted people. And now she was a nervous wreck.

'What about him?'

She looked at the lead in her hand and sobbed. 'He was kicked in front of a train by a madman.'

'Is he dead?'

She exhaled deeply, unable to do anything rational. She couldn't keep walking, couldn't just stand here, couldn't answer. In the end she was startled by an angry bus driver hooting at an SUV to get out of his bus lane.

'I managed to get hold of his lead at the last moment and pull him up.'

*Jesus. So close.*

Alina bent down and patted the back of TomTom's soaked head. He joyfully licked at her hand.

'Thank God,' Zorbach said, breathing a sigh of relief. 'Did anything happen to you?'

She too felt a burden fall from her shoulders. As if she'd confessed something to Zorbach. 'No, I'm fine. Both of us are. We're unharmed. I'm just in a complete tizzy. I mean, the madman was already gunning for me on the train. First he nicked my phone.'

'The one you're calling me on now?'

She nodded so vigorously that her wig almost slipped. It didn't stay in place so well when it was wet.

'That's the weird thing. He gave it back to me.'

'Your phone? After kicking TomTom onto the tracks?'

Zorbach sounded bewildered. Understandably so. She couldn't make head or tail of it either; all she could do was speculate.

'Are you saying that your attacker first kicked TomTom onto the tracks and then disappeared into the crowd?' he said.

'Yes.'

'Sounds like a psychopath.'

*Or like a performance.*

'I can't be sure, but I think the guy wanted to lure me out of the underground. Unsettle me.'

Her strength seemed to return with every step that took her closer to Lietzenburger Strasse. TomTom too pulled on the lead, as if his near-death experience had filled him with new zest for action. But probably he just wanted to get out of the wet and into the warmth.

'Do you think he knows you?' Zorbach asked. 'Maybe it's got something to do with our case.'

'Your case,' she corrected him. 'I don't know, but maybe I found something out that could help you in your search for Feline.' That was the only reason she'd answered the phone; she'd ignored all the other callers who'd tried to contact her in the meantime.

'What?'

'I'll tell you when you pick me up. How quickly can you get here?'

# 19

## NILS

The phone rang at kilometre number forty-eight, speed fourteen and incline four. Nils took the incoming call by gently pressing the right earpiece without interrupting his training programme.

'Could I speak to Frau Gregoriev?'

'Who is this?'

'Dr Rej, I'm—'

'Alina's therapist. Yes, I know.'

Nils focused on the eastern tower of Ludwig Kirche, of which he had a magnificent view from the treadmill through the tinted panorama window. His pulse was unchanged at 110; he was breathing more easily than his friend Timo did during his evening stroll. But Timo's BMI was thirty-one, unlike Nils's, which came in at just under twenty-one.

'She's told you about our sessions, then,' the psychiatrist said.

*Not directly.*

Alina had been very tight-lipped about her therapy since

the eye operation, but Nils had done his research into the therapist. He'd also accompanied her to the first session in Bleibtreustrasse.

'Why are you calling me on my mobile, doctor?'

'I can't get hold of your fiancée. She gave me your number for emergencies.'

'Emergencies?'

Nils wondered whether he should slow down, but he maintained the pace for the time being.

'I'd prefer to talk to my patient personally.'

'Fine. This evening I'll tell her you called.'

'I fear it can't wait that long.'

'That sounds rather dramatic. Should I be worried?'

'I don't know.'

Somewhat reluctantly, Nils now activated the cool-down phase. 'I'm sure you understand that I can't just hang up and continue with my day, Dr Rej. What is this emergency you're talking about?'

'I think I had a break-in.'

'Oh dear.'

'Yesterday. I can't be sure, but I have good reason to believe that someone broke into my practice while I was deliberately trapped in the lift.'

'I'm very sorry to hear that, but I don't understand what it's got to—'

The treadmill droned as the incline came down one level.

'It happened just before my appointment with her. When I was finally freed after an hour I found scratches on the lock to my door and I got the feeling...' The doctor hesitated.

'What sort of feeling?'

'Well, your fiancée always sits on a particular spot on

the couch. She arranges the cushions, which are only there for decoration, behind her back. After she gets up they're crumpled in a very particular way. And when I entered my practice yesterday, they looked exactly as they do after she's spent a session with me.'

'Are you insinuating that Alina broke into your office?'

The psychiatrist cleared his throat. 'No, God forbid. It's more that I'm worried about her. I don't think the intruder molested Frau Gregoriev in my practice. All I'm saying is that, if he broke in and then opened the door to her, because of her impaired vision she might—'

'I know what you're getting at. But Alina's fine. She came back home safe and sound yesterday, and in good spirits.'

'So she told you the session didn't take place because I wasn't there?'

*No, she didn't say anything. But...*

'Yes, of course...' Nils lied.

'I'm pleased to hear she's okay. I'm just wondering whether Frau Gregoriev might have bumped into anyone on the stairs or in the lift?'

*No, she didn't say anything... But she came home with this Zorbach guy in tow.*

'She didn't mention anything out of the ordinary, but I can ask Alina when she comes back.'

'Please do that. If she did see anything I might go to the police after all. Even though nothing was taken.'

'There was no robbery?' Nils stopped the cool-down, but remained on the treadmill.

'No, that's the weird thing,' Rej said. 'In fact it's what I find most unsettling about it all. But, oh well, I'll be expecting your fiancée at three o'clock tomorrow afternoon.'

Dr Rej sounded as if he wanted to finish the call.

'Oh, didn't you get the email?' Nils said.

'What email?' The psychiatrist sounded alarmed.

'Alina doesn't want to continue her treatment with you.'

A pause. This news seemed to have tied Dr Rej's vocal cords into a knot, and it took him some effort to disentangle them.

'What? I, er, um… No, she hasn't, er, said anything to me about this. And, like I said, we didn't talk yesterday.'

Nils picked up his mobile, which was connected to his Bluetooth headphones, and the towel he'd laid over the handle of the treadmill.

'Then please check your spam folder, Dr Rej. So far as I'm aware Alina was going to write to you. She's got too much on her plate at the moment and wants to get over the physical side of the operation first before she addresses the psychological consequences.'

'That might sound reasonable, but I think it's a mistake.'

'Perhaps, but it's her decision.'

Nils heard the lift opening at the entrance to the apartment, then TomTom panting, followed by footsteps. His voice lowered, Nils said, 'I've got to go. She'll get back in touch when she wants to continue the therapy.'

He hung up before Alina appeared at the glass door. TomTom had presumably headed for his usual place beside the sofa and let his mistress enter the fitness room on her own. She appeared slightly out of breath and from the colour of her face it looked as if she'd taken the stairs rather than the lift.

'Who was that?' she asked. Alina wasn't normally so nosy, but she knew that Nils rarely interrupted his fitness routine to take a phone call, so it must have been something important.

'Your psychiatrist. Are you alright? You look the worse for wear.'

Pale. Her eyes sat deeper in their sockets than usual.

'Yes, everything's fine,' she said. He got the impression she was being evasive. 'I'm just completely drenched. What did Rej want?'

Nils wandered over to a water dispenser beside the weights bench and filled a cardboard cup with chilled water.

'Oh, he wanted to tell you himself, but he couldn't get through to you.'

'*What* did he want to tell me?'

Alina's mobile rang, interrupting their conversation.

'Go on, answer it!' Nils said.

She shook her head. 'That was just the signal that he's here.'

'Who?'

'Zorbach. I've got to go again.'

'I see.' Nils scrunched up the cup and tossed it into a bin beside the door. 'You've only just got back.'

'Only to fetch something.' Alina came and gave him a peck on the cheek. 'It won't take long, trust me,' she said.

He cocked his head, wondering whether to ask what had so rattled Alina that her face couldn't hide the unease, but it wasn't going to stop her from leaving the apartment again in this godawful weather. With a man she was connected to by something he didn't understand. Her time with Zorbach had left her with visible physical scars as well as the psychological ones.

'We'll talk as soon as I'm back. In the meantime would

you give TomTom one of his favourite treats? He's deserved it,' she said as he followed her into the study they shared, where she took the box with the bits and bobs from the bottom shelf.

'Oh, and you still haven't told me what Rej wanted.' She lifted off the cardboard lid and began searching for something.

'Oh, yes. I'm sorry, he wanted to tell you himself.'

'What?' She took something from the bottom of the box; he couldn't make out what.

'That you shouldn't go to see him any more.'

'I'm sorry?' she said, perplexed.

Nils sighed. 'I'm sorry, Alina, I don't understand it either, but he doesn't want to treat you any more. You need to find yourself a different psychiatrist.'

## 20

### ZORBACH

I was pleased the drive was over. The cool air outside felt good and for a moment allowed me to take deep breaths without feeling that I had to take an ibuprofen with each inhalation. In the car I'd had a throbbing headache and asked Alina to turn down the volume of the songs on Feline's playlist before my eyes filled with tears.

The blow that knocked me out yesterday wasn't particularly hard. In the past it wouldn't have made me lose consciousness; I might have even stayed on my feet. It certainly wouldn't have put me in an MRI scanner. But ever since I'd tried to take my life two years ago by slotting a bullet in my head, some days my skull felt like it was bursting if I just scratched the spot where the exit wound had been.

The doctors thought it a miracle that I'd managed to aim the gun so the bullet didn't damage any essential areas of my brain. But it was pure chance. The Eye Collector hadn't given me a choice; I had to commit suicide so my son could live.

'What exactly are you planning?' I asked Alina.

'Wait,' she said, leaving my question unanswered, and so I rang the bell without knowing what we were actually doing here at Feline's parents'. We had at least telephoned in advance, which meant that Emilia Jagow wasn't surprised when she opened the door. Only the bandage I had around my head made her eyebrows twitch briefly.

She let us in with the words: 'My husband's at a parents' evening.'

The interior of the bungalow looked strangely unlived in, its key feature being what was missing from a normal family house. There was no jumble of keys on the key rack; there were no letters in the wicker basket, no shoes on the drip tray, no fingerprints on the white surfaces of the fitted cupboards. And of course no hats, scarves or even coats on the coat stand.

No mess, nothing to upset the eye. Only Emilia, in her faded apron, looked out of place in this excessively tidy environment. Her hair was straggly, her fingernails cracked, while a cold sore on her lip had won its battle with the concealer.

'Would you mind wearing these?' she asked, her eyes on our shoes that we'd already wiped thoroughly on the mat. She handed us some green overshoes like I'd seen in operating theatres. 'I got these from work,' she said.

'No problem.'

I was going to help Alina, but she scowled at me and put them on herself.

We followed Emilia into the sitting room, our feet rustling. She was wearing hotel slippers.

'It's nice here,' I lied. Although the dark furniture wasn't to my taste, at least the chunky leather sofa went with the massive coffee table and the huge wall of built-in cupboards. But even someone like Alina, who wasn't able to make any visual comparisons, couldn't feel cosy here on a sofa covered with a milky plastic sheet.

*Obsession with cleanliness?* I ventured a diagnosis in my mind.

After Alina and I sat down next to each other, I allowed my gaze to wander. From the freshly hoovered grey carpet and the gleaming black piano, to the meticulously cleaned windows that led out into the back garden. Nowhere could I find a blemish that would have excited an eye scouring the room for signs of dirt.

'Do you have a cleaning lady?' I asked as innocently as possible.

'No.' Emilia, who'd sat in a chair opposite us, shook her head. 'It looks dreadful here, doesn't it?'

'On the contrary. I'm asking because everything's so tidy.'

*Almost clinically clean.*

'That's what I'm saying. It's not a home; there's nothing cosy about it. We're not allowed to leave anything lying around. Since Thomas cleared away Feline's photos we haven't had anything personal on the shelves.'

Emilia had adopted the typical posture of an insecure girl: knees pressed tightly together, shoulders hunched forwards, hands clasped in prayer in her lap.

'Sometimes I wonder if Feline simply ran away from home because she couldn't put up with Thomas's perfectionism any longer.'

'It's his wish that everything's so tidy here, is it?' I asked.

She looked at me. 'Wish? He flips out when he sees the

tiniest speck of dust. Look at the books on the shelf. Not only are they ordered alphabetically, but I have to adjust the spines with a spirit level.'

Alina shook her head. 'You must spend day and night just cleaning the place, Emilia!'

'Me, less. My husband does most of it. He's the pedant who can't stand the slightest mess. Before Feline was kidnapped he even power-hosed the path outside several times a day. And that was in autumn!'

I was briefly confused when Alina and Emilia called each other by their first names, but then I remembered that they knew each other from Feline's physiotherapy at Friedberg hospital.

Emilia gave me a sad smile. 'You must be wondering how I can put up being married to a man like that. But he's not a bad person. On the contrary, he's the love of my life. I was twenty-eight when I met him and on the verge of chucking in my anaesthesia care training. I was so shy, insecure and pessimistic. And he...' – now the smile was dreamy – '... Thomas built me up, gave me confidence and drove me to college himself to make sure I didn't bunk off.'

She couldn't know this, but Emilia's words had literally struck a chord inside me or, more accurately, an entire song. In 'Silver Lining' from Feline's playlist, Tom Walker sang almost uncannily about the beginning of Emilia's and Thomas's relationship: *I'm the glass half empty, darling, you're the glass half full. I'm twenty-eight years old and you're still taking me to school.'*

While I pondered whether this could be a coincidence, Emilia said gloomily, 'Since then our relationship has flipped and now I'm the stronger of us two. Thomas, on the other hand, has become more and more insecure over the years. The world out there drives him crazy. The chaos, as he calls it. Rude pupils, complaining parents, violence in the playground. Hostility online – everyone judging everyone else, even the teachers are being rated these days. He wants our house to be the perfect refuge where nothing is tainted.'

I couldn't help but think wistfully of my houseboat.

'That's why we don't have a TV and only one computer with an internet connection. It's in the study where Feline does her homework. Thomas doesn't want to stop her having fun, but nor does he want her to get access to bad news.'

'Was it his decision for Feline to go to his school?' I asked.

Emilia nodded. 'He wanted her to be nearby. I always saw it as a sign of his love…'

*Or of his obsessive-compulsive disorder.*

But could a father eager to monitor every move his daughter made be involved in her abduction? Unlikely. Unless there had been some tragic accident that Thomas was trying to cover up.

'When will he be back from the parents' evening?' Alina asked.

'No idea. Thomas said he might be late.'

Eyeing my head bandage suspiciously, Emilia asked, 'Have your investigations turned up anything new, Herr Zorbach?'

I nodded and tried to outline what had happened at the Ambrosia-Resort without upsetting her. Unsuccessfully.

'You left Feline there?' she cried in disbelief, leaping to her feet.

I attempted to placate her. 'We don't know if it really was Feline.'

'Where is it?' Emilia said, asking the only question relevant in this situation. 'I have to go there.'

God, I could understand this impulse. I remembered my own helplessness when Julian was kidnapped and I was desperate to do something merely because I couldn't put up with my inaction.

'And suffer the same fate as Zorbach?' Alina asked. I instinctively touched my bandage. 'What do you expect to achieve there?'

'Alina's right,' I said. 'As I said, it's diplomatic territory. There are cameras everywhere and probably other alarm systems too. Besides, it's a huge area and we've no idea where to start looking.'

'But you found the hut?'

'It was demolished first thing this morning. The MP3 signal has gone dead.'

Over the phone Stoya had filled me in about his visit to Lieberstett.

'Good God,' Emilia said, slapping her hand over her mouth.

'We think Ambrosia's a sort of women's refuge where they only take in victims of serious violence,' I explained. 'Hence the security.'

And the attack on me. They probably thought I was a husband stalking his wife who'd sought protection at Ambrosia.

'So, what now?' Emilia's eyes turned to Alina, who clearly sensed she was the one being addressed. 'What can we do?'

'I don't have a plan, Emilia. But I do have a hunch,' she said, making me as curious as Feline's mother.

'A hunch?'

Alina got up, took off her glasses and said, 'Yes. And to confirm it I need to take a look at your daughter's room!'

## 21

## ALINA

*It's so futile,* Alina cursed to herself, desperate to howl as she entered Feline's room because she felt so helpless. No matter how hard she tried, she couldn't identify the individual items of furniture precisely. What might have been a bed, table, cupboard or chair were mere shapeless shadows to her. The only way she could tell they were furniture was that they weren't moving. Unlike Emilia beside her.

'Are you looking for anything in particular?'

When Alina turned to her she almost gasped, finding herself face to face with someone so abysmally ugly. She knew she was certainly being unfair on Emilia, whose features might be symmetrical to eyes trained since childhood. To Alina, however, she looked like a monster, especially when she opened her mouth to speak.

'The police already looked at everything in here,' Emilia said, and Alina had to turn away because the woman's hand movements were making her nervous.

*How ludicrous of me to think I could use my eyes to confirm my hunch!*

Although so far she'd managed to refuse Zorbach's help, she needed it now.

'Notice anything?' she said.

'If you tell me what you're searching for I might be of more help,' Zorbach said.

'Look for something that's missing.'

'I can tell you that,' Emilia replied. 'What's missing is the usual girly stuff. Even in here Thomas makes sure nothing's left lying around and that the bed's made like in the army.'

A shadow from Emilia's body, presumably her arm, pointed to another long shadow, presumably the bed.

'He didn't want Feline to waste her time with make-up or music instead of learning. He let her have books, of course. But no pictures of pop stars or anything like that on the walls. The only thing he allowed was this – because he's a physics and geography teacher.'

All Alina could see was a patch on the wall to her left, but when Zorbach read the title of the poster she could imagine what it depicted: 'My very educated mother just showed us nothing.'

'Mercury, Venus, Earth, Mars, Jupiter, Saturn, Uranus and Neptune!' Alina said. She knew the mnemonic for remembering the sequence of the eight planets in the Solar System. The initial letters of the words in the sentence stood for the initial letters of the celestial bodies.

'I thought it went, "My very educated mother just showed us *nine planets*",' Zorbach said.

'That was until Pluto lost its status as a planet, partly because it's too small,' Emilia said, seemingly happy for the discussion to move away from what might have happened to her daughter.

But Alina didn't let this emotional breather last long. 'Feline told me her chest had a secret compartment,' she said.

'Do you mean her old wooden box?'

Alina saw Emilia's shadow move towards the window and open a chest-like object.

'She uses it as a seat. But a secret compartment?'

'What's inside?' Alina asked.

'Nothing the police would have thought relevant.'

Zorbach, whose shadow also bent over the chest beside Emilia's, was more specific: 'Pens, expired passes and IDs, ballet and youth games certificates, a photo album, another one. Old copies of *Bravo*.'

'Take everything out,' Alina said, asking Emilia to remove the bottom of the chest.

'I didn't know anything about this,' the bewildered mother said, opening up the secret compartment where Feline had stored her 'treasures', something she'd revealed during one of her therapy sessions.

'Do you see her MP3 player?'

'What player?' Emilia asked.

Feline must have kept it secret from her mother too.

Alina explained all about the watch and why she'd given Feline the MP3 player.

'I didn't know about that either,' Emilia said sadly. 'And obviously Thomas didn't, or he'd have taken it away from her.'

There was a hint of self-recrimination in Emilia's voice. Not for the first time she must be wondering to what extent her husband's controlling nature had alienated their daughter.

'No, there's no MP3 player here. Just this.'

Emilia bent over the chest again and took out something that Alina couldn't describe or compare to anything else, simply because she'd never seen anything like it in her life.

Although she could make out a chunky, greyish-green object, she had to touch it to really understand its significance.

'A cassette recorder?' Zorbach said as Alina held the handle of the ancient device, which must have been for children to listen to stories on, and ran her other hand over the lid.

Then she placed the recorder on a surface she assumed was a desk.

'Could you put this in for me?' she asked. Zorbach pre-empted Emilia by grabbing from Alina's hand the cassette she'd picked up from the box in the study when she'd popped by Nils's apartment earlier. Without further ado he pressed play and Feline's voice filled the room.

## 22

*'Hey, Alina. Thanks for giving me your MP3 player.
I really don't mind that the watch has a fault. As you
know, I don't have my own Wi-Fi at home and I'm no
technological expert. So it's really cool you've helped
me put together a playlist. I told you I've got unusual
musical tastes for someone of my age. I might be the
biggest—'*

The recording broke off abruptly because Emilia, or the
shadow that Alina took to be her, had pressed Stop.

Emilia cleared her throat. Where she guessed Feline's
mother's eyes to be Alina saw something shining silver.
When she realised Emilia had started to cry silently, she
closed her eyes.

'I'm sorry, hearing her voice was... was just so
unexpected.'

'No, *I'm* sorry,' Alina countered, ashamed at her
insensitivity and having played the cassette without warning.

'Where did you get this recording?' Emilia asked.

'Feline gave me the names of fifteen albums and around forty individual songs. As I obviously wasn't able to read her handwriting, she read out the titles and artists on this cassette. I kept it because I found her choice so particular. In the end her requested playlist ran to more than two hundred songs.'

She passed Emilia her mobile phone, which had a screenshot of Feline's playlist.

'Eyelids?' Feline's mother said.

'That's what I called the playlist. You can't edit text on the MP3 player I gave your daughter – that's how it's faulty. So Feline couldn't change the name of the playlist, but she could choose other songs. And that's what she must have done.'

Her voice hushed, Emilia read out the names of the artists from the mobile phone:

'Majan, Namika, Lotte, Kool Savas, Justin Jesso, Rea Garvey, Tom Walker, Joris, Charlotte Jane, Silbermond, Alle Farben with Hanne Mjøen, Johannes Oerding, Beth Ditto, Tim Bendzko, VIZE with R4GE and Emie.'

'Okay, so Feline has put together a new playlist,' Zorbach said. 'But it's not unusual for a young girl's tastes to change.'

'No, it isn't,' Alina said. 'But while she's being held captive? I checked: the playlist was last updated two days ago.'

'And you think she's trying to tell us something with her choice of titles?' In Zorbach's mind the penny seemed to be dropping.

'If she is, then it's definitely with the songs she *hasn't* chosen. I mean, there are only fifteen left. And a very particular one is missing...'

'Which one?' Zorbach and Emilia asked as if of one voice.

'Listen for yourselves,' Alina said.

She closed her eyes and pressed the Play button. Feline's bright voice rang out once more:

*'I might be the biggest Depeche Mode fan in Berlin even though I don't own a single one of their albums. Could you upload as much of their stuff as possible? I don't care what. Actually, wait! My absolute favourite Depeche Mode song is "World in My Eyes". I absolutely have to have that one.'* Feline giggled in anticipation at her joke, which at the time of the recording she couldn't have known would become deadly serious: *'If that song ever disappears from my playlist, Alina, then you'll know I'm in big trouble.'*

# 23

Alina asked Zorbach to stop the recording before Feline began listing the albums and songs she'd wanted.

For a while there was nothing but silence in the girl's bedroom, eventually broken by Emilia.

'But… but that might mean that Feline's still alive?' she said with the hope of a mother clutching at the faintest of straws. 'She must be where you were yesterday, Herr Zorbach. We've got to go there!'

Alina decided not to object. What use would it be for her to point out that another person could have modified the playlist? That it was more likely that someone else had the watch now rather than Feline having internet access to stream songs while she was locked up?

'It could be a message,' she said. 'But it might also be a trap. Or a warning. Before we go rushing back to the Ambrosia-Resort we have to consider all the possibilities. So let's assume Feline is trying to send us a message. Via the choice of songs or the artists. Or the content of the songs. Perhaps it's her only way of being able to communicate with the outside world. That's why I'm here, Emilia. To ask, given what I've said, if anything strikes you when you take a look at Feline's playlist.'

The mother sniffed and snuffled. The shadow was probably shaking its head. 'I'm sorry. Besides the horror of her disappearance, it's terrible to have to face the truth of how badly I know my own daughter. I didn't even know that Depeche Mode is her favourite band.'

'It's not typical for a girl of her age. Don't beat yourself up about it, just concentrate. Is there anything in these songs that stands out?'

'Maybe, yes.' Emilia cleared her throat, but still sounded hoarse. '"Rose".'

'Track 6. By Rea Garvey. What about it?'

'When Feline was little we had an Irish au pair girl. She was besotted with Feli and always said things like, "One day you're going to blossom like an Irish rose."'

In her mind Alina heard the chorus from Rea Garvey's hit: *'She's like a wild, wild Irish rose.'*

'Hence her nickname: Rose. It's what we called her till she started secondary school and Thomas thought it was too childish.'

'I see,' Alina said, excited. This was more than a sign. Maybe it was a first real hint that Feline was still alive: nobody else could know the significance of these lyrics. On the other hand, she didn't want to think too hard about the second line of the chorus: *'She leaves a trail of death wherever she goes.'*

'Anything else that catches your attention?' Alina asked the mother.

'I hate to interrupt,' said Zorbach, who'd been

remarkably quiet. Alina thought he'd been mulling over Feline's potential hidden messages in the playlist, but now it looked as if he'd been on his mobile, if that's what was in his hand.

'Your husband's parents' evening is at his school, right?' he asked Emilia. There was more than just impatience in his voice; he sounded alarmed.

'In Grunewald?' Emilia replied interrogatively. Zorbach cursed to himself.

Then he said, 'In that case I fear your husband's been lying to you. He's definitely not there.'

# 24

## ZORBACH

'You've bugged him?'

Alina put the glasses back on when she got into the passenger seat.

'Tracking him. GPS,' I replied as we belted up.

It was the first thing I did after promising to help Emilia when she visited me on my houseboat. Even before setting out to find Alina, I drove to the school car park and fixed the transmitter beneath the rear right wheelhouse of Thomas's black Golf.

'So where are we going now?'

Even though Alina couldn't see it, I pointed to the screen of my mobile, which I'd wedged into the dashboard. 'Right now Thomas is heading east in his car through Wedding.'

Alina harrumphed disapprovingly, as I manoeuvred out of the parking space outside the Jagows' house. 'Where's he going?'

'Not to his school in Grunewald, that's for sure.'

Feline's father was just passing Osloer Strasse underground station.

'I could take you home,' I offered.

To Nils's.

'And let Thomas slip through our fingers?'

She said *our*. And from the tone of her voice I could tell that her fighting spirit had been stirred. It was sad that this alone was sufficient to lighten my gloomy mood.

'I've got him on the monitor,' I said. 'He won't get away.'

'But maybe you won't be there when he stops.'

*Point for you.*

'Okay, let's start the pursuit,' I said, glancing at the temperature: six degrees. On account of the fresh wind and drizzle I'd thought it was colder when we left the bungalow. As soon as we got to the A115 slip road I had to switch on the windscreen wipers.

Soon afterwards I was driving my Volvo alongside the sound barriers that weren't adequate to shield the well-heeled residents of Schlachtensee from the racket made by my dilapidated exhaust. Nor from the roar of the lorry behind. It was beyond me why anyone would shell out millions for a villa, only to spend their lives under smog next to the city motorway and with a view of a grey concrete wall. But who was I to criticise other people's lifestyles? Maybe the families behind this wall were enjoying supper together and looking forward to a game of Monopoly in front of the fire, while I drove through the cold night, shadowing a man whose daughter had disappeared, instead of spending my last few hours of freedom with my son.

Lost in thought, it didn't occur to me as I sped along the quiet motorway that Alina and I hadn't said a word to each other for several minutes. I hadn't even noticed that she'd put the earphones in and was listening to music via her mobile.

'Feline's playlist?' I asked her.

'Hmm?'

She took out one earphone.

'The music. Is that from Feline's MP3 player?'

Alina nodded.

'You think she's sending us a secret message with her selection.'

'You heard what she said.'

*If that song ever disappears from my playlist, Alina, then you'll know I'm in big trouble.*

'Okay, let's go through the fifteen songs on her playlist again. What else stands out?'

'They're new. None of these songs was on the original list,' she remarked.

We headed north when we got to the International Congress Center. The traffic was heavier now and I no longer had to keep an eye on the speedometer, as we'd slowed to a crawl.

'Lots of German artists,' Alina added.

Although I'd heard of the names of all the musicians and bands, I wasn't sure of the songs so I asked Alina to play extracts from them all. She disconnected the earphones, turned up the volume and moved on from each track after just a few bars, like an impatient teenager searching for the right Netflix film.

'Any idea what significance this selection might have?' I asked at the end, then cursed because I'd almost taken the Tegel airport turn-off rather than continuing along the A100 to Westhafen.

'I'm struck by how many of the songs are about prison or something like that. Lotte, for example, sings about walls and a maze you can't get out of, while Johannes Oerding sings about a place beneath the world where no light comes in.'

*Which in the worst-case scenario could be a grave.*

'A place that's somewhere *below*,' I added, referring to Justin Jesso's 'Under'. 'And what I find remarkable is that the playlist may have changed, but the title "Eyelids" is still quite apt.'

'What do you mean?'

'The lyrics are very visual, not just in Johannes Oerding's song. "I see you, even though it's pitch black,"' I said, quoting Silbermond. 'In "Erlking", Kool Savas raps, "I see you, but I can't see you." Or, "Can't make out who you are even when I look." Tim Bendzko even has "Open Eyes" in the title.'

Alina nodded. 'But what's it telling us?'

I pondered this. These could all be hidden clues relating to her kidnapper, who only revealed themself to Feline in the darkness. In a mask. Here my imagination might have been playing a trick on me, turning wishful thinking into the truth. There were dozens of possible interpretations, particularly of the Kool Savas song, the fourth in the playlist, which I could twist to match my situation and emotional state. For example, on the first hearing of 'Erlking' I couldn't help thinking of my former mentee Frank Lahmann: *'I opened doors for you, even before you thought about becoming someone.'* That's how I felt when I wrongly believed that Frank had betrayed, used and tricked me. *'You act the nice guy, who everybody likes.'* In fact it was the Eye Collector who murdered my wife, abducted Julian and tried to kill me. A line from Kool Savas fitted the bill: *'When the mask cracks I see the real man. It's all eyewash like a sleight of hand.'*

My head was spinning. I had to stop analysing the lyrics for the moment and focus on another question to get my thoughts back in order.

'Maybe we should take a step back,' I said to Alina. 'Let's assume Feline has sent out a musical SOS. How did she do it?'

'Do you mean how was she able to keep the MP3 player hidden the whole time?'

I nodded.

'She managed to hoodwink her father. After all, it looks like a watch.'

'Okay, but how come she has internet access?' I asked.

'If her kidnapper didn't know about the MP3 player, then maybe they'd have no reason to turn off the Wi-Fi,' Alina speculated.

I shook my head. 'It's all too implausible. That scenario means Feline must have been kidnapped, she must still be alive, she must have hidden the MP3 player and she must have cracked the password of her abductor's router. Or got access to a computer connected to the internet and used it to rework her playlist.'

'That's one thing we can definitely rule out,' Alina said promptly.

'Why?'

'Because then she could have sent us a message or at least changed the playlist's title. But it's still called "Eyelids", which shows that Feline must have modified the list with the watch. Because that's the problem with the scratched display: you can change an existing playlist – delete or add new songs – but you can't put together new playlists or change the title.'

I agreed with her as I braked fairly sharply; the traffic had thinned out and I'd been driving much too quickly.

'As for the Wi-Fi password, she might have been near an open, unsecured network when she changed the songs. I mean, these days every other café advertises its free hotspot. Maybe she's being held above a Starbucks, or in a hotel,' Alina said, alluding to the Ambrosia-Resort.

'We're getting lost in speculation here,' I said.

Alina sighed. 'You may be right, Alex. I'm probably just wasting my time and we should wait for the search warrant for that diplomat's crude sanatorium. But I feel responsible for Feline somehow. I don't want to give up hope just like that. Isn't it better to analyse the playlist rather than simply wait?'

'But we're not waiting. Besides the playlist, we have a very promising, concrete lead. And one that's just changed course.'

'What do you mean?'

Again I instinctively pointed at the screen of my mobile. Once upon a time Alina had made me realise how we sighted people assume that others are able to interpret gestures and facial expressions. And how we take our sight for granted when we just nod or shake our heads in response to a question.

'Thomas Jagow has turned around,' I said. 'When we were listening to Feline's playlist he briefly stopped at the junction of Bornholmer Strasse and Schönhauser Allee.

Now he appears to be going back in the direction of where he came from.'

'Back home?'

'Maybe,' I said, turning right at Seestrasse to stop. Jagow did indeed seem to be on his way back (from wherever he'd been). When I was certain he was coming our way, I moved to a parking spot on the other side of the road so we could tail him as soon as he passed us. Twenty minutes later – we'd now been on the road for almost an hour – it happened. Feline's father, who till now I'd only seen in the newspapers and pictures Emilia had given me, drove past, looking tense and hunched. I let him pass through one set of lights before pulling out.

Exactly one set of lights too late.

# 25

One phase of lights. A mere three minutes, during which a police motorbike escort drove past and blocked the junction at Virchow hospital. A high-profile patient must be arriving, or a politician to deliver a lecture in the Charité's auditorium. This cost us a further five minutes. When we were finally able to drive off again, Jagow was several kilometres ahead of us, and I was convinced our pursuit would be fruitless, because until the Spanische Allee turn-off, it looked as if Feline's father really was on his way home. *But then…*

'He's going on,' I said.

'Out of the city?'

'Yes.'

'Potsdam?'

'That direction.'

One of the many things I liked about Alina was her habit of staying silent in stressful situations. Unlike Emilia Jagow she didn't fill the time with unnecessary chatter, but used the lull to think. I could virtually hear her smart brain rattling away like a rickety car on cobblestones. I wondered if she was asking herself the same questions that I was. For example, why I was going after Jagow. Did I really hope he might have something to do with his daughter's disappearance? Did I think I'd be able to solve the case tonight? The fact that he'd lied to his wife about the parents' evening didn't mean he would lead us to his daughter.

*Dead. Or alive.*

Although... the place he chose to next make a stop suggested the former.

Alina asked me to repeat the location of Jagow's Golf, which was at least fifteen minutes away.

'Albrechts Teerofen.'

'A factory?'

'No, that's what the area is called.'

'Never heard of it. Is it still in Berlin?'

'Hard to say,' I replied. 'Officially it's in Wannsee. But Jagow's parking roughly where the wall used to be. Could also be in Teltow.'

Alina scratched her neck in the place where part of a strangely drawn tattoo flashed above the collar of her sweatshirt. An ambigram: a word picture that had a different meaning depending on the angle it was seen from, if you were able to glimpse the tattoo in its entirety. I had been granted a view of it on that one and only night when Alina and I had been intimate on my houseboat. More an act of desperation rather than desire; both of us, after all, had just narrowly escaped death. If you stood facing Alina, the tattoo read 'luck'. But when I embraced her from behind on that occasion and glanced over her shoulder, the tattoo transformed into the word 'fate' before my eyes.

*Luck or fate?*

This question, which defined Alina's life like no other, was etched into her skin forever.

**LUCK**

**FATE**

Was it chance that we'd met, a stroke of luck, or had fate determined that once again we should be in pursuit of a suspect as we searched for a missing child?

'Okay, we know that Thomas Jagow definitely wasn't at a parents' evening,' Alina said. 'But he could be meeting colleagues for a drink afterwards, couldn't he?'

'Unlikely.'

'Why do you say that?'

'Hold on a sec,' I said, and again we spent the next few minutes side by side in silence as we drove down an unlit track parallel to a canal, which got ever narrower until it came to a dead end and we had to stop.

'Tell me what you can see!' Alina begged after we got out. She stretched after the long drive – almost one and a half hours – which had taken us to an unpleasant wasteland. I cupped my hands and blew warm air into them. Out here it was couple of degrees colder than in Nikolassee, itself one of the chilliest districts of Berlin with its sparse population and large proportion of woodland and lakes.

'We're parked right below the motorway bridge,' I told her softly. According to the GPS, Thomas's car was still a few hundred metres away, but because the receiver wasn't that precise, he might be closer and I simply couldn't see him in the darkness.

'The bridge is on huge, graffitied concrete pillars. The road crosses the canal at least thirty metres above our heads.'

'So why can't I hear any tyres or engines?' Alina said, also in hushed tones.

'Because they shut the bridge after reunification.'

'Okay, what else is here?'

'All manner of things. In front of us is a wood. To our right, beneath the former motorway bridge, are garages. Judging by the sign, cars used to be repaired here.'

'*Used* to be?'

'Looks empty and abandoned, though it's hard to tell in the dark.'

It felt as if we were far from civilisation. All I could see was what my headlights lit up: a number of huts with flat roofs beyond the pillars.

'No one works here any more.' Before us lay a vandal's paradise. 'All the windows are smashed and the building's missing half its roof. Come on.'

I took Alina by the hand – this time she didn't resist – and led her closer to the garages, avoiding mountains of scrap and rubbish. Besides wrecks of cars there were heaps of old batteries, rolls of cable and household rubbish spilling from torn bin bags. Screws, broken glass and empty beer cans dug into the soles of our shoes, slowing our progress.

'It's so dark out here you could take off your glasses, Alina.'

I expected her to say no, but she actually heeded my suggestion, although she kept her eyes closed at first.

'I assume you want to take a look at the garages?' she said.

'The ruins, more like. But yes.' I stopped briefly. 'Would you like to stay here till I come back? If there's as much crap inside as there is out here, I—'

'Shhhh!' she said, raising her hand.

'What is it?' I whispered.

'Is that someone crying?'

I'd heard nothing apart from the rustling of the leaves in the trees and of course the ever-present noise of the city, which you never escaped, not even at its margins. Somewhere there was always an engine droning.

But the fact I hadn't detected any human sounds didn't mean anything, for compared to Alina's bat-like sonar hearing I was practically deaf. I did, however, see something that she probably hadn't noticed as quickly as me, even though her eyes were no longer closed.

*A light!*

It had flickered only momentarily, inside the garage closest to us, around twenty metres away.

Like the glow of a mobile phone activated by an incoming call before the owner declines to take it, the light had flared through the only intact window.

And now it was out again.

'What is it?' Alina said, sensing my tension.

Before I could reply, fright gripped her body too when an excruciating cry tore through the night.

*The cry of a baby.*

# 26

The plexiglass door of the garage, dimly illuminated by my headlights, finally came off its hinges.

Before, it had been half hanging on; now it crashed onto me just as I was reaching to open it.

And with the door came the pain. I felt my jaw dislocate, heard it crunch and was sure it was broken, but all of that faded into insignificance when something as hard as an elbow jabbed my liver.

All of a sudden it was bright – only in my mind, obviously; the surges of pain flashed like sheet lightning.

I gasped to draw air into my burning lungs, and was in danger of toppling backwards. Desperate to hold onto something, I grabbed a piece of material. Then an arm, which must be attached to the heavily breathing man who was trying to knock me to the ground. He shook me off and I fell onto some hard rods that once might have belonged to some metal steps or a radiator grille.

I smelled damp earth, tasted blood and forced myself to open my eyes. Between the flashes, now fading, I could see the escaping man had run into Alina too; she was on her knees, coughing and holding her head. Struggling to my feet, I felt my throbbing head and realised that my bandage was now hanging like a scarf around my neck. Then I saw the light.

To my right.

The man had made a mistake, which made me think he had little experience in crime. Although he'd parked the car in one of the darkest spots beneath the decommissioned motorway bridge, he'd forgotten to switch off the courtesy light to prevent it from coming on the moment the door was opened.

The door of a VW Golf. Into which – there was no mistaking him – Thomas Jagow climbed, started the ignition and sped towards the canal, his tyres spinning and squealing.

'Was that him?' Alina asked. As I stared at Feline's father's tail lights she did the sensible thing and wandered slowly up to the garage Thomas had just come from.

'Yes, it was,' I said and got moving too.

I had to clear the door lying by the entrance to the workshop so Alina didn't trip up, having ignored my pleas to stay outside. Although she could probably find her way around these dim surroundings better than me.

In the weak light of my phone's torch I saw a dusty counter; we'd obviously entered the sales area of the former workshop.

I felt a drop on my forehead. In the hope it was only rainwater, I shone the torch at the ceiling. A tangle of cables hung down and an overhead light was half torn off.

'Can you see anything?' Alina said.

I pointed the torch to the right, past a pile of rusty wheel rims.

*Yes. Unfortunately.*

If, somewhere within our brains, there is an archive for terrible, fear-inducing sequences and images that a director of nightmares can access and edit into a film that wrenches us from our sleep, screaming, then this director had just obtained some new, horrific material from my head.

On the floor in front of me I saw something I wished was a perverse art installation. Tasteless, but not real. But the woman sitting half-naked beneath a smashed window did indeed exist. And the baby in her arms was real too. Filthy and defiled, hopefully from the blood dripping onto the infant from the wound in her neck. Hopefully, because the other option would have been even worse: the baby itself bleeding from every pore.

Feeling my legs buckling, I kneeled and put out a hand. My head would not let me go over to them, to the motionless, blood-soaked woman pressing the baby to her bare breast as if feeding it. The child wasn't moving either and had stopped making any sound.

*Didn't I hear it scream? Just after I saw a mobile flash in this ruin of a garage that stinks of rancid oil and iron?*

'Who's there?' Alina asked. She was standing behind me, thank goodness unable to see what I could. In spite of the operation, which I'd never have consented to if there were a risk I'd have to look at something like *that* afterwards.

'Is the baby dead?' she asked, clearly suspecting something of the sort. Maybe she could smell the blood. Or see that the shadow in front of the wall wasn't moving at all.

Edging forwards on my knees, I reached for the woman's

neck, a completely futile undertaking as I could now see from close up.

'Someone's slashed her jugular,' I croaked.

'Her?' Alina said, but I couldn't give an answer.

First I had to know what was wrong with the baby, whose head fitted into my hand and who didn't react when I took it from its dead mother.

# 27

## BECKY

She'd never been inside such a house, nor could she imagine coming somewhere like this of her own free will.

Having said that, she thought 'free will' was an elastic concept in our society. Most people she knew would give up their job tomorrow if they won the lottery. They worked only out of fear, because they had to, because otherwise they couldn't afford their lifestyle. Money replaced free will. This might be a luxury problem for those with qualifications who could pick and choose on the job market. But not for those pitiful creatures who for a mere handful of euros destroyed their body and soul in 'Supermarket 69'.

'What the hell do you want?' asked the bearded face which had appeared in the opened flap. The reinforced pub door was one of the many structural changes the new owner had made. But these were only noticeable close up. From a distance the building near Westkreuz station still looked like the discount supermarket that had gone bust years ago. Fake rust-red bricks, a brown tiled roof and the obligatory car park outside the entrance, its sliding glass doors taped over. The well-known blue sign with the firm's logo was missing, of course. But the car park was as full as the evening before a public holiday.

'I want what everyone does,' she replied to the bearded man, whose eyes gleamed red at her, which might have been down to the lighting inside.

She prayed she wouldn't fall over. Her knees had the consistency of lukewarm jelly and her impaired balance had been getting worse by the second since she'd got out of the car.

'Men only here,' he said through the small flap.

'I *need* men,' she said, which elicited a grin from the doorman.

'Oh, really?'

First the flap shut, then the security door unlocked and swung outwards. She had to take a step back before she could go in.

One step back, two steps forward. So this was the path to hell.

In the gloomy light the man who'd opened the door resembled a bad waxwork copy of an unshaven Donald Trump. The same side parting that looked like a bonnet, baby-pink shimmering eyelids, deep furrows around his nose and a huge body in a poorly fitting blue suit. All that was missing was the red tie, but he was wearing two signet rings that presumably were handy in a fight.

'Welcome to the most awesome supermarket in the word.' He laughed and invited her to go with him. But the first impression of the establishment gave her such a shock that she found it hard to follow the doorman's instructions.

It looked like a discount store inside the multifunctional

building too, although instead of bananas or lettuces in the fruit and veg aisle by the entrance, there were dildos, vibrators and other sex toys.

'You don't need a shopping trolley.' Trump laughed.

Several trolleys – for decoration – were in fact beside the original checkout, where bored-looking topless girls sat. Hardcore porn films were playing on the screens of the electronic tills.

'Hey, I told you to come with me,' Trump said, having already passed the 'fruit and vegetable' section. They turned into an aisle of supermarket shelves, coldly decorated with streamers, naked Greek plaster statues, empty magnums of sparkling wine, and condoms.

The aisle led them into the centre of the former shop, where only the meat counter had survived, including the labelling, which no doubt elicited a wolfish smile from oversexed, misogynistic first-time visitors to this brothel, but only made her feel sad. As did the sight of the stark-naked teenage girls dancing behind the counter to top-forty hits booming from the ceiling speakers.

One of them was even lying in the glass cabinet with a sign between her legs that read: 'Special Offer'.

She noticed how the girls' wandering gaze changed when she appeared on the scene with Trump. Some had been hoping for custom, others dreading it. All of them saw her as a new competitor, which explained the scorn in their eyes.

'Calm down, she's not taking any of your business,' Trump said.

She hurried up, unsettled by the looks she was getting from the men too. These were drinking champagne on plush sofas, some already with 'ladies' they'd picked out on their laps. There must have been ten of them, if not more. Although the dimmed light meant she couldn't see their eyes, she still sensed she was being sized up. A group of young men, all in identical white T-shirts, whistled as she went past. It must be a stag do where the groom-in-waiting was being given one last opportunity to humiliate a prostitute before getting hitched.

'Keep going!'

She followed the doorman through a glitter curtain into the rear of the former supermarket, where a handyman had jerry-built some square pens from sheets of plywood. The boxes were open at the top, which meant you could hear everything going on inside them despite the music blaring. She wanted to cover her ears to block out all the groaning, squealing and grunting, but she was already holding her nose because of the unsavoury smell of sweat and semen.

Trump turned to the left and opened a door that led into a proper office with brick walls and a plastered ceiling. Here he left her alone with a man who at first glance looked shy. Then like a psychopath.

'She's looking for men, Pete,' Trump said to the slightly hunched boss sitting behind a large desk, then closed the door behind him. The longer she looked into the shifty eyes of the tall, thin, bald man, the more the temperature seemed to drop in the office.

'Okay, darling, what exactly is it you're after?' Pete asked, having invited her to sit on the sofa opposite the desk.

She racked her brains for the word of a sexual practice she'd recently read about in a medical journal, one categorised as highly dangerous. When she remembered it she could scarcely believe she'd allowed the word to pass her lips. Then she wasn't sure if Pete knew what she was talking about because he was looking at her in such bewilderment. But when he licked his lips salaciously, she realised he was a master of the language of perversion.

'Why?' he asked her.

'Because it makes me so horny,' she said, wanting to throw up. There was every likelihood this was exactly what she'd do repeatedly once the evening here was over.

'What makes you think we offer something like that?'

'Well, your online slogan is: "Here in the sex supermarket you can buy anything. If we don't have it, it doesn't exist."'

'It's just advertising. You'd be the first person to take that waffle seriously,' Pete said, laughing.

She could smell his coffee-breath, but oddly this didn't make her feel more nauseous. Maybe she was already so panicky that her body was incapable of producing another reaction.

'Alright, then. Trampling. Let's say I could arrange that for you. How would you like it?'

'One man, or even several. Hard.' She swallowed.

'How far can they go?'

'No taboos. There's only one condition: you have to drop me off at this address afterwards.'

She handed him a small piece of paper she'd prepared.

'That's not exactly round the corner,' he said.

'I'll pay well.'

Pete's eyes flashed. 'Five hundred? Cash?'

Nodding, she took out the banknotes that were loose in her trouser pocket. Pete grinned like a mischievous little boy. Maybe he thought she'd been pulling his leg before, but now he was rustling the notes between his fingers he seemed most satisfied with himself and the world.

'Right then,' he said, reaching for the telephone on his desk. 'Slobo? Tell Pali. We'll meet in the old cold store in five minutes. I've got someone with me here who we can stamp the shit out of. A woman, she's just paid. For real. What...? Hold on a sec.' He put the receiver on his shoulder and bent forwards to her. 'What's your name, darling?'

'My...?'

Shit. She was so worked up she'd forgotten her cover name. *Becky*. After her middle name, Rebecca. *Shit*, that's what she'd meant to call herself, but it would only occur to her later. When the men were hitting her so hard she wet herself with pain.

But now, in her panic, she couldn't think of anything apart from her true identity. And so she stammered, 'Emilia. My name is Emilia Jagow.'

# 28

## ZORBACH

'Have you lost the last of your fucking marbles?' Stoya screamed so loudly down the phone that it shook in my hand.

'What's wrong?' I asked innocently, getting out of my car that I'd parked illegally just before the junction of Alt-Moabit and Gotzkowskystrasse.

'Don't play the fool with me. You're fleeing a crime scene?'

With the answer 'I don't know what you're talking about,' I finally pushed my former police colleague over the edge of fury.

'Of course you do.'

I heard voices in the background, car doors closing. Something crunched beneath Stoya's leather soles, from which I inferred that he'd arrived at the crime scene himself and was making use of the time until Forensics had finished to give me hell.

'I'm talking about the dead woman in Albrechts Teerofen and her baby with hypothermia.'

*Thank God.* Breathing a sigh of relief, I stepped under the porch of the apartment block on Gotzkowskybrücke to get out of the drizzle. I almost said, *'So the infant's still alive'*, which would have properly given me away.

I'd wrapped the silent baby, its breathing hardly detectible, in a blanket I'd found in my boot and waited until the ambulance arrived, having watched its flashing lights approach from a distance. When it parked in front of the garages, I handed the torpid baby to Alina, jumped into my car and sped off, which cannot have escaped the notice of the paramedics.

'Don't insult my intelligence!' Stoya barked.

I was about to unlock the front door with the key Alina had given me – but it was already open. Grateful that she'd lent me her former apartment as a bolthole, I wandered past the mailboxes. A few days ago I'd opened the third one from the left, labelled with her name, to get hold of Dr Rej's letter.

'Your girlfriend's already been lying through her teeth. I don't want to hear the same crap from you.' Stoya kept going with his tirade, and me with my lies.

'I haven't seen Alina since yesterday.'

'Oh, how do you know I was referring to Alina?'

'I've only got one girlfriend,' I said. Strictly speaking, that wasn't the truth; in fact I hadn't had a girlfriend ever since she said she didn't want anything to do with me.

'You're not expecting me to believe that a blind woman walks to Albrechts Teerofen and rummages around abandoned garages just for fun, are you?'

'Alina isn't blind any more.'

The sign on the grille door of the ancient lift in the stairwell was probably the bestselling one in Berlin: 'out of order'. So I had to take the stairs, whether I wanted to or not.

'She had a retina transplant.'

'And still she sees less than a mole in a blindfold. Stop taking the piss, Alex! I know full well that you drove out here with Alina. And I can understand you not wanting to spend your last hours before prison in my interrogation room. But we're talking about the life of a child here, for God's sake. I need your witness statement!'

With every second step I climbed, my left knee cracked as if bubble wrap were being squashed inside it. 'Put out a search for Thomas Jagow,' I said.

'Alina already told us that. Apparently she recognised Feline's father's VW Golf from its ignition.'

'She's got elephant ears.'

On the third floor I stood by a door and couldn't tell if it was originally brown then poorly painted over in white, or the opposite. It said 'Gregoriev' in indelible ink on the packing tape stuck below the handle in place of a nameplate.

'But you *saw* him,' Stoya said, getting worked up again. 'And if that's the case, your statement is much more useful in court.'

'You have to catch Jagow and bring him to trial first. By then I'll be in the nick and have plenty of time to comb back over my memories thoroughly.'

I hung up and opened the door to Alina's apartment. A musty smell assailed me from the darkness of the hallway. It was so chilly that I was certain I'd be able to see my own breath as soon as I'd found the bloody light switch.

Once I'd groped my way into the sitting room I found it right beside the door, but it didn't get me any further. When

I pressed it, the bulb hanging from the ceiling flickered briefly then blew.

I sat in the murky light on an upholstered armchair beside a sofa. When I first visited Alina at her flat in Prenzlauer Berg, I was amazed she had any lights plugged in at all, as well a mirror in the bathroom. She'd even hung pictures on the wall. It was another example of her opening my eyes to the world of blind people, which I'd known nothing about before our fateful meeting. Because of course visually impaired people had lightbulbs, pictures and mirrors – so that their sighted guests didn't end up staring at bare walls in the dark.

I wondered whether I should remove the SIM card from my mobile, but then decided to place my trust in the chronic staff shortage of the Berlin police force. Nobody would go to the bother of locating me tonight. Besides, I wanted to be contactable for Alina when Stoya released her after the interrogation.

*Who is the dead woman with the baby?*

*Did Thomas kill her?*

*What connection does she have to Feline?*

Tired and pumped up in equal measure, I closed my eyes and believed I could understand why Alina felt more secure with her protective glasses. Not being able to see at all sharpened my other senses almost immediately. I could hear the blood rushing in my ears, feel goose pimples beneath my coat and suddenly realised how urgently I needed to empty my bladder.

I found the bathroom in which a motion-activated nightlight beneath the basin came on automatically. It was bright enough for me to be able to see the dust lines in the sink that hadn't been used for weeks. They matched the dark bags beneath my eyes that had grown bigger in the past few hours.

I closed my eyes, not because I couldn't bear the sight of my haggard face, but because I needed to order my thoughts. Had I heard Alina correctly?

*Yes, I had.*

I was almost one hundred per cent sure that she'd said she hadn't been in her flat for weeks. And yet in the bathroom I didn't just smell the stale, rotten stench of sanitary facilities that hadn't been used in ages.

But also a pungent, expensive aftershave.

*How is that possible?*

The scent was woody, with notes of pepper and a spice I couldn't place. If I'd had to describe the aftershave I'd have said the smell of a forest after a brief summer storm.

A fragrance someone had sprayed here only recently, or must have already been wearing.

Presumably the same person who'd drawn a gallows on the dusty mirror.

# 29

## EMILIA

*'Fist-sized bruises on the arms, chest and back. Bite marks with subcutaneous bleeding on the right thigh. Palpable bruising on the back of the head, deep scratches and further bite marks on the back. A cigarette burn on the inner left thigh.'*

The list of Emilia's injuries enumerated by the elderly female doctor with the severe expression was endless. As was the pain, even though she'd been given an injection. Half an hour after she'd been found in a puddle outside the front entrance. Barely conscious. Booted out of her tormentors' car. Just as Emilia had ordered and paid for.

'We'll do a more thorough dental examination tomorrow, when our dentist is here. So far I can see that your front right incisor is broken. Will you cope until tomorrow, Becky?'

Emilia nodded to the grey-haired woman who'd introduced herself as Dr Lieberstett and whose American accent was far more suited to the false name she'd given to the doctor.

At least she'd remembered her cover name this time,

unlike in the 'supermarket'. She'd had plenty of time to do so after coming round in the hospital room, furnished in old-fashioned style with white enamelled medicine and filing cabinets, a meticulously tidied steel desk with a laminate top and a rather antiquated-looking gynaecological chair beneath a circular lamp.

Emilia had lost all recall from the moment when strong hands grabbed her and placed her on a stretcher to when she woke up in this treatment room. She couldn't even remember how she'd got out of her filthy rain- and blood-soaked clothes and into this coarse linen nightshirt.

'Are you well enough to talk about what happened to you, Becky?' Lieberstett asked, making notes by hand while Emilia sat on the edge of the treatment couch where the doctor had just been seeing to her wounds.

*'My child's been kidnapped. I believe she's being held here. I couldn't think of another way to get to Feline than by having myself get beaten up by perverted strangers, as apparently you only take in victims of violent crime.'*

Of course there was no question of revealing the truth, so she said evasively, 'Nothing happened, actually.'

Not because she really was ashamed. But because somewhere online she'd read that denial was a typical symptom of female victims of male violence. For this reason she lowered her eyes too and answered in curt, timid sentences. 'I'm absolutely fine.'

Lieberstett removed the glasses she'd put on to write her doctor's report. 'I understand you find it difficult. But look, Becky, I've been running the Ambrosia-Resort for a while now. I can tell when someone's inflicted an injury on themselves. I can tell when someone's had an accidental fall. And I can also tell when a man's hand has slipped – apologies for the dreadful expression – just once, which is never an excuse. I hate abusive men. But there is a medical difference between a red mark on the cheek and the brutal injuries you suffered. Your wounds, abrasions and bruises are so fresh they must have happened in the last few hours. If you tell me who did this to you we might be able to apprehend the bastard today.'

'I don't know,' Emilia said, telling the truth just for once. She couldn't even remember the faces of the men in the 'supermarket' who she'd paid to kick, punch and jump on her and torture her in every conceivable way until they carried her unconscious to the car and drove her to Schwielowsee.

'You're safe here. We protect all our guests from their tormentors with fences, video surveillance and an infrared alarm. The moment an unauthorised person steps onto the premises, whether from the lake, the woods or the road, I get an immediate notification on my mobile.'

So Zorbach was right. This really was a high-security block.

'I don't know,' Emilia said, embarking on the story she'd concocted. 'I was in a bar.'

'Where?'

'In Potsdam, some pub in the Dutch Quarter.'

'Were you alone?'

'I was lonely. My husband's left me.'

'What happened?'

Emilia touched a bump on her head. 'It's the sort of place where later in the evening they clear away the tables for dancing.'

'So you danced?'

'Yes. And drank.'

'I assume you left your drink unguarded on the bar.'

*Good, very good*, Emilia thought, feeling slightly relieved for the first time in ages. She didn't have to recount her scrappily put-together story without help. Lieberstett was voluntarily guiding Emilia through her false statement. All she had to do was nod and confirm the possibility that someone had mixed knockout drops in her gin and tonic.

'So you don't know how you left the bar or who you left it with?'

'No. I only regained consciousness outside your gates when someone picked me up and brought me in.'

'Jakob, my right-hand man.'

Lieberstett put two fingers to her lips, as if asking Emilia to be quiet – probably an unconscious gesture.

'How do you know about Ambrosia?'

*Zorbach and Alina told me about it.*

'I... I'm not sure.'

Lieberstett sighed and put her glasses back on. 'Okay, I understand. Let's not delve any further right now. Jakob will take you back to your room. You have a rest and tomorrow, after the morning group session, we can speak again just as soon I'm free.'

The doctor closed the file on her desk and got up.

'That's very kind of you,' Emilia said, 'but I think I'd rather go home.' In her head she'd already rehearsed the dialogue that would begin with Lieberstett trying to convince her it was necessary to stay, at least until the wounds had been treated and the police notified. She would offer a brief protest but then acquiesce, at least for a night, in case the men were still waiting outside.

What Emilia hadn't counted on, however, was that Lieberstett wouldn't even enter into a discussion, for all she said was, 'Under no circumstances. You won't be leaving Ambrosia for the time being.'

'I'm sorry? Isn't that my decision?'

'No.'

'No?'

'Not while I still don't know what to make of you.'

'What's that supposed to mean?' Emilia felt a menacing numbness spread through her body, brought on by what Lieberstett had said rather than the painkiller she'd just been administered.

'You know what, Becky? It's all a bit strange. Hardly anybody knows us and this place here. Our establishment places great emphasis on discretion. We don't advertise; everything is by word of mouth. For this reason it's highly unlikely that the men who abused you would drop you off here after their bout of sadism. In fact, it's impossible.'

'Are you asking me a question?'

Shaking her head, Lieberstett came closer. 'No, I'm just stating that the CCTV pictures have left me scratching my head, Becky. Because they show you being pulled from the boot of a dark BMW estate by two men and chucked in front of the gate like a carcass of meat. Without ID, without a mobile. Without anything we can identify you with. Unfortunately the BMW's number plate was too filthy to send out a courier.'

*A courier?*

'But then you must have seen that I'm telling the truth. And that it was several men.'

Lieberstett nodded. 'As I said, it's inconceivable that the abusers themselves would bring you to the Ambrosia-Resort. It makes no sense. Unless you told the men where to come, which would also explain the little note with our address that we found in your trouser pocket.'

Emilia closed her eyes and felt the blood rush to her cheeks.

*They searched me.*

'But why would you do that, Becky? You see, until I've solved this puzzle, until I know who you really are, I'm afraid I can't let you go.'

The shoes of this strange doctor who ran this even stranger 'resort' squeaked as she went to the door. Before opening it and calling for her 'right-hand man', she said, 'Oh, and before you get any silly ideas, Becky, you ought to know that the surveillance system I was talking about doesn't only mean you're perfectly safe in here. It works in both directions.'

'What do you mean?' The numbness was intensifying.

'Well, it doesn't just stop unauthorised people from getting in here.'

*It doesn't allow anyone to get out either!*

Lieberstett didn't have to finish her sentence for Emilia to understand just how fatal the mistake was she'd made tonight.

# 30

## ALINA

'A little contribution for *Motz*?'

It was just after one in the morning, that time when Berlin city centre showed its second, broken face, and Alina was standing outside the Moabit apartment block where she'd spent the saddest months of her life. On her own, her evenings filled with overproof schnapps and concentrated self-pity, she wouldn't have stood out from the peculiar night-time figures if she'd left her own four walls at night rather than drinking herself to sleep.

*Until I met Nils.*

Before midnight the capital endeavoured to preserve a semblance of civilisation, but as soon as the theatres and restaurants were closed, the last politicians, managers and lawyers had gone home after their business dinners, and families of tourists had made their way back to their hotel rooms, the hour of the nightriders, as Alina called them, struck. Adolescent gang members, prostitutes, pimps, drug addicts, dealers, drunks and those with visible mental illnesses were a far more common sight on the streets than those citizens who'd just popped out to take the dog for a walk, even though the endless heaps of shit by the side of the road might suggest a different story.

Alina wasn't in the least surprised, therefore, when the poor guy with the gravelly voice asked her for a donation to the homeless newspaper.

'I wrote the story on the centre pages myself.'

*That's good to know.*

'Here.' It took her a while to fish the change from the taxi out of her trouser pocket.

'That much?'

He seemed reluctant to accept it, even though it couldn't be more than three euros eighty.

'Please take it.'

'Great, thanks!'

The entry door hadn't closed again so she pushed it with her shoulder. If the homeless man had worked out by now that she was visually impaired it didn't seem to bother him. She couldn't prevent him from stuffing *Motz* rather awkwardly into the outer pocket of her rucksack before stepping back, coughing. Soon afterwards she rang at the door on the third floor, having wisely opted for the stairs. The lift had never worked in this building.

'Alina? What are you doing here?'

She recognised Zorbach in the doorway solely by his voice. In Albrechts Teerofen she'd put her glasses back on in the hope that the atrocity of what had taken place there would be easier to stomach. The floodlights the police had set up at the crime scene had created nebulous shadows, diffuse reflections of light and shapeless blots, which together had triggered her imagination of the horror that must have played out in the workshop. The blurred stimuli sharpened the image of the horribly battered mother's body, her mouth wide open, perhaps contorted into a scream. Alina even 'saw' the child's heartbeat, which was worryingly irregular, beneath the babygrow that wasn't thick enough. But thanks to the glasses, the images before her eyes had vanished again.

*Darkness*, Alina had found out since the operation, *is very often a great comfort.*

'Are you asking what I'm doing in my own flat?' She pushed past him into the hallway of her former apartment, which was familiar but not a nice place to be.

*Too many hours on my own. Too many bad memories.*

'Weren't you going to call?' he asked as she put down the rucksack.

'Yes.'

That was the plan: to tell Zorbach about her conversation with Stoya as soon as she'd signed her statement.

'I...'

She hesitated. It was none of Zorbach's business that she and Nils had rowed over the phone. He was pissed off that Alina had been out of contact for so long. If there was one thing that made them incompatible as a couple, it was that they were both obstinate; neither was willing to concede if they thought they were in the right. An argument could quickly escalate, for example if Nils didn't understand why she should spend her nights with a man who'd once put her in a situation where she'd been so badly injured that she couldn't have children any more. And if she screamed at Nils that he'd never wanted kids anyway, which was why his ex had left him.

'I need to crash here. Don't ask any questions,' was all Alina said, hoping that Zorbach hadn't put anything in the way to the kitchen.

Although she was incredible thirsty from all the talking in the interrogation room at the station, she let the tap run for ages to get rid of the stale water in the pipes. She didn't want to crown the emotional suffering she'd experienced this evening with a touch of legionella.

'As we agreed, I stated that I was there on my own and recognised Jagow's car by the noise of its engine. Stoya didn't believe me, of course, but, then again, he's not the best interrogator. The way he formulated his questions meant that I got more information out of him than he did out of me.'

'Such as?'

'Did you know Mathilda Jahn? Did you have contact with her baby?' she said, repeating Stoya's question.

'Mathilda Jahn?' Zorbach said.

She bet he was googling the name, just as she'd done in the taxi.

'There's not much about her,' Alina said. 'Apart from an interesting school photo. I'll give you three guesses as to which school she attended.'

'No way!'

'Oh yes. My speech assistant said it to me loud and clear: Mathilda was in Feline's father's physics class!'

'Are you saying the two of them had a relationship? Maybe Thomas is the father of the baby.'

'It's possible. But why did he kill her and leave the baby alive? I don't know, Alex. The more information we get, the more mysterious I find it.'

Alina took off her glasses, then her wig, a short bob, beneath which she was suddenly sweating. She was just about to hold her shaven head under the tap when Zorbach said, 'Talking of mysterious – there was someone here in your flat.'

'What?'

Alina turned around to his shadow approaching her; she'd forgotten she was thirsty.

'Who?'

Instinctively she moved out of the way, worried that Zorbach would grab her after his unexpected remark had set her on edge. But he was just going to turn off the tap that was still gushing.

'No idea. A man, judging by the smell.'

Alina shuddered when Zorbach described the scent he'd detected in her bathroom. When he then told her about the macabre message on the dusty mirror, she felt as if someone had tipped icy water down the back of her neck.

'I searched all the rooms. There's nobody here, unless you've got a hidden floor, secret room or something like that.'

Alina shook her head and moved away from the kitchen counter.

'Where are you going?'

She didn't bother with an answer as it was so obvious what she had to do now. Besides, he would see it with his own eyes.

*Four steps forwards, three to the left and a half turn to the bathroom.*

When Alina opened the door it felt as if the memory was going to explode inside her head like a firecracker.

'You're right!' she panted.

'Can you smell it too?'

'Just about, yes.' Enough to launch a horror film in her mind. About a man hassling her on the underground. Patting her knee.

'It's the scent of the guy who kicked TomTom onto the tracks.'

'Maybe he was trying to intimidate you?'

'In what way?'

'Well, he did draw a gallows on your mirror.'

'More likely he wants to kill me then.'

'If that's the case he'd have pushed you in front of the train or lain in wait for you here in the dark.'

*True. I can't dismiss that possibility.*

'But why's he trying to intimidate me?'

'Maybe this is about Feline and he wants you to keep your nose out.'

Alina shook her head. 'How on earth would he know I'm involved?'

'Good point. He must know you. Maybe very well. The door was double-locked and I didn't see any signs of a break-in. So I'm asking: who apart from you has got a key to this flat?'

'Nobody, only...' Alina paused. Once more she felt a burning desire for a drink, this time an alcoholic one.

She didn't dare say his name. But there was only one person she'd given a spare key to after her move and hadn't yet asked for it back.

*Nils.*

'No, nobody.' She decided to change the subject. 'Let's not waste any time; let's focus on Feline instead. There's plenty of stuff about Thomas Jagow and the playlist that we haven't worked out yet.'

'Don't say that,' Zorbach countered as he followed her out of the bathroom and back into the kitchen.

'What do you mean?'

'I went over the songs in Feline's playlist again. And now I think I know what she's trying to tell us.'

'Really?'

'Yes. But I fear it's not what we want to hear.'

'Too vague?' Alina said.

'Too horrific,' Zorbach replied.

# 31

## ZORBACH

'Do you remember what was on the poster in Feline's bedroom?'

'The mnemonic for the planets?'

We were back in the kitchen, standing at the wooden work surface because there weren't any seats. Alina was by the recess where probably the sink once stood. I was in the corner with a bulb dangling from a cable above me.

'My very educated mother just showed us planets,' I said.

'Nothing,' Alina corrected me. 'Nothing for Neptune. But how are the planets going to help us decipher Feline's playlist?'

'Let's go through the songs together and you'll work it out yourself. I sent your screenshot of the playlist to my phone.'

Alina sighed. 'Okay, read it out, then.'

Junkie – MAJAN
Evermore – Namika

Maze – LOTTE
Erlking – Kool Savas
Under – Justin Jesso
Rose – Rea Garvey
Silver Lining – Tom Walker
Live in Peace – JORIS
Alone in a Crowded Room – Charlotte Jane
Million Tweets – Silbermond
85 Minutes of Your Love – Alle Farben, Hanne Mjøen
Under the World – Johannes Oerding
I Need You – Beth Ditto
Open Eyes – Tim Bendzko
Para Paradise – VIZE, R4GE, Emie

I looked up from my phone and saw Alina blinking hard, as if something had flown into her eyes.

'Wait, are you saying that the order of the initial letters in the playlist is important?'

I grinned with pride at having solved the puzzle, but immediately found my behaviour so childish that I hoped Alina wasn't able to guess the expression on my face. Given Feline's message, which I'd at least partly deciphered, my pleasure was totally inappropriate.

'Precisely,' I said. 'It's all about the initial letters. But not of the artists. If you write these down you get something completely unpronounceable.'

*MNLKJRTJCSAJBTV*

'It's gibberish, meaningless,' Alina said, shaking her bare head, and I wondered if she wasn't freezing with the heating off. But maybe the excitement of my discovery was keeping her as warm as me.

'No it isn't – listen! The initial letters of the songs are: J, E, M, E, U, R, S, L and A. Put them together and you get...'

'JEMEURSLA?' Alina coughed drily into the crook of her arm. 'I don't understand.'

'Because you didn't do French at school. You need to put gaps in the right places between the letters. Then it reads: *Je meurs là.*'

'Can *you* speak French?' she asked in disbelief.

'No. And I don't know if the phrase is grammatically correct either, but I did put the words into Google Translate—'

'And what came out?' Alina interrupted me.

I took a step backwards and scratched my neck. Reading it was one thing. Saying it out loud was quite another.

'As I said, Alina, you're not going to like it.'

She actually rolled her eyes, something I'd never seen her do before, so I hurried to tell her the gloomy message.

'According to the translator, it means: *I'm dying there.*'

'Seriously?' She breathed in sharply. Then she nodded as if I'd been the one to ask a question. She was also wiggling her fingers, which I took as another sign of her growing nervousness, and counting something in her head, as I soon realised.

'Hold on a moment. *Je meurs là.* That's only nine songs. Feline had fifteen on her playlist.'

She was right. 'Million Tweets', '85 Minutes of Your Love', 'Under the World', 'I Need You', 'Open Eyes' and 'Para Paradise' were missing.

'I'm afraid I can't make head or tail of those initial letters or the numbers.'

M

85

U

I

O

P

'With "85 Minutes" I don't even know if we should be looking at the number 8 or the letter E for eight, assuming either is significant.'

Alina cocked her head and for a moment looked like she was scanning the ceiling for spiderwebs. 'Feline once told me that twice a week she used to go to riding near Dallogow before she had the accident, which was why she came to me for treatment.'

'So?'

'I think she said it took exactly eighty-five minutes to drive there.'

'That could be a clue.'

'Yes, but to what? To the stables? Well, the lyrics fit.'

Alina sang a few lines of the hit by Alle Farben and Hanne Mjøen:

> *Feet above the ground,*
> *Head up in the clouds,*
> *You're my adrenaline.*

'That's what I imagine it's like to ride on a horse.'

'Okay, but what do the letters after it mean? Have you googled that?'

'Yes, but I can't find anything for UIOP that points to a place.' I rubbed my tired eyes. 'UIO, on the other hand, is according to Wikipedia the abbreviation for a university in Oslo or an airport in Ecuador. If she were in either of these places she'd have gone for Scandinavian or Latin American songs, wouldn't she? Quite apart from the fact that Ecuador or Oslo wouldn't exactly narrow down our search area.'

'Shit!' Alina said, slamming her fist on the counter and offloading her pent-up tension. 'It feels like we're so close to solving the playlist puzzle,' she cursed. 'And yet we're no further.'

I didn't contradict her; there was no reason to. My discovery about the initial letters was interesting, but useless. Because the fact that Feline was going to die somewhere very soon was something we could have concluded with almost one hundred per cent certainty anyway.

The question was: *where?*

Where was 'there'?

This puzzle, the most important of all, remained unsolved.

All the same, I deliberately tried to remain optimistic by saying, 'At least we know that Feline was alive two days ago when she changed the playlist.'

'Or her abductor did.'

I saw Alina wrap her arms around her body. Her lips too looked bluer than a few minutes ago; she seemed to be cold now after all.

'We can't stay here,' I decided. 'You ought to go home and I'll find a hotel with heating.'

'We could light the stove in the sitting room.'

'Have you got any paper?' I'd seen a pile of wood in the sitting room as well as a lighter on the windowsill. But no firelighters or any paper to get the fire going.

'Would you fetch my rucksack, please? We could use the newspaper I just bought.'

'Newspaper?'

'A homeless man sold me a *Motz*.'

I found her rucksack by the door and removed the newspaper. A postcard fell from from the thin pages, which I took to be advertising. It might help get the stove alight too so I picked it up and carried my spoils back to the kitchen. Only now did I realise what was in my hand.

'Who did you get this from?' I asked Alina, who'd been drinking straight from the tap.

'What do you mean?' she said, clearly alarmed by the severity in my voice.

'Who gave you this?'

'I told you: a homeless man. Some poor bastard.'

'He wasn't a homeless man,' I told her.

'How do you know?'

'Because he left a message for you in the *Motz*.'

I looked again at the postcard that had fallen from the newspaper. An advertising card like the ones you find in racks in cafés. They carry funny sayings or images in the hope you'll stick them up on the wall or fridge at home or, even better, send them to someone. This card was from a bookshop and it said: 'Reading can harm your stupidity!'

'This card fell out of the newspaper.'

'Is my name on it?'

'I can't tell.'

'Huh? How do you know it's for me, then?'

I moved right up to Alina, grabbed her fingers, which felt dreadfully cold, and put the card in her hand. She immediately understood what I was trying to do. As if automatically, her fingers felt the tiny bumps on the back.

'That's why,' she mumbled.

'That's why, what?'

'The guy said he'd written the centre-page story and I had to read it.'

'Is that braille?' I asked.

She nodded.

'Can you read it?'

She nodded again.

Alina's eyes closed and her lids began to flutter; she was in a state of high concentration as she felt the bumps on the back of the postcard once more. As if wanting to make sure she hadn't misread it the first time.

Then she read out a telephone number.

'That's on it?'

'And the words: "Ring me as soon as you read this."'

'Is there a sender? Any sort of signature?'

'No, only the name of the person this is about.'

'Who?' I asked impatiently.

Alina's silence was interrupted by the noise of a tap that hadn't been properly turned off. In my ears the plopping of the drops in the steel sink sounded like a metronome urgently trying to tell us we were running out of time.

'Feline?' I finally asked.

'Ambrosia,' she corrected me.

# 32

## EMILIA

Her fists were burning as if they'd been dipped in acid. For the lacerations on her hands alone she would need all the ibuprofen Lieberstett had given her for the night. But Emilia wouldn't stop hammering wildly against the locked door of her prison.

'Hey, come back. Hey…!'

The small square room she'd been locked in was on the top floor of the main building and looked how Emilia imagined a monastery cell to be. Sparsely furnished with a hard wooden stool, a tiny table made from the cross-section of a tree trunk, with a metal carafe of water on it, and a pallet-like single bed with stone-grey sheets that matched the walls of her jail. Jakob, Dr Lieberstett's right-hand man, had brought her up here.

The toxic cocktail of painkillers and sedatives in her blood had prevented her from even considering an escape. Emilia had silently followed her minder through the park to the 'lobby', which had turned out to be an empty hall, and then up the stairs to the roof. Jakob was at least two metres tall, bald and with the body of an out-of-shape removal man. He wore something that looked like a mixture between a kimono and a judo suit. It must be made to measure; his ankle boots were outsized too.

'*Try to get some sleep. Tomorrow's going to be a long day.*' With these words Jakob had taken his leave of her and then locked the door from the outside.

Now it was half past two. This meant the day had scarcely begun and yet for Emilia it was already unbearable.

'Jakob? Can you hear me? Let me out of here!' she screamed at the door, having already given up hope that her alternating curses, pleas and threats would be heard. But then, as she paused to draw breath, she heard footsteps.

'Jakob?' she exclaimed euphorically, momentarily overwhelmed by emotion when he actually entered the room.

Tall and well-fed, he wore a white coat fastened only by a black cloth belt. This made him look faintly simple and awkward, which was at odds with his alert, clever eyes. He had a slightly rounded back, like many tall men who are used to bending down to talk to others.

He came straight to the point: 'I can't let you go.'

'Why not?'

He asked Emilia to sit on the bed, whereas he stayed standing, emphasising the power dynamic even further now she had to look up at him.

'First of all, because you're not well.'

'I've been given good treatment. My injuries can heal at home.'

'The external ones, perhaps. But here at Ambrosia we

focus primarily on the emotional consequences rather than just the physical ones.'

'So this is a loony bin, then?'

*Good God. I'm locked up in a secure facility and nobody knows I'm here.*

'No, this isn't a psychiatric clinic in the conventional sense.'

'What is it, then?'

'First and foremost, Ambrosia is a well-kept secret, and that's how it must remain for us to be able to help many more people.'

'You're worried I might damage you?' Emilia asked hastily. She felt as if she were choking on her own voice.

Jakob went over to the desk and filled a tin mug with water from the jug. 'If I'm being honest, yes. I think Dr Lieberstett is right: there's something dodgy about your story.'

'What's dodgy is being kept prisoner here.'

'This isn't a prison!' he said, handing her the mug.

'So I can leave, then?'

'Just as soon as you've told us the truth and we know who you really are.'

Emilia turned away from him, glanced up at the hatch in the ceiling and took a sip.

*How long can I stick to my story?*

*How long will it take them to identify the BMW and trace my steps back to the 'supermarket'? And from there, where I gave my real name, back to our house in Nikolassee?*

Emilia was annoyed that she'd overreacted again, shouting at Jakob without having worked out a plausible story. For want of any alternative she kept going with the yarn she'd been spinning so far.

'I was given knockout drops. I can't remember anything.'

'Knockout drops don't erase your memory of everything that happened *before* you were given them.' Now the expression on Jakob's face was severe. 'How do you know about us?'

She just shrugged. 'Maybe the men felt remorse and knew I'd get help here. Why don't you believe they just drove me here?'

'Because that doesn't happen.'

'Why not? Please explain.'

Jakob glanced at his watch. 'Are you saying you're not lying? That you really don't have any idea of how you got here?'

'Not at the moment, no.' Emilia left open the possibility that she might be able to 'remember' at some point.

'Okay.'

Jakob pulled up the stool, which looked much too small for him but was sturdy enough to take his weight.

'Ambrosia is a community of like-minded doctors, nurses, orderlies, psychologists and couriers.'

'Couriers?'

'I'll come to that in a moment.' His lecture sounded rehearsed; he must have already delivered it to plenty of people he'd locked up before. 'We see body and soul as a single entity, although the damaged soul undergoes a considerably longer healing process than physical wounds. But it's only when the psyche recovers that the patients are properly cured.'

Emilia gave a hollow laugh. 'Do you really think that

locking me up against my will is going to help my healing process?'

'The point is, Becky, you don't know what you want. Look, at the moment you're behaving like a tiger caught in a trap. The jaws have sprung shut and the beast is unable to free its paw without outside help. If this help comes in the form of a person, the tiger bares its teeth and drives them away. The animal, who doesn't know what it really wants, struggles against being freed.'

'I'm not an animal.'

'Of course not. But nor do you know what you really need to free yourself from the manacles of violence you've been shackled in.'

In agitation, Emilia felt the hairs on the back of her neck stand on end. Jakob had hit a nerve even though he'd been describing a different hopeless situation from the one she was in.

'If we were to let you go now, Becky, before the treatment's finished, you'd be going back to the same surroundings where you'd bump into the same people who tortured you. And worse than this vicious circle of violence and humiliation would be the fact that those criminals would feel their behaviour vindicated by your return. They would have learned how to abuse their victims without fear of reprisal. More souls would be ravaged as a consequence and the cycle of violence would never stop.'

*Treatment?*

Emilia touched the bandage on her thigh, beneath which it now felt terribly itchy and said, 'What sort of treatment are you talking about?'

She couldn't help but think of bad psycho-thriller films

in which patients are tortured by electric shock or locked in water tanks.

Jakob leaned forwards and the stool creaked worryingly. 'You've misunderstood me, Becky. It's not just about *your* treatment.'

'Who else is involved then?'

'Your tormentors. We need their names so we can find them and bring about a settlement between culprits and victim.'

'What does that look like?'

'It varies from case to case. Sometimes we don't need to apply any pressure to make the perpetrator see sense. Sometimes the victims themselves are hands-on.

'Are we talking about an eye for an eye here?'

Jakob nodded. 'I know it must sound slightly archaic, but believe me, it's incredibly cathartic when you see that your tormentors can feel suffering, fear and hopelessness too. Besides, this is how we finance ourselves. We find the perpetrators, confront them with the misery they've inflicted and make them compensate financially for the harm they've caused.'

Emilia's throat felt so constricted that she was amazed she could swallow the water at all when she took another sip. 'That's what you need the couriers for, is it?' she asked Jakob. 'To drag the offenders back here?'

*Where revenge is exacted on them.*

Her guard stood up. 'I see you've grasped the principle.'

Emilia nodded involuntarily. She felt like hurling the mug across the room.

*Yes, unfortunately.*

No culprit who knew about Ambrosia would willingly

bring their victim anywhere near this place. Nobody would hand themselves over like that.

*Christ!* Only now did Emilia realise the complete hopelessness of the situation she'd put herself in. Lieberstett wouldn't let her go until she could be sure Emilia wasn't playing games with her and didn't represent a threat to her organisation.

*Which meant: never.*

*And you will say:*
*'There are the police and laws.*
*An eye for an eye, a tooth for a tooth*
*What's the cause?'*
*Injured pride is like a shadow*
*That reveals itself at night.*
*Do something about it,*
*Get up and fight.*

**Namika – 'Evermore'**

# 33

## ALINA

'Hello, Alina? Alina Gregoriev?'

The man whose number was scrawled on the postcard answered after one ring. Judging by his voice he'd been a smoker all his life. She recognised the growl, even though earlier she hadn't paid particular attention to the supposed newspaper seller on the street. Nor to the lack of smell, as she only now realised. This mysterious man, who must be around forty, hadn't reeked of alcohol, sweat, tobacco, or any of the other odours that usually lingered around homeless people.

'I hadn't expected you to call so soon. To be honest, I wasn't sure you'd even look inside the paper.'

'Who are you?' Alina asked curtly.

'Not on the phone. We need to meet.'

Alina raised her head and looked at the shadow Zorbach's head cast on the kitchen counter. She'd put her phone on speaker.

'We *have* already met,' she said. 'You know where I live.

You could have spoken to me directly. Why all the fuss with the postcard?'

The man gave a dry cough. 'When I saw you I wasn't sure.'

'Sure of what?'

'Whether I could trust you.'

Alina frowned. 'And now you are?'

'Yes.'

'Why?'

'Because you called. That was the test.'

'Test?'

Alina heard Zorbach whisper something to her, but was so focused on the conversation that she didn't understand what he wanted.

'When I investigated you I started to have my doubts. It's scarcely possible you could have done what you're accused of. My client didn't tell me you were blind, you see. I only discovered this through my own research. But I don't want to say any more now. We should meet straight away.'

*Investigated? Client? Research?*

Alina's patience was wearing thin. 'Look, mate, as you now know I can't *see* anyone.'

'Touché.'

'And besides, how likely do you think it is that in the middle of the night I'm going to meet up with a stranger who skulks around my block then tells me later on the phone that I've passed a *test*.'

'Very likely.' The stranger's answer came promptly. 'Because if not, this conversation won't be the end of it. Ambrosia will...'

When the line fell silent Alina was worried the call had

broken off at a crucial moment. Then the man suddenly said, 'Are you on your own?'

Zorbach made a hand gesture she couldn't decipher. Alina decided to opt for the truth: 'No, I'm not.'

'You have to come on your own.' The man panted. 'In fifteen minutes, no later. I'll meet you by the river. Take the alley beside the building at the end of Alt-Moabit that looks like a boat sail. If you're not there in twenty minutes you'll never hear from me again. This telephone number will be out of service. So come.'

Alina took a deep breath. Deeply unnerved she said, 'What if I don't?'

'Then Ambrosia will send another courier who'll no doubt be less sympathetic and complete his mission.'

# 34

There used to be a Greek restaurant in the sail building by the Spree, which Alina would frequent from time to time when she'd had enough of tinned ravioli and cheap ready-made pizzas, and could be bothered to drag herself a couple of hundred metres down the road. Giorgio, the owner, had always given her a window seat with a view of the river, even though he knew she was blind. He must have grasped intuitively that visually impaired people appreciated it when they weren't treated like second-class citizens, but sensitive emotional beings who could distinguish between sunlight angling through the window and being parked in the far corner.

Sadly Giorgio's empathy and care wasn't enough to protect him from insolvency during the second Covid wave, and the curved glass tower on the ground floor had remained empty ever since.

'Stay here. I don't want him to see you!' she said to Zorbach when he was about to take her hand as they were passing the sail building on the path that sloped down to the embankment.

The path was about three metres above the level of the river, which at this point was roughly the width of a canal. During the daytime it was filled with joggers and baby buggies, but at night it was deserted, apart from a few unfortunate homeless people who used cardboard boxes, blankets and plastic bags to turn the park benches into tent-like camps.

Alina didn't have a problem avoiding the few obstacles in her path, but she found it far more difficult to cope with various night-time lights. On the other side of the river, empty yet fully lit office blocks cast their glow onto the black surface of the water, where this mingled with the headlight beams of the cars darting across Gotzkowskybrücke. Added to the lights of the street lamps and park lanterns, the jumble of reflections made Alina's operated eyes see a confusing flicker; everything around her looked as if she were on a hallucinogenic trip.

*Why does everyone always rave about the world of colours?* she thought as she searched for a human shadow moving towards her.

The disturbing patches of colour were a reason why every morning she wondered if she really ought to continue taking the medicine that was supposed to prevent her transplanted retina from being rejected.

'Alina?'

The voice made her whip around.

*Shit!* She'd actually failed to spot the man. Something that would never have happened with closed eyes, before the operation in Hanover. When she was still blind she'd sensed changes in the reflection of sounds. The echo produced by her shoes on the hard ground would have told her that a man was standing beside the tree.

She closed her eyes to concentrate fully on his voice. That, at least, she'd recognised.

'You're the courier!'

'Who came with you?'

Shit.

Either Zorbach hadn't hidden himself properly on the road or the man had kept her under surveillance ever since she left her block.

'I told you to come alone.'

'And because you were so insistent I brought reinforcement,' Alina replied. 'What do you want from me?'

'My orders are to abduct you.'

'And take me to the Ambrosia?'

'Correct.'

'Who gave you your orders?'

'I'm not going to tell you that. All I'll say is that you're in great danger.'

'Why?'

She heard him clear his throat. 'Listen. Ambrosia is a good institution. We look after victims of serious crimes and see to it that they get justice.'

'What would my abduction have to do with justice?'

'I was told you'd caused a woman great suffering.'

'Who?'

'I only know her first name. Tabea.'

'Never heard of her.'

The shadow moved a step closer. His voice became softer and more urgent. 'Tabea attracts pain and violence like a magnet. She's the victim of repeated violence. A few days ago someone dripped acid in her eyes.'

'Who?'

'You.'

Alina tapped her forehead. 'Rubbish. I'm not a psychopath, but I am visually impaired. From a purely technical point of view, how could I manage that?'

'Exactly. That's why we're talking now. That's why I'm not going to take you back with me. I wasn't told you were blind and had only just recently undergone an eye operation.'

He sighed like a man at odds with himself. 'But nor do I know why I'm doing this, why I'm warning you. Perhaps because till now I'd always been convinced that Ambrosia was doing the right thing. But then you...' He paused. 'Go to ground if you can. It's very possible they'll send someone else to look for you.'

'I'm a big girl. I can look after myself,' Alina said, although she no longer felt as confident as she sounded.

'As you wish.'

Alina saw the shadow move. Away from her.

'One last question.'

The courier stopped and turned back round to her.

'Yes?'

'How did you know that I'd come to my flat this evening? I haven't been here in months.'

'What did you say?' The gravelly voice sounded alarmed.

'I don't live here any more. Until a few hours ago I didn't even know myself that I'd pop back.'

'My God!' Alina heard the courier say, then, 'That means you're in bigger danger than I thought.'

'Why?'

A gust of wind freshened by the water tugged at Alina's collar.

'Because the informer who claims you were the one who injured Tabea said almost exactly when I'd be able to meet you here.'

'Which means?'

'That he must be watching you around the clock.'

Alina felt tempted to look around. 'How can he do that?'

'Have you had a strange encounter recently?'

*A strange encounter? I've visited the mother of a missing girl, been to a place where a woman died, and this here is anything but an everyday chinwag.*

'I mean, has anyone followed you?' the courier said, being more specific. 'Or got too close.'

Alina briefly closed her eyes and at once the scent of the aftershave filled her nostrils again, maybe because eerily she'd just smelled it in her bathroom.

'Actually, yes. I was hassled on the underground yesterday.'

'Was something planted on you by any chance?'

'No, on the contrary. A guy was going to nick my mobile, but...'

*Fuck!*

'But what?' the courier asked impatiently. Alina felt a vibration produced by an underground train a few metres below them.

'He gave it back to me.'

She coughed and gasped; in her anxiety she'd forgotten to breathe. Then she took the mobile from her coat pocket and removed the rubber case. A shiny metallic object immediately fell by her feet. It must have been hidden beneath the cover. Alina couldn't see it, but the courier bent down. 'A tracking device,' he said, confirming Alina's worst fears.

He put the tiny object, which felt like a watch battery, into her hand and ran off.

# 35

After flinging the tracking device into the Spree, Alina hurried after the courier. When she got to the road Zorbach blocked her path.

'What did he say?'

She pointed in the direction of her former flat. 'I'll tell you when we're back inside. Which way did he go?'

'There. Heading for the petrol station. Can you see him?'

Alina nodded, even though the blurry shape Zorbach was pointing at could have been anything. A tree, a bollard – or a person.

'He was running up the pavement. Now he's got a phone to his ear,' Zorbach told her. 'He must be talking to someone. Wait.'

The shadow, a mere ten metres away from them, started moving again. Alina saw him peel away from the darkness of the pavement and onto the road.

'He's turning around. Looking towards us. Moving. Faster now. I think he's running towards us. He's waving. Looks as if he's trying to warn us.'

Alina's heart started beating faster. 'I was being tracked!' she said. 'He told me I was in danger. Let's get out of here.'

But it was too late.

The courier was in the middle of the road when two lights flared up. Alina stared at the slip road – a mistake, as she was staring straight into the blazing light, which felt as if hot needles had been thrust into her pupils.

'Shit, no!' she heard Zorbach say.

Then she heard an engine roaring. A heavy car accelerating. Alina saw the headlights shooting towards her from the slip road, heard the vehicle revving, and closed her eyes. Which was why she didn't see the shadow of the man who'd called himself a courier get hit front-on by the car and go flying in a high arc. But she heard even more acutely his body crash onto the hard asphalt like a sack full of glass. And his bones crunch again when the car ran over him.

# 36

## ZORBACH

'What a mean, fucking coward you are!' Alina yelled at me the moment we were back inside her flat. 'We didn't help the poor bastard. That's a crime!'

'He was beyond help,' I protested, collapsing on the sofa in the sitting room. 'He's dead.'

'You can't have seen that so quickly. You didn't even go to check on him. And even if he was dead, we ought to have rung emergency services.'

'The others did that.'

'Which others?'

'The taxi driver and his passengers – you didn't see them.' Immediately after the crash they'd stopped on Alt-Moabit and got out.

'When we were around the corner the taxi driver was kneeling beside the horribly contorted body and the woman of the couple he was ferrying was already on her phone.'

'All the same,' Alina snorted defiantly.

'All the same, *what*? Should we have put our names down as witnesses? "A stranger was run over by someone else we don't know. We've no idea what he wanted from us and why he had to die. But, heigh-ho, it's probably just some silly coincidence that we've wandered past a crime scene twice in the past six hours."'

Leaning back against the white cushion, I stretched my neck and stared up at the stuccoed period ceiling.

'What did you talk about?' I asked her after a while.

'It was completely surreal. The guy said he was a courier and had been instructed to take me to Ambrosia because I'd badly injured a woman called Tabea.'

'Tabea?' I interrupted. 'Not Feline?'

'I may be visually impaired, but I'm not stupid. Yes, Tabea. And like you I've no idea who that is. Just like I've no idea who was spying on me.'

'What do you mean?'

'The guy who snatched my mobile and kicked TomTom onto the tracks put a tracker in my phone case. The courier found it. Then he scarpered.'

*And was murdered.* I got up and went over to the window overlooking the street. The glass shook even though there were no cars passing beneath.

'Someone must have got wind of the fact that you're causing trouble and they're desperate to stop you investigating any further,' I said as the vibrations from the window frame spread to my fingers.

'Someone who drives over bodies,' Alina said. 'The question is: why not over mine?'

I nodded. *Another question mark in a line of unsolved questions. Why has the culprit been content to give Alina warnings, but killed Mathilda Jahn in Albrechts Teerofen and the courier on the road?*

Although ordering a 'courier' to abduct her clearly went beyond a mere warning…

*Fuck, what are we getting ourselves into here again?*

There was a droning in my head as if someone had struck a tuning fork and held it to my ear. I'd have loved to switch my brain onto idle for an hour, just to be able to think about nothing. But I knew that no autogenic training in the world would be able to help me relax right now. Not after everything that had happened today. Especially not considering the theory I'd come up with while waiting for Alina on the street and which had given me such a thrill that I had to share it with her. 'While you were with the courier down by the Spree I hid in the entrance of a travel agent's.'

'What's *that* got to do with the price of eggs?'

'They had an advert for a fjord cruise in the window, which made me think of the playlist.'

*Track 12: Under the World – Johannes Oerding*
*Track 13: I Need You – Beth Ditto*
*Track 14: Open Eyes – Tim Bendzko*

'UIO,' I said, putting together the initial letters of the songs.

Alina gesticulated with open arms like someone trying to surrender to their opponent. 'I've lost you.'

'Maybe the initials do stand for Oslo.'

'Are you being serious?'

I shrugged. Of course I wasn't sure. And now I was talking about my theory, I realised that it had sounded more plausible in my mind.

'I found a class photo of Feline on the internet. It was taken one year ago, but I didn't recognise her straight away. She's holding hands with a boy. Guess what his name is.'

'I suspect you're going to tell me.'

'Olaf Norweg.'

'And?'

'As I said earlier, UIO stands for Oslo University. The capital of Norway. And the surname of Feline's classmate is Norweg.'

Alina sighed, shaking her head.

'Okay, okay. What's the time?'

I looked at my mobile.

'2:52.'

'Right then, this is the plan. At seven on the dot we're going to pay Olaf Norweg a breakfast visit. Until then we'll try to get a bit of shuteye here.'

She pointed to the old armchair she'd earmarked as my sleeping place, while she headed for the sofa.

'Do you think there's something in this, then?' I asked.

She shook her head. 'No, I think it's totally far-fetched. But there's not much time until you have to go to prison tomorrow. So…'

She swallowed loudly.

'… even if it's most unlikely that this UIO Oslo lead will get us anywhere, what have we got to lose if we follow it up?'

# 37

## EMILIA

Early in the morning the view over the Schwielowsee looked like the inside of a steam room. Clouds of grey ground fog drifted across the shore – so low that you might think they were going to have a rest on the surface of the lake.

Like virtually everything, this view also reminded Emilia of her daughter, who loved cycling to the Wannsee lido even though nobody would join the class misfit there, apart from her friend Olaf, perhaps.

*What I would give to sit on that shore now. To hold Feline. Embrace her. Never let go.*

The clear, cold air that breezed into the hall through the open window smelled of grass and cooled Emilia's tired eyes. The first pleasant sensation she'd had since arriving at Ambrosia. And so she was all the more disappointed when Jakob closed the windows at the request of several people present, before he sat down on the unused beanbag.

Including Emilia there were seven patients in this rectangular room on the ground floor of the main building. All of them women, even though Jakob had assured her that male victims of violence were staying at Ambrosia too. One wall was mirrored as in a dance school or a ballet hall. This went with the sprung floor that gave a little with every step. The only thing missing was the handrail for the dancers.

*And they don't lock the door at a dance school*, Emilia noted.

After Jakob had left her alone last night, she was on the verge of killing herself. But there was probably good reason why her monastic cell was kitted out so spartanly, without any mirrors, coat hangers or glasses that could be used as knives, blades or other stabbing instruments. In a small wooden chest cupboard were her cleaned clothes and shoes. But no belt or laces. And the hatch in the ceiling could only be opened a crack. There was no chance of leaping from it.

*Hopeless.*

Emilia would never have imagined that the despair she felt on account of her missing daughter could get any worse.

*And now look where I've ended up.*

Once more she thought of Feline, especially the playlist her daughter had compiled, perhaps in sheer desperation. And the song by Charlotte Jane. She knew why Feline had chosen this one; it corresponded exactly with the emotional turmoil her teenage daughter had revealed to her in one of her darkest moments.

'I feel so alone, Mum. Dad is making me an outcast. I'm alone, even in a classroom full of other pupils.'

*I'm so alone in a crowded room*
*I'm invisible*
*Misunderstood*
*I'm so alone sitting next to you*

And now Emilia herself was sitting in a room full of people, feeling more alone than she ever had before, as Jakob introduced the morning group session.

'It's great that everyone's here, apart from three members. Because today we're welcoming a new comrade.' Jakob smiled as Emilia tried to find a position on the beanbag where it didn't feel as if her back was broken. Now she realised it was a mistake to have taken off her nightie and swapped it for her own clothes that were dry. The tight jeans were a particular problem. She'd tried to sit cross-legged and almost screamed. Like someone with a trapped nerve, she had to find a position that minimised the pain from the bruises on her legs, which throbbed and chafed with every step. Her broken tooth ached permanently and a spasm would shoot down her dental nerve whenever she knocked it with her tongue, which now she was doing on purpose.

*Because the pain*, she thought, full of self-loathing, *is the punishment for my stupidity.*

For her crackpot, ill-thought-out plan that had landed her in a situation from which there appeared to be no escape.

'Becky arrived here only last night. She was given knockout drops before being badly abused. She's still under the influence of the drug and her memory is very hazy, so it might take her time to fully integrate into our community. I think it would be a good idea, therefore, if someone who's been with us for a while could say something to her.'

As if Jakob had given them the order to study the floor, eyes shot downwards. Like at a parents' evening when the school is looking for volunteers for the parent-teacher association.

Only one pair of eyes remained fixed on Emilia, seemingly intent on puncturing her and yet looking straight through her.

*I'm so alone sitting next to you*
*You just look right through me*

The woman, who was about her age, was sitting to Jakob's left and she was so petite that she barely made an imprint in her beanbag. Beside the massive figure of Lieberstett's assistant she looked like a doll. She wore a grey tracksuit with a hoodie, her hands thrust grimly in the pocket at the front. Her short black hair extended across her round head like a motorbike helmet, and so in her head Emilia baptised the woman 'Harley'. The fringe would soon need cutting to prevent it from hanging over the eyes, her most striking feature.

For they were blind.

'Hi, I'm Louise,' a woman opposite her said, but Emilia couldn't take her eyes off the blind woman staring at her with a painfully empty gaze.

'I've been here for half a year now and I'm very grateful for everything they've done for me.'

'Thanks, Louise. Would you tell Becky your story?' Jakob asked the woman diagonally to his right. She was one of those people who appear taller sitting down. Her legs seemed strangely short in relation to her body, which was larger than anybody else's here save for Jakob's.

'Sure.' She seemed quite shy, but clearly delighted to be able to say her piece. 'I'm a courier patient. Which means a courier brought me here. Like most normal mortals I didn't know about Ambrosia before I was admitted.' She smiled coyly. 'But somebody – and to this day I don't know who – found out I was being stalked. His name is Edgar and I made the mistake of meeting him through Tinder. After that I couldn't shake him off. It was harmless to begin with.'

The beanbag made a loud squeak when Louise changed position. 'He wrote me hundreds of letters and put them under my windscreen wipers. Scattered roses outside the front door. And he hired a private detective to spy on me. He sent me photos of other men I was meeting. Before– after photos as he called them. Then he stalked them too. Friends, colleagues, dates. And beat them up so badly they needed hospitalisation.'

Her subdued smile had disappeared and Louise sped up, as if trying to be done with an unpleasant report as quickly as possible.

'Edgar never raised a hand against me, but he broke my soul. I didn't dare have contact with anyone else because I was worried he'd hurt them. It got really bad when he started killing pets, even those of men I had only fleeting contact with. In the end I was close to killing myself just to get rid of Edgar for good. Because the police couldn't help me.

'Only Ambrosia,' Jakob said with a smile.

Louise looked at him gratefully. 'Exactly. Ambrosia gave me the opportunity to inflict on my tormentor what he made me suffer.'

'How?' Emilia asked, having finally turned away from the blind woman.

'My best friend had a horse he absolutely worshipped. Shania. A white horse. My stalker crept into the stable and injured the poor animal so badly that poor Shania had to be put down.'

'What about you?' Emilia probed. 'How did you confront your stalker?'

'Me?' Louise rose another few centimetres as she puffed out her chest and stated assuredly, 'I was allowed to break Edgar's leg.'

Shocked, Emilia held her breath until she asked the group, 'So are we talking about revenge and vigilantism?'

'We're talking about karma,' Jakob corrected her. 'At some point when the healing process is at an advanced stage, the meeting between victim and perpetrator takes place.'

'Which is also arranged by the courier you told me about?'

'Exactly.'

Emilia shook her head and stood up.

All the Ambrosia patients bar three were here.

*Seventy per cent. I'll probably never get a better proportion again.*

And so she did what she'd been contemplating over the past few hours: she grabbed the bull by the horns.

'Listen to me, every one of you. What I'm hearing is all very well, but I don't want to be part of it. I don't know exactly what you lot are. A sect, a religious community, an asylum, rehab, hotel, clique of diplomats. And I don't care either.'

She raised a hand to pacify the group and looked Louise in the eye. 'I can understand your approach: quid pro quo. The victim suffers all their life whereas the perpetrator gets off with probation. Maybe. And maybe you're in the right.

I don't intend to dissuade you from fighting your fight. But that's not why I'm here.'

Emilia avoided catching Jakob's eye. She was sure he'd try to interrupt her any second now.

'I'd rather talk to you about my daughter. Her name is Feline and she's fifteen years old.'

'Becky!'

*There it was.* Jakob's vocal intervention. 'This isn't the forum for—'

'Here's a photo of her,' Emilia went on, undeterred by Jakob's warning to keep quiet. 'It's crumpled because I always keep it in my trouser pocket.'

'Becky!' Jakob got to his feet.

Emilia took a step backwards and presented the photo to the group with her arm outstretched, like a warrior displaying an enemy's scalp. With all eyes now on her, she spoke faster. 'I have just one question for you, all of you, then I'll disappear again and you'll never hear another word from me. I also promise I won't tell anyone about this place here. I just want to know…'

Jakob was now beside her.

He grabbed her arm and pulled her to one side. 'We have our rules here in the morning group session,' he said firmly, but not impolitely. 'You don't speak until you're invited to.'

'But I have to know—'

A scream behind Jakob made her stop. When Lieberstett's assistant turned back to the group Emilia too could see why the other women had leaped up from their beanbags.

All apart from one.

'Jakob! Tabea needs help!' Louise said, stating the obvious.

The blind woman, who Emilia had baptised Harley and who must be Tabea, lay convulsed on the floor and let out a protracted, animal-like groan.

'Get out of here! All of you back to your rooms at once!' Jakob tried to make some room but nobody was listening. Nobody could tear their eyes away from the woman who was having the dangerous-looking fit.

'Get Lieberstett!' one of them barked.

'She's popped out to town,' Jakob said, kneeling beside Tabea. He didn't particularly look like he knew what he was doing; clearly he had no experience of medical emergencies.

'What about the duty doctor?' Louise said.

'He's stuck in traffic...' Jakob wiped his sweaty brow with his sleeve as Tabea's spasms became even wilder.

'Shit, there's nobody here at the moment.'

'Yes there is!' Emilia heard herself exclaim. She felt all eyes on her. 'I can help. I'm a nurse.'

The group immediately broke up, making room for her. Kneeling beside Jakob she forbade him from holding Tabea's hand.

'In cases like this it's the wrong thing to do,' she explained calmly.

'In cases like *this*? What's wrong with her?'

Lips smacking, twitching, convulsions. Eyes so skewed you could only see the whites.

All typical signs of an epileptic fit.

Something didn't fit with the diagnosis.

The moaning. It was only quiet and yet Emilia, who was up very close, could clearly make out a melody.

# 38

## ZORBACH

It was reasonable to assume that Olaf Norweg was a good pupil.

The private school he attended with Feline in Grunewald admitted pupils on the basis of their grades or the size of the parents' wallets. And nothing suggested that the Norwegs had coffers full of riches. Least of all where they lived.

Even non-Berliners knew the tower block in Schöneberg's Pallasstrasse from many a documentary on domestic violence, dilapidation or the drug use of its residents. The place had more visits from the police each year than sunsets.

It was thus a reasonable security measure that Olaf's mum had the chain on when she opened the door to her flat.

'Yes?' she asked through the crack, sounding as if she had a cold.

'Good morning. Sorry for disturbing you so early,' I said, introducing Alina and myself. 'We're investigating on behalf of Emilia Jagow. I'm sure you know Feline has disappeared and we'd like to speak to your son.'

'My son?'

'Olaf, yes. Is he at home?'

'In a manner of speaking,' the mother said, shutting the door in our noses again. I was slightly taken aback as she'd sounded tired but not unfriendly. But then I realised she was just taking off the chain.

'Feline Jagow?' she asked, rubbing her eyes. Frau Norweg looked as if she'd slept in the black linen dress that was almost as wrinkled as her face. But she was in pretty much the same state as us; we were both exhausted too, having spent the night merely dozing. At least Alina's opaque glasses and well-styled short wig disguised the fact she'd been on the sofa. Unlike my real, unkempt hair, her wig allowed her to make a halfway decent impression.

'Do you think we could ask Olaf a question or two?' Alina enquired.

'I fear you won't get an answer out of him,' the mother said.

'Couldn't we try at least?' I asked.

I noticed Frau Norweg was avoiding eye contact with me.

'Sure, be my guest,' she said, then asked us to follow her. Alina took my hand so I could help her navigate the unknown interior.

The small, square flat, with a tiny hallway that led to three rooms and a kitchen, was impeccably tidy. But it didn't look as sterile as the Jagows' bungalow, which was chiefly down to the personal things that caught my eye, such as the family photos on the walls. They only ever depicted mother and son, never a father, which led me to the not very bold theory that Frau Norweg was a single mum or maybe even a widow. Most of the pictures were holiday snaps showing

Olaf's mother looking far less tense than now. Tanned, smiling and with alert eyes. Which afforded a stark contrast to Olaf's melancholic teenage aura – most of the time he was scowling at the camera.

'I can't offer you anything, I'm afraid. I'm not used to visitors,' Frau Norweg apologised on the way to the sitting room.

'Is Olaf still asleep?' Alina asked.

'Most probably, yes,' the mother said, pointing to the wall with shelves where I was expecting to see a door to Olaf's bedroom. Then I realised what she was really pointing at.

*Oh my God!*

I instinctively raised my hand to my mouth in a gesture of embarrassment. 'Oh my goodness, we had no idea. We're dreadfully sorry. We'd never have bothered you had we known.'

# 39

For a while Frau Norweg didn't say another word. I even got the impression she was holding her breath while she looked at the container on the shelf with her son's ashes. She stared silently and still at the matt-black urn, as if trying to move it by sheer force of will.

After a few seconds had passed I cleared my throat in embarrassment. 'How did he die?'

'Of life.'

Alina squeezed my hand. Now she too had understood how thoroughly inappropriate our visit to the grieving mother was.

'I could make it easy for myself and give the names of those who destroyed him,' Olaf's mother said. 'But I've been grieving too long not to realise that this would make it too simple for me.'

*The names of those who destroyed him...*

'Was he bullied?' Alina said, asking the most obvious question.

Frau Norweg gave a weary shrug. 'If you mean there

wasn't a single day when he wasn't afraid to go to school because he didn't know what they'd do to him. Then, yes, he was bullied.' She stepped over to the shelves and picked up the black-and-white photo in a dark frame she'd placed beside the urn. The first picture in which I'd seen the boy, who appeared slightly too tall for his age, smile. And yet even in this photo he looked sad, which might be down to the fact that through the thick lenses of his glasses it was impossible to tell whether the smile had spread to his eyes.

'He was different,' Olaf's mother said, looking at Alina. 'You know what that's like, don't you, Frau Gregoriev?'

Alina nodded.

'I know you from the papers. I once read something about you that really impressed me. That time at school you applied to be a lollipop girl because you were able to prove to the school board that as a blind person you could regulate the traffic with your sense of hearing. Did you really do that?'

Alina said yes.

'Hmm, there's different and then there's different, isn't there? Even at primary school my son was teased because of his glasses. But although you couldn't see anything, Frau Gregoriev, I bet you earned the respect of the entire school.'

She put the photograph back. 'Olaf once explained to me the difference between a loner like Feline and a victim like himself. Feline wanted to be alone and that was seen as a sign of strength. He, on the other hand, was different but wanted to belong. Which in the eyes of the cool kids made him a weakling. First they'd beat him up in the playground, then ridicule him online when they uploaded the videos.'

Her lower lip was quivering and it seemed to be just a

matter of time before the dam broke and the tears came flooding out.

'I really blame myself. When his father left us I shouldn't have been so stubborn, thinking I could cope with it on my own. I ought to have moved out of the city and into the countryside. Or at least taken him out of that snobby school, which I needed three jobs to afford, despite Olaf's bursary.' She rubbed her tired eyes. 'I'm sorry, you didn't come here to listen to me moan. I shouldn't have invited you in just to give me the chance to talk to someone else apart from myself.'

We told her that it was we who ought to be apologising and accepted her invitation to sit on the sofa. 'Do you have any idea who might have abducted Feline?' Alina said, boldly steering the conversation to the real reason for our visit.

Olaf's mother, who was on a chair, patted her hair nervously. 'No, sorry. I wish she'd eloped with Olaf. They made a good pair, the two of them did.'

'Was he taught by Feline's father?' I said, venturing a shot in the dark. After all, he was our only suspect so far.

'Herr Jagow?'

I nodded.

'Sadly not.'

'Why sadly?'

'Herr Jagow is a good man. Olaf was never courageous enough to go to him with his problems – as I'm sure you know he's the teacher in charge of pastoral care. But Herr Jagow took it on himself to approach Olaf on a number of occasions and he also got in touch with me, which I give him great credit for. He took his responsibilities seriously and was genuinely interested in his pupils' problems, even when they avoided him and his office hours.' She cleared her throat. 'I know people talk behind his back, especially because of his dislike of technology. Apparently he wouldn't allow Feline to have a mobile. But do you know what? I think that's right. If I'd taken Olaf's silly smartphone away he wouldn't have had to read all those terrible things his classmates had put on the internet about him.'

I cursed myself for not having prepared ourselves better and done some research into Olaf Norweg before turning up here. I didn't even know how the boy died and I didn't dare ask the key question: *Are you absolutely certain that your son took his own life?*

As if Olaf's mother were able to read my mind she said, 'The police were here too, by the way. They thought it was suspicious that two pupils from the same school had disappeared within only a few weeks of each other. My son for good, Feline only temporarily, I hope. She was...' The mother bit her lip. 'She is such a good girl. Feline was the only one who stuck with Olaf.'

'Were they a couple?' Alina asked.

'No, I don't think so. But she was nice to him. I think she only did the train thing for his sake.'

'Train thing?'

She looked at me. 'Olaf was what you'd call a trainspotter.'

'He hung around railways?'

'That too. But his great passion was underground trains.'

I was getting goosebumps. A few moments ago I still thought we were at a dead end, but right now I felt as if this information was crucial, even though I didn't understand its significance for the time being.

'Olaf wanted to become an engineer, building tunnels and stations. Not a weekend went by when he wasn't riding the Berlin underground network. Feline went with him sometimes. It was his passion. And his undoing.' She looked at the urn again. 'For his first birthday party at secondary school he tried to make himself popular with his classmates by inviting them all to a convertible underground ride.'

'What's that?' I asked.

'A trip through Berlin's underworld in a wagon without a roof. There's nothing like it anywhere else in the world. Olaf was so proud that he'd got tickets for everybody. But disaster struck as soon as they got on at Deutsche Oper station. Someone poured the cola he'd bought for everyone all over his trousers. It looked as if he'd wet himself, though this didn't stop him from giving the talk he'd prepared for his classmates on the Berlin underground system. Someone filmed it and put it online with the comment: "Olaf has got the hots for trains, he even comes on the underground."'

I nodded. That sort of story was repeated thousands of times every day on social media. Violence breeds violence, they say. Statistically a victim of abuse has a much higher chance of becoming an abuser themselves than someone who enjoys a violence-free childhood.

I wondered what sort of a world we'd be living in a few years down the line once all those people whose souls were scarred by hatred and bullying in childhood had grown up. If they got that far.

'After that first video Olaf actually stuck it out for another three years,' Frau Norweg said, her voice getting softer. 'Until after the last horrid Instagram post when he entered a station for the last time and threw himself in front of the U7.'

'*Under the World*' flashed in my mind. And when I thought of Johannes Oerding's song and track 12 on Feline's playlist I had an idea.

'Did he leave a note?' asked Alina, who must have been thinking of the incident with TomTom on the underground platform and wanted to be sure that nobody had given Olaf a helping hand.

'No, but he called me shortly before and left a voicemail message explaining why he was doing it and saying he was sorry.'

Now the tears flowed and Olaf's mother did nothing to stop them. Sobbing, she kept on: 'You've been a policeman and crime reporter, Herr Zorbach. What do you think? If someone's hit by a train it's all rather quick, isn't it?'

'He didn't feel a thing,' I assured her by saying what she wanted to hear.

Then, after sitting there in silence for what must have been at least five excruciating minutes, we said goodbye. I was in a hurry to take the lift back down to get out of that concrete block.

Partly because I'd found the visit so depressing and urgently needed some fresh air. But more importantly because I could hardly wait to tell Alina about having solved another piece of Feline's playlist puzzle.

# 40

## EMILIA

In next to no time Jakob had organised a brand-new patient trolley, with which they transported Tabea from the main building into the annex where Emilia had been examined by Lieberstett upon admission yesterday.

Once there, Emilia first put the patient in the recovery position and flipped up the bars at the side of the bed to prevent her from rolling off the mattress. Then she made sure that her airways were free, and she removed all sharp and angular objects which Tabea might knock against and injure herself on if the convulsions got worse again. When the sleeves of Tabea's hoodie rolled up, Emilia could see that her forearms were covered in scratches.

'Here's our emergency kit,' Jakob said after he'd unlocked the medicine cupboard for Emilia.

Although the Ambrosia-Resort was lacking in doctors, nurses and orderlies, its in-house pharmacy was comparable to that of a university hospital.

'What do you need?' Jakob asked, again revealing that he wasn't here on account of his medical skills.

'Nothing.'

Jakob looked first at Tabea, her body still clenched and shaking on the trolley, then at Emilia. His harried eyes became suspicious.

'All the medicines in question would have to be administered via the rectum,' she explained. 'They wouldn't take effect for twenty minutes. An epileptic fit is usually over much more quickly. Look...'

Indeed, Tabea was already much calmer than she had been at the meeting. Emilia took her hand, which felt cold but wasn't so tense. 'Has anything like this happened to her before?' she asked Jakob.

'Not that I know. And I definitely *would* know because Tabea is something like a permanent resident here.'

'What does that mean?'

'She always ends up with the wrong men. Till now, however, her injuries had never been irreversible.'

'Her eyes were corroded?'

'With acid, yes.'

Jakob glanced at Tabea, whose chest was rising and falling as if she'd just completed a sprint. 'She was always a little confused, but ever since the injury to her eyes she seems to be living completely in her own world.'

'Who did it to her?'

'It's none of your business and I'm not going to discuss it. But maybe I should organise a radio.'

'Why?'

'In case it flares up again. Music has a soothing effect on Tabea. That's why we let her keep the thing we found on her.'

'What thing?'

'I'll show you.' Jakob went over to the desk and opened the drawer.

Emilia felt as if an ice cube were sliding down her spine. She shuddered in anticipation of what she was about to set eyes on.

'We didn't know that it could be used to locate Tabea,' Jakob said as he took the device out. 'That's why we confiscated it yesterday and switched the thing off. Since then she's been humming the songs of the playlist that was on it.'

*Feline!*

Emilia came within a whisker of calling out her daughter's name and slapping her hand over her mouth. For at first glance the device in Jakob's hand looked like a normal modern watch – had there not been a white earphone lead sticking out of it.

*Jesus Christ...*

Emilia was just about to grab Feline's MP3 player when Tabea's spasms started again. Worse and fiercer than before.

# 41

## ZORBACH

'I suppose that's that, then,' Alina said.

We were standing beside my car, two wheels of which I'd had to park up on the pavement. Today was market day on nearby Winterfeldplatz and most places were occupied by stallholders' or visitors' cars. The only free space I'd found might have been alright for a Smart, but not a Volvo.

I shook my head. 'Maybe not completely. Frau Norweg gave me an idea when she talked about her son's trainspotting.'

'What's this one, then?' Freezing, Alina turned her collar up. The fine drizzle was spoiling everyone's morning, but she wouldn't get into my car.

'Tell me quickly, then I'm going to jump on the underground and go to Nils's. He'll be sick to death with worry and I'll get there quicker than in your Volvo.'

'Underground is the key word,' I said excitedly.

'How?'

'As we know, the twelfth song in Feline's playlist begins with the letter U.'

'*Under the World*' – *Johannes Oerding.*

'So?'

'So, that could stand for underground!'

'I see,' she remarked flatly. '*Je meurs là.* In an underground station?'

'I know it sounds a bit far-fetched, but two other songs on the playlist point in the same direction.'

'Which ones?'

'Humour me, and think about the I of "I Need You" and the O of "Open Eyes".'

'I and O?' she said. 'Alright, where's the connection to the underground?'

Our faces glistened in the drizzle.

'What if you read the initial letters as numbers?' I said.

'I and O?' Alina repeated sceptically, then her eyebrows popped above the rim of her glasses and I saw she'd got it.

'Ten!'

IO.

'Correct.!

'And U – I O stands for…'

'… U ten,' I said with a broad grin.

A car hooted at three youngsters crossing the parallel road without paying attention to the traffic. Two of them stuck their middle finger up at the woman without looking to see who'd had to brake so suddenly for them.

'Oh, Zorbach…' Alina said, almost with pity in her voice, which made me angry as I was sure I was close to solving the playlist puzzle now, whereas she didn't seem to be making any effort to follow my thought processes. 'The whole Olaf thing was a real long shot and I ought to have known better than to go along with you. But now you've got completely carried away.'

'What do you mean?' I said huffily, running a hand through my wet hair. 'I think there's a lot of evidence. Quite apart from the fact that Olaf was an underground trainspotter and Feline used to accompany him on his trips, just listen to the playlist again.'

From my mobile I read:

'Track 3: Lotte sings about someone who's trapped behind a thousand walls in a maze. Track 5: Justin Jesso is more specific: "Under". And even more clearly, track 12: "Under the World". Right at the start Johannes Oerding even sings something about being on track. Feline hasn't chosen all of this purely by chance.'

Alina shook her head as I put my phone away. 'You're trying to see connections where there aren't any.'

I stuck to my guns. '*I'm dying there*,' I said, again citing Feline's cryptic message in French produced by the initial letters of the first nine songs. 'What if the place she's being held captive is somewhere on the U10 line?'

Alina was clearly struggling to suppress a tired yawn. Wearily she said, 'I don't want to disappoint you, Alex. But there's one massive problem with your theory.'

'What's that?'

'It's evident you don't take public transport very often. Otherwise you'd know that Berlin doesn't have a U10 line. The network stops at U9.'

*Shit!*

I could practically hear the bubble burst inside my head.

My euphoria disappeared as quickly as the excitement about my underground theory had been sparked.

*JE MEURS LA*
*UIO*
*U ten.*

'Sorry, Zorbach,' Alina said. 'I wish there was more we could give Emilia Jagow and Stoya, but we have to accept that this isn't going to get us any further.'

I nodded even though I sensed I was on the right road and had merely taken the wrong fork at some point. But I had no time to retrace my steps and start thinking about this from scratch again, which distressed me as I felt that Feline's life depended on our investigation. Maybe it was arrogance and I had too high an opinion of myself, but I knew I'd blame myself for having given up too early when I heard later in prison that they'd found her body.

But what else could I do today?

In less than six hours I was going to be locked up. Too little time to solve the playlist puzzle, find Feline and bring her back to her mother. Shit, there was barely enough time to do what I'd been chickening out of for weeks. Because I was scared.

'I'm sorry,' Alina said again, now in that tone of voice that Nicci used to adopt when after our separation I told her I'd never wanted it to come to that.

She pressed her lips together sadly and shrugged. I didn't know whether she was regretful about our farewell or our failure to find Feline – both, probably.

'Alright, then,' I said and wondered whether to embrace Alina one final time. I decided to keep my distance because whichever way she reacted, it would have made me sad. Both the potential rebuff and the feeling that I wouldn't be able to hold her again for ages, assuming she let me, which I thought unlikely.

'Are you going to the prison now?' she asked.

I shook my head. 'No.'

Over the past few hours I'd driven to the wreckage of a workshop in Albrechts Teerofen to encounter a murdered woman who even in her dying moments had clutched her baby protectively. In Moabit I'd seen a man knocked down and killed before my very eyes. And I'd just spoken to a mother whose life had lost all its meaning. All that was dreadful.

And yet, as Alina and I went our separate ways for good, I knew that something far worse awaited me. And I didn't mean my prison sentence.

# 42

## EMILIA

Emilia gazed through the window at the park where she saw Jakob hurrying towards the main building.

'You've got to get Tabea to hospital immediately,' she'd urged Lieberstett's right-hand man, before adding, 'This needs to be cleared up,' as Tabea went into even wilder spasms.

'We *are* a hospital,' Jakob tried to protest.

'With no doctors or care staff.'

'We can't afford them round the clock. It's just a bit of bad luck that both Dr Lieberstett and the duty doctor happen to be indisposed at the same time. Shit.' Clearly Jakob had been in two minds as to whether he could leave his charges here on their own. But when Tabea began choking, he made a quick decision. 'Stay with her. I'm going to see where the doctor's got to.'

Emilia didn't hear Jakob lock the door behind him.

Yesterday he'd locked her up. Today, either he was sure that an escape from this high-surveillance compound was impossible, or in the commotion he'd forgotten to do it.

She watched him enter the main building.

*Not so fast*, Emilia urged him. Even though she herself was gripped by anxiety that felt like a shivering fit. Her worry about Feline was manifesting itself psychosomatically. Feverish hot flushes alternated with the sensation that she was suffering from hypothermia.

*Where are you, my darling?*

When Jakob had disappeared from her field of vision, Emilia turned to the woman who was still thrashing around on the patient trolley and said icily, 'You can stop your play-acting now, Tabea.'

# 43

Emilia undid the bedrail on Tabea's trolley, then went to the desk where Jakob had left Feline's 'watch'. He must have thought it was useless without a charged battery.

'Where did you get my daughter's MP3 player?' she asked Tabea.

The fake patient hesitated before sitting up. She sat on the edge of the trolley, her legs dangling, and immediately started scratching her left forearm with the fingers of her right hand. She appeared to be looking straight past Emilia. Her pupils, which in the slightly colder light of the treatment room looked like a scratched screen, were fixed on something between the door and the basin on the wall. Emilia came closer and made a windscreen-wiper gesture with the watch in her hand. Tabea didn't react.

Maybe she's faking now too?

*Maybe she's no blinder than she is epileptic and is merely wearing special contact lenses?*

'At the group session this morning you reacted to the name Feline and pretended to have an epileptic fit. Why? What were you trying to say to me?'

*Say*, as Emilia was to learn, was the wrong word when it came to Tabea. If she were trying to communicate at all it was in another way which unsettled Emilia at first. For Tabea started to sing: '... *your walls won't stop me...*'

Emilia felt the hairs on her arms stand up.

*Wait. Is that...*

'Is that a song from Feline's playlist?'

In the car on the way to the supermarket Emilia had googled most of the songs on the printout Alina had given her, but she couldn't remember all the titles and artists.

'Talk to me! Where's my daughter? What do you know about her?'

Emilia pressed all the buttons on the side of the watch but none had the desired effect. Jakob must be right. The screen remained blank.

Tabea, however, became more animated. She sang louder. Flat, but the lyrics were intelligible: '*Every path leads in, but none leads out.*'

'What are you trying to tell me now? Is Feline locked up? Behind walls?'

*Stupid question. Of course she is.*

Emilia felt like slapping herself. She mustn't waste a single question with this crazed woman. If Tabea were going to answer at all then it should be something relevant and before Jakob returned.

'How is Feline?'

*Is she still alive?*

Tabea took a deep breath as if she were about to dive

underwater and scratched herself even harder. Then she began to sing again:

'… *We arrive alone. We leave alone…*'

'That's from the playlist too, isn't it? Tim Bendzko?'

Emilia thought she'd heard this hit on the radio once.

'So you were together but now she's alone. Can you tell me where? Where were you kept prisoner?'

Tabea answered with another riddle. A new song. Another cryptic lyric.

'… *but I couldn't find a light!*'

*Dark? Is my little girl all alone in the dark behind walls?*

Was that what Tabea was trying to tell her?

Emilia had an idea.

She went back to the desk and yanked open the drawer Jakob had taken the watch from. It was a complete mess. Old batteries, lighters, cigarettes, aspirins and other medicines, paperclips, receipts and pieces of paper. But no USB lead to charge the watch. Nor a power bank or anything similar. So she was even more surprised when she suddenly heard a piano. Quiet and tinny, because the sound had to press itself through the tiny in-ear headphones that Tabea was plugging into her ears.

'How did you manage *that*?' Emilia asked in astonishment.

The blind woman must have found a combination of buttons that squeezed something like the last bit of battery from the watch. Whatever it was, she'd activated the playlist.

'*Why are you doing this to yourself? You must never forgive!*' Tabea began singing along to the track she was listening to through the earphones. She visibly relaxed to the music and stopped running her fingernails across her sore skin.

'Do you know where my daughter is?' Emilia tried again.

'Yes.'

Good God.

A clear answer. Spoken by a raw, throaty, sandpaper voice. No sooner had Tabea uttered 'Yes' than Emilia's body was flushed with heat, accompanied by an unpleasant prickly sensation from her head to her toes, urging her to scratch. The exhilaration of hope remained even when Tabea uttered her first full sentence: 'I'll tell you, but there's a price.'

# 44

## ZORBACH

The ferry set me down on the shore of Scharfwerder island. It had been a mere three-minute trip from the DLRG river rescue station and yet when I got off I again felt as if I'd left Berlin and arrived at the end of a long journey.

Everything here seemed quiet and peaceful. The dense woodland stretching from the middle of the island into the water, its trees devoid of leaves in the winter, which made the mighty boughs of the lime trees, oaks and chestnuts appear even more majestic. The paths lovingly laid with dark cobbles on this island that was car-free, save for the odd e-vehicle.

And of course the schoolhouse with its red-tiled roof; beside it the new building housing the dormitories, which by Berlin standards was unusually in harmony with the architecture of the boarding school that had stood here for almost a century.

Fortunately there was a pause in the drizzle.

I headed along the jetty flanked by reeds straight for the school building, pleased that it was Reformation Day. A normal working day in Berlin, but in the private Protestant school a holiday; I didn't have to take Julian out of lessons.

*How serene it is here*, I thought naively, thinking of the warm opening lines of 'Live in Peace', perhaps the saddest song on Feline's playlist. If I hadn't known better I might have thought she'd chosen it specially for me, as a soundtrack for saying goodbye to my son before starting my prison sentence.

*I hope your life is happy and bright*
*And that you find someone to hold you tight*

As I took a deep breath of cold air, I wondered what it said about our society and the world in which we lived that we often put our children through emotional hell only to plonk them later in wonderful places such as this, in the hope that they'll be able to shake off their demons.

*I hope your curiosity wins the day*
*Spread your wings and fly away*

How much suffering we could spare them if we saw to it from the beginning that the little things enjoyed a peaceful childhood rather than being sent to graffiti-smeared schools where nobody dared enter the filthy loos apart from the junkies who scored their gear from the playground dealer.

*That's too cheap, Zorbach*, was my next thought, now just a few metres away from the entrance to the main building that housed the headmistress's office. A little over a year ago I'd entrusted Julian to her care – she was an expert in traumatised children.

Because when a child had a problem, of course it was too easy to shift the blame onto the school, incompetent teachers or an idle youth welfare office. The responsibility always began with the parents. *Which meant me.*

There was no point pretending – if I hadn't kept setting the wrong priorities in life, if I hadn't kept focusing on my work, my marriage wouldn't have broken down. My wife wouldn't have died. And the sadist who called himself the 'Eye Collector' would never have got his hands on my son if I'd looked after him better instead of chasing after a serial killer with Alina.

*Julian.*

My heart was in my mouth as I climbed the steps to the school building. For days now I'd been terrified of this final visit. I was worried I'd say the wrong thing. Or maybe even not be able to say anything at all because I'd start crying my eyes out at the prospect of being locked away from my son for the next couple of years.

*Julian!*

I was thinking so intensely of him that I didn't realise I wasn't just hearing the name in my mind.

*'JULIAN!'*

A girl. She was yelling her head off and her voice was so high and shrill that it was impossible to tell her age. I dropped the bag with the presents I'd bought for Julian as a parting gift and ran to my right, around the main building. Here I ended up by the fence of a multipurpose sports pitch. The girl's screaming got louder.

She had long hair that wafted in the wind. I only noticed its dyed platinum-blond colour because of the sharp contrast it made with her shiny black jacket. She was prancing around in the vicinity of the penalty spot, gesticulating wildly beside two figures wrestling each other.

*'JULIAN! STOP!'*

Shoving open a wire mesh gate I ran over to the group of three. With every metre I got closer, the colour of the all-weather pitch where the boys were fighting seemed to become more intense. From light red to claret to blood red.

*Blood?*

Yes. The red wasn't just beside the head of the boy lying on the ground, it was also on the fist of the one sitting on top and aiming another punch.

'JULIAN!' I now shouted myself, having recognised him. Despite his face contorted with anger, despite his crazed look and despite the fact that he was furiously beating a fellow pupil to death.

*'JULIAN!'* I was about to yell again, but it wasn't necessary. As if my voice had flicked a switch inside him, he froze, looked up at me and rolled, panting, off his bloodied opponent, who immediately put both hands in front of his face, screaming when he touched his nose, which must be broken.

*Thank God. He's still alive. He can move. He's not paralysed. My son hasn't killed or crippled anyone.*

These were my first thoughts when I crouched down to Julian. The second, when he bashed my arm away, was: 'What the hell's going on here?'

I must have spoken these words out loud, because Julian answered, 'None of your business. Shit, Dad. What are you doing here?'

'Thanks,' said the blond girl who'd alerted me. For a moment I'd forgotten she was there.

'Get lost, Stella!' Julian barked as he got to his feet. She gave him the finger, then turned away and stomped off the pitch.

I watched her go then looked up at the windows of the main building and annexes, from which some pupils must have been watching us, although I couldn't see anyone. Then I checked out Julian's victim, who was around the same age. He'd also got to his feet now and was desperately trying to stop his nose bleeding.

The boy, who looked a bit taller and stronger than Julian, had made the mistake of running a hand through his blond hair, giving his carefully blow-dried quiff a red streak.

I handed him a tissue and turned back to Julian.

'For Christ's sake, what got into you? Do you want to be kicked out?'

He just waved his hand dismissively and walked off.

'Hey, wait,' I shouted after him, then started walking too and caught him up by the gate. 'What was that just now? What was it all about?'

Julian stopped. Apart from a small scratch on his right cheek, he'd come out of the fight unscathed. I was in shock. Not because he looked paler than when we'd last met, but because I'd never seen so much of myself in him before. The same chin jutting out aggressively when something didn't suit him. The same dark rings around his eyes that looked as if they'd been painted on. The world-weariness that was already afflicting him. Far too intensely and far too early.

'You want to know what it was about?' he asked.

I nodded.

'What do you think? What it's always about? Every fucking day after day after day after day. There's only one topic they ever go on about. Laugh at me for, tease me about, whisper about behind my back or – like Ansgar – permanently diss me for.'

As if God had a pronounced sense of drama, the sky, sunny till now, darkened as a raincloud drifted over our heads.

'It's about you, Dad,' Julian said. His words hit me like punches. As did the ones that followed, which I took on the body without putting up any guard: 'You killed an innocent man. You're going to prison. How popular do you think I am here with a father like you? Every idiot challenges me to a fight.'

I cleared my throat and opened my mouth without knowing what to say. Without knowing if I could say anything because my tongue suddenly felt paralysed.

'Oh dear... have I shattered your idyllic world?' Julian asked, sniffing. 'You think you're coming to visit me in the South Seas and the fucking school here is Villa Villekulla. But for me it's like a cage in which there's a fight every day. And today's fight, against Ansgar, I would've won.'

'Would have?' I croaked aghast, pointing at the figure staggering slowly from the sports pitch, who just a couple of minutes ago Julian was beating to a pulp. 'You *did* win the fight. For God's sake, you almost killed that boy.'

'Sure, that's what it looks like in your world. But in my world my prison daddy came to the rescue. That's what they'll be saying in the playground tomorrow.'

I felt winded. The conversation was like a continuation of the unequal struggle between my son and Ansgar. All of a sudden I realised why his words had hit me so hard.

*Because they're true.*

It's often said that nothing hurts more than a lie. But that's wrong. The deepest wounds are caused by the blunt, unsparing truth – when it's brought home to you that you've made a mistake that cannot ever be rectified.

'Was that your parting gift to me?' Julian asked. 'Popping in here briefly to destroy my reputation even more before disappearing again for a few years? Thanks a bloody bunch. Like everything else in life you've nailed that too.'

Then I noticed we were being watched.

# 45

The figure keeping an eye on us was sitting on a park bench about thirty metres away.

*A teacher?*

The age would be about right, but he was too far away for me to be able to recognise him.

I wondered whether he'd been watching the fight the whole time and, if so, why he hadn't responded to Stella's cry for help and stepped in. But I didn't have time to confront the man if I wanted to avoid parting from Julian like this.

'Hey, wait. Please,' I called after my son, but he didn't even turn around. He ran past the bag of presents I'd dropped, up the steps to the main building and went in the entrance. In two minds as to whether to follow him, I looked around helplessly. Rarely had I felt so empty and alone.

Ansgar had left the sports pitch on the other side. Even the man on the bench had gone.

*Like everything else in life you've nailed that too.*

I decided against making things worse and more embarrassing for the two of us, so I went back to the ferry.

A video camera icon appeared on my phone. I opened the WhatsApp when I got to the jetty. The file began with black, juddery pictures, followed by what looked like a comet's tail because the groaning camerawoman had panned across a street lamp before focusing on the body. A body I'd seen a few hours ago with my own eyes lying on the tarmac in this position. Albeit from a different angle.

I'd seen about a third of the clip when the sender called me.

'Why are you sending me this?' I asked Stoya.

'I think the question we should be asking is: Why are you and Alina on a video captured by a chance witness in Moabit? Not long after you'd already fled from one crime scene in Albrechts Teerofen?'

'We can talk about this in an hour. I'm heading to the prison now,' I said, hanging up.

Less than five minutes later the ferry dropped me back at the school car park on the mainland. As soon as I got off the boat I sensed something wasn't right with the Volvo. My hunch became a certainty when I got closer.

The driver's door was open.

Not wide open, but enough for me to know I hadn't left it like that.

I opened the door and leaned in to see if anything had been nicked.

*No, but...*

At first glance it appeared that nothing had been taken. Even the bag I'd packed for prison a few days ago was still on the back seat.

And yet I felt as if my sombre thoughts had found a way

out of my body to transform into a grey, toxic fog I was becoming lost in.

For the culprit *(a man, a woman?)* had done something far more worrying than break into my car.

As I looked around, scanning the deserted car park for witnesses or anyone who might have been secretly watching, I recalled the man who'd been observing me on the island from the park bench. This time I couldn't see anything apart from a carelessly discarded plastic bottle rolling across the tarmac in the wind.

There was only me and this female singing voice, almost supplicatory, who in the chorus rolled her Rs like a Spaniard.

... *Parrra, Parrradise...*

Somewhere I'd never felt so far away from as now.

*VIZE, R4GE, Emie.*

Track 15 on Feline's playlist rang out muffled and distorted from the speakers in the dashboard. But the person who'd put the CD on repeat in my old car stereo was long gone.

# 46

## EMILIA

*'Do you know where my daughter is?'*

*'I'll tell you, but there's a price.'*

To begin with, what Tabea was asking for in return seemed impossible to satisfy. Then she recalled that she'd had the object of Tabea's desire in her hands only a few minutes ago.

*'Give me a cigarette,'* Tabea had demanded. And there were some in the desk, along with the lighter that Emilia had to help Tabea with because of her acid-damaged eyes.

'Thanks,' Tabea said, coughing the tangy smoke into the room. She was still scratching her arms between drags, but nowhere near as severely as before.

'Where's Feline?' Emilia asked for what must have been the tenth time. Only a minute or so ago she was sure she was dealing with a wild, psychologically disoriented and spaced-out woman. Now she clung to the hope that Tabea would help her discover the truth.

About Feline.

'Where is she?'

She had to speak at the top of her voice to be heard over the music Tabea was still listening to with earphones and which continued to relax her, it seemed.

But Emilia had clearly got through to her, for Tabea answered and not just with song lyrics.

Although not in complete sentences.

'My boyfriend.'

'She's with your boyfriend? Did your *boyfriend* abduct my Feline?'

Tabea nodded.

'Where is she? Where did he take her?'

'Tank.'

'To a tank?'

Another perfectly normal word. But from this day onwards its meaning would be changed for Emilia forever.

Tabea put her hand out to Emilia, who took a step backwards, as she didn't want to be touched in this moment of extreme emotional tension.

'Give me the mobile, please.'

This *was* a full sentence, but Emilia didn't grasp what the patient wanted from her. 'I don't have a mobile.'

Tabea began singing again.

'... *you know your way around your maze.*'

'What sort of maze? I don't know my way around here. I don't know how to get hold of a mobile.' She grabbed Tabea by her bony arm, really wanting to shake the answers out of her.

'Out there. Porter. Toilet. He hid it.'

'Who?'

'My boyfriend.'

Emilia shrank back again. Puzzled, she asked, 'Are you

saying that your boyfriend, who abducted Feline, has hidden a mobile phone in a loo here?'

Tabea nodded.

'Who is it? Tell me his name.'

Tabea shook her head defiantly, at which Emilia took away the MP3 player by disconnecting the lead from the watch that was in Tabea's lap.

The blind woman began crying at once. Like a baby that's had its toy taken away.

'Tell me who your boyfriend is and you'll get your music back!'

Another cough followed more frantic puffs on the cigarette that was almost finished. 'I'll light you another one,' Emilia said. 'And I'll give you back your music. All you have to do is answer my questions.'

'Okay, okay, okay,' Tabea said, nodding hectically, no longer like an infant but an addict in search of the necessary hit.

When the watch was reconnected to the earphones she relaxed again, as if the music had flipped a switch inside her. From unpredictable to disturbed, but approachable at least.

'The name!' Emilia demanded once more, grabbing Tabea by the elbows as if she were about to snatch the watch again. Tabea crossed her arms in front of her chest and put the MP3 player out of Emilia's reach.

Her lower lip quivering, she whispered.

A single short word.

# 47

## ALINA

Black coffee, a croissant straight from the oven and his aftershave that smelled of ginger.

Three of her favourite aromas delighted her nose simultaneously when Nils bought breakfast to her improvised bed. He put the tray on the coffee table, which TomTom was lying beneath. It was a peace offering, although Alina knew that she was the one who ought to be making an approach to him. It was she, not Nils, who after a heated argument had been out all night with her ex-partner and then crept silently back into the apartment, falling asleep with exhaustion on the sofa while Nils was still in the shower.

'I would have let you sleep on,' he said softly. 'But you've got to take your pills.'

At the thought of her medicine Alina pressed her eyelids together more tightly.

'Nils...' she began in a gnarled voice. After sleeping her vocal cords often felt like rusty bicycle chains that had trouble getting going. Today it was even worse. Two dead people in just one night, followed by interrogations, discussions and disturbing messages someone had left in her own flat, was too much for her suppression mechanism that was operating at full stretch. Even after she'd gulped down the glass of water Nils had also brought, the words still sounded as if they were being transported from the depths of her throat by a faulty conveyor belt.

'You were right. I should never have allowed myself to get mixed up with Zorbach again.'

'Did he hurt you?'

'No, he didn't. But he attracts evil like a drain does water. If you don't stay far enough away from him you get sucked in and then it's impossible to get out of the whirlpool.'

Nils sat beside her on the edge of the sofa. 'Would you tell me what happened?'

'First I want to say that I'm not going to take my pills any more.'

'But—'

Alina interrupted him; she didn't have the strength for a discussion. 'I know what you're going to say. If I stop taking them my eyes will reject the retinas. The operation would have been in vain, I can't have a second one and I'll remain blind forever. But...'

'But what?'

She couldn't help thinking of Tim Bendzko, track 14 on Feline's playlist. A song that seemed to have been composed especially for her and her situation.

*Do you see the world as it is?*
*How can you bear*

*That its dark sides*
*Eclipse all that is fair?*

'I just think I find the world more tolerable in the dark,' Alina said quietly. 'I don't want to see all of that.'

'What? What don't you want to see?'

She wished she were able to cry; she urgently needed an outlet for her pent-up despair. But not a single tear ran from her painful eyes. Maybe her mind was too preoccupied with whether she could take Nils into her confidence. She hated her reluctance, felt ashamed of her fear, for her boyfriend had never given her reason to doubt him. The fact that he had the key to her flat and knew her habits didn't justify her suspicion that he might have been the one who'd harassed her on the underground or been the intruder in her flat.

Besides, she needed someone to talk to. And so she silenced the warning voices inside her head and replaced them with another track from Feline's playlist, one of the few happy songs.

*I need you!*

*Yes, I do need you.* Beth Ditto's longing was nothing compared to how desperate Alina was to confide in Nils, and so she gave him a full and frank account of what had happened to her in a matter of a few hours the previous night.

When she began talking about the murder of the 'courier', Nils took her hand. She felt like withdrawing it because she didn't think she deserved to be treated so kindly. Not after abandoning the dead man on the road. She was expecting Nils to criticise her too. As an engineer it was second nature to him to examine every single aspect of the circumstances with the utmost precision. Every calculation was checked three times to ensure that the control units actually worked later. He'd never be able to overlook the fact that they hadn't stuck to the rules, not even calling an ambulance. But to her astonishment he asked only one question, which was about Zorbach's underground theory.

'So he thinks the last songs are a clue to a stretch of the underground?

'Yes, U10. But it doesn't exist.'

'Yes, it does.'

In amazement Alina opened her eyes for the first time since she awoke and got a fright from the image she saw. She'd once heard Edvard Munch's famous painting *The Scream* described in a podcast: painful colours in waves, and a blood-red sky above an emaciated face, contorted into the scream.

Against the background of the rising winter sun through the window, Nils's face looked equally disturbing.

*Another reason to stop taking the medicine.*

'U10 does exist,' Nils explained. 'But it's not in operation. I know that because I was brought in as part of a feasibility study looking into what was required to accomplish the construction of the line.'

'So it was planned but never built?'

'Hold on.' Nils went away and came back with his laptop, a hulking, shatterproof thing that could survive being dropped on construction sites. With just a few mouse clicks he found the plans he'd been sent for the study.

'Here it is. Originally it was going to run from Weissensee via Alexanderplatz to Potsdamer Platz, and later to Lichterfelde in the western part of the city. Since 1972 it's been known as U10. But in 1993 the plan was abandoned in favour of the new U3 line.'

*Trainspotter.*

Alina couldn't help think of Olaf and the conversation with his grieving mother. She propped herself up on the sofa with her elbows and then sat. 'That might be really interesting for rail freaks like you, and Berlin historians, but a girl can't be hidden in a plan.'

'She can in ghost stations.'

Alina felt queasy. 'What did you say?'

'The U10 line is one of those fascinating Berlin underworlds that barely anybody knows about but which actually exist. Because of all the preparatory works, skeleton tunnels and ghost stations that were never put into operation, the U10 is also known as a phantom line.'

It felt as if thousands of ants were crawling up her arms to her neck. Alina shook herself, but could not cast off the excitement triggered by what Nils was saying.

'Have you got a plan of the proposed line from back then on your computer?' she asked.

'Of course.'

Alina closed her eyes again. In her head she heard the choruses from tracks 10 and 11 on Feline's playlist. She thought of the song titles. The M from 'Million Tweets' and the number '85'.

Then she asked Nils what was perhaps the key question. 'Does the abbreviation M85 have anything to do with the underground too?'

He shook his head. 'No, but...'

'But what?'

'So far as I know that's a bus line.'

# 48

## Emilia

The wind whipping up from the lake flew down the back of her neck, causing Emilia to shudder as much as Tabea's voice still ringing in her ears, having revealed the nickname of Feline's abductor.

'You said he was your boyfriend?

'Yes.'

'Your boyfriend abducted my daughter?'

But then Tabea had started to sing again: '... *When you lie on the floor, I lie down beside you...*'

'How can someone who abducts children and destroys their eyes be your boyfriend?'

'... *I saw heaven in your eyes, now I see empty skies, don't let me down...*'

If this was an answer it was as bizarre as the entire situation Emilia found herself in. Locked up on the premises of a sect-like community of vigilantes, searching for answers in the cryptic songs of an other-worldly woman.

Tabea was evidently so mad that she didn't appear to hold it against her 'boyfriend' that he'd taken away her sight. The way she talked *(and sang?)* about him, she sounded sympathetic, as if her disability, which had been caused deliberately, were an unavoidable part of a larger plan; Tabea wouldn't have been admitted to Ambrosia had her injuries not been so severe. And the mobile phone she'd talked about also seemed to play an important role in the execution of this shady plan.

*'Out there. Porter. Toilet. He hid it.'*

When Tabea had stopped uttering anything meaningful and Jakob still wasn't back, Emilia went to check whether this telephone actually existed where Tabea said it was. Without her coat, which she'd left behind in the room where they'd had their morning session, and without gloves and hat, which she could have done with in this frosty weather, even though it was only a short walk to the exit. The only thing wrapped around her head was a cloud of dark thoughts.

*Feline is in a tank. Abducted by a beast.*

Wet gravel crunched beneath her feet on her way through the park. She looked around in vain for the security cameras she'd been threatened with. They must be somewhere here in the trees.

Emilia quickened her pace.

From a distance the porter's lodge looked like a half-timbered building. As she got closer, however, Emilia realised that the wooden beams had merely been painted on, like the windows facing the park. The porter could only see out of the side of the lodge to the entrance barrier, where the perverts from the 'supermarket' had dumped her from the car only yesterday.

Emilia walked around the hut.

'Where do you think you're going, eh?'

The porter, who'd stepped outside, was wearing grey flannel trousers and a blue blazer, on which she spotted the logo of a well-known security firm. So he was a contractor, which might make this a little easier. Although he would have had his instructions drilled into him – nobody must be allowed to leave the grounds – he wasn't an Ambrosia employee and thus no more loyal, perhaps, than you might expect him to be at twelve euros an hour.

'To the loo!' Emilia said, pointing to the grey door at the back of the porter's building. It had a wheelchair and baby sign.

Licking his front teeth, which were slightly too long for his narrow lips, the porter said, 'Why don't you go in your room?'

'My period's just come on this minute while I was out for a walk,' Emilia said, rattling off her lie. 'One of the other patients said there were sanitary pads in the disabled loo.'

'Really? I never noticed,' the porter muttered, and before it could occur to him to take a look himself, Emilia had already dashed into the toilet, which she locked from the inside.

Inside the WC it unsurprisingly smelled of citrus detergent and disinfectant, and it looked as Emilia suspected it would. Tiles hardly ever stepped on, not even a hint of them being scuffed, were reflected in unscratched enamel and chrome fittings. The handles beside the disabled toilet were padded with shiny plastic, and the mirror above the sink even had some masking tape stuck to it that the painter had forgotten there.

*Where can it be?*

Emilia first looked for the mobile in the obvious places, although without tools she couldn't get into the cistern that was built into the wall. Her pulse got faster when she saw a recessed joint in the floor, right beside the changing table. But this was just careless work by the builders. No secret hiding place beneath the tiles that could be opened by hand.

*Shit.*

Emilia spent a fair while in a fruitless attempt to open the soap dispenser on the wall, but it could only be changed with a particular Allen key, which meant it was hardly likely to be the hiding place for an emergency mobile.

All she'd achieved was to cover her hands in soap.

She pushed up the lever for the mixer tap and held her sticky fingers under the jet of water. Emilia stared thoughtfully at the waste, where the water was swirling and running away very slowly.

'Why's that?' Emilia thought out loud, unable to take her eyes off the gently spinning whirlpool. *I only turned on the tap for a bit. This loo is hardly ever used, and yet...*

... there were several centimetres of water in the sink and it was barely draining away.

Emilia kneeled and her suspicion hardened. The siphon was easy to unscrew. When she removed the larger vertical pipe from its fitting, what was left in the sink immediately emptied onto the floor. Her jeans were soaked by the water that now headed for the floor drain in the tiles.

*Heavy*, Emilia thought as she weighed up the unscrewed stainless-steel tube in her hands. *Too heavy*, unless there was something inside that shouldn't be there.

*Like a plastic bag wrapped in packing tape to make it waterproof!*

Emilia pulled excitedly on a flap and out came the object hidden in the pipe.

Her hands were trembling and she'd lost all sense of time, which was why she almost jumped out of her skin when she heard a loud noise and the door shook.

'Hey, you in there,' roared the porter who must have slapped the door.

'Yes?'

'Come out, now!'

'Just a minute!'

Emilia ripped open the bag like a greedy child would a packet of gummi bears. First an object like a lighter came out, followed by a something the size of a slim packet of cigarettes.

For a split second she wondered if she'd just found one of the employees' secret tobacco stash, but then she saw the cable glistening damply and knew she was holding a power bank.

And a mobile phone!

'Almost done!'

Emilia pumped her fist in childish delight at her discovery.

'No, not almost. Now! Doctor Lieberstett's looking for you. If you don't open up I'm coming in.' Despite the porter's threats Emilia felt like whooping loudly and dancing with joy. Even the painful wounds covering her body were forgotten for the moment.

She'd rarely felt so full of energy. And rarely had she been brought crashing back to earth so fast by the cold, terrifying truth.

For when she took the mobile out of its protective wrapping, she realised exactly who it belonged to.

*Thomas!*

The moment Emilia saw the shattered screen that looked like an outsize snowflake Emilia recognised the phone that her husband had said he'd lost weeks ago. Her hands shaking badly, she connected the mobile to the power bank. Outside the porter was cursing, probably because the key he'd selected didn't fit. She switched the phone on and immediately entered the PIN she had in her head. It worked, and when she found her own number in the address book, she had the definitive, shocking proof. She and Thomas had twin SIMs; their saved contacts were identical.

'I'm coming in now!' the porter shouted at the very moment the mobile connected to a network.

# 49

## ALINA

'Emilia?'

She'd just been examining the planned but never finished U10 line with Nils for the umpteenth time when her mobile rang, announcing Feline's mother's name. Alina had saved the contact ages ago in case any appointments for Feline's physiotherapy sessions had to be changed.

'I can't talk for long.'

Yes, it was Emilia.

Although she hadn't put it on speaker, Alina turned to the side on the sofa for privacy.

She couldn't bear anyone listening to her when she was on the phone. For some reason it always made her feel hampered and she found it hard to speak openly, even if the person in earshot was one of her nearest and dearest like Nils.

'Where are you?' Alina asked. Before Emilia replied she heard a dull thud and the muffled angry cries of a man in the background.

'In the Ambrosia-Resort. I'm locked in a loo here. There's

just a short section of waste pipe separating me from the guy who's trying to get in. I've jammed it between the door and the wall. So please listen carefully. I've got barely any time.'

Alina leaned forwards as if she had stomach cramps, but it was merely a subconscious reaction from her body, which was too weak to get up, but too restless to stay sitting.

'I'll call the police. We'll get you out of there, Emilia. Stay where—'

'No, don't waste any time on me. I've got news about Feline.'

'Do you know where she is?'

'Somewhere inside a tank. Behind walls.'

*'Your walls won't stop me...'* Alina thought of Lotte's song and automatically turned her head towards Nils.

He just shrugged.

'We're wondering whether she might be in a ghost station on a non-operational underground line,' Alina said.

'Possibly,' Emilia panted. It sounded as if she was using her entire body to try to prevent the man from opening the door. 'I'm afraid Tabea talks and sings in riddles.'

'Tabea?'

Alina recalled the noises when the courier was killed. Once again she heard the splintering like glass after the man was flung across the tarmac by the car that hit him. Shortly after he'd mentioned a blind woman with this name.

'That's the woman who was locked up with Feline.'

'You spoke to her?'

'Yes. And listen to this. Tabea told me her boyfriend abducted Feline.'

'What's he called?' Alina asked.

'Tabea only told me his nickname.

'Which is?'

When Emilia answered, Alina felt as if the man's name had metamorphosised into an insect inside her ear. A ferocious scorpion eating through her eardrum and into her brain where it would sting her with its poisonous tail.

*No, please for heaven's sake, no. That can't be true!*

The toxin seemed to paralyse her physically, but mentally take her to the limits of her imagination.

'That can't be true!' Alina replied, finally recovering her voice, although all her hope and confidence had gone. She was in such anguish she didn't realise Nils was holding her hand. Nor that the ambience on the phone had changed.

'Can you still hear me, Emilia?'

No.

Feline's mother was no longer there.

The line was exactly how Alina felt since Emilia uttered the name: numb, empty and dead.

# 50

## ZORBACH

'Where are you?'

'Almost there!'

Gate 1 of Tegel prison looked a little like the entrance to an old-fashioned factory.

With Stoya's voice in my ear I walked the last few metres along the cobbled street, through two brick columns topped with art nouveau-style lanterns. They weren't on even though it was already dark, but the red light on the fortress-like, iron-barred gate shone with an almost unnatural brightness. As if trying to signal to me: STOP. DO NOT GO ANY FURTHER. YOU ARE IN DANGER.

Which of course was true. Nobody knew better than I did what awaited me behind the prison walls. A former policeman and crime reporter? I wasn't in the same category as paedophiles and child killers, of course, but nor was I much higher up in the pecking order.

Another ten metres at most. I could already see Stoya behind the bars. He'd come in person, keen not to miss out on my admission. From a distance he looked scrawnier than when we'd last met. When he saw me wave he pulled his shoulders back and tried to stand more upright. I heard the signal of someone trying to call me and I paused.

'Why have you stopped?' Stoya asked suspiciously.

'Wait a sec.' I put him on hold and switched to the incoming call.

'Alex?'

*Alina?*

'I wasn't expecting this,' I said merrily.

Her tone sounded anything but cheerful. 'I'm not calling to say goodbye.'

'Why then?'

Stoya waved at me from the prison gate and shook his head. His gesture was that of the sports teacher imploring their pupils to stop bloody dawdling. But I was so alarmed by the strain in Alina's voice that I wasn't going to take one step further before I knew what she was so worked up about.

'There are three things you really must know.'

'Which are?'

'First, you were right. A U10 line does exist. It's not in operation, but there are some skeleton works.'

'And?'

'And then there's an M85 bus line.'

*Track 10 by Silbermond begins with M. Track 11 by Alle Farben with the number 85. And it's also got M as its first letter in the title!*

'Does the M85 route cross the U10 line?'

'Yes, and I'll give you three guesses what's there.'

'An underground ghost station?'

'Yes, exactly at Innsbrucker Platz. Completed but never used.'

Wiping the drizzle from my eyes I looked at Gate 1.

'I'll tell Stoya. He's beckoning me just a few metres away.'

'You can tell him the name of Feline's abductor too then.'

'How…?'

'That's the third thing you have to know. Emilia got in touch. I don't know how, but she must have smuggled herself into the Ambrosia and called me from there. A woman, the girlfriend of the abductor, apparently, is there too. Emilia talked to her and found out his name.'

'Go on.' I scratched my forehead, which had started to itch with anxiety.

'It's a far too harmless a nickname for that monster.'

*Oh God.*

I could hear how difficult it was for Alina to say it out loud. She, the strongest woman I'd ever met, feared to even utter it.

'Scholle?'

'Exactly.'

'Michael Scholokowsky?'

'She didn't give me his full name, but…'

*… it can't be a coincidence.*

'Are you sure?' I asked, just to have something to say.

Scholokowsky. Alias Scholle.

Also known as the Eye Collector.

'Yes. He's playing his games again. Abducting children.'

*And driving us to distraction. Making us all lose if we get in his way.*

Mike 'Scholle' Scholokowsky was the devil who'd murdered my wife and kidnapped my son. The epitome of evil who caused me to kill an innocent man I thought was guilty, because Scholle had framed him for his own crimes.

He was the reason why I was now standing here in the rain, on the way to losing my freedom.

'I can't,' I groaned.

'I know, you've got to start your sentence,' Alina said.

'That's what I'm saying. I can't go into the prison.'

I looked at Stoya, who was now just a couple of car lengths away, staring at me from the open gate and sensing something ominous.

'Hold on a sec.'

I switched back to the inspector. 'You've got to do something for me,' I told him.

'Okay, let's talk about it when you're here.'

'That won't work. I can't come.'

'Are you out of your mind?'

'Julian. This is about my son at boarding school. Please do exactly what I'm about to ask you.'

'Zorbach, if you turn around now you're screwed.'

'Please, I'll text you everything you need to know. Do me this favour. I beg you!'

I cut Stoya off and switched to Alina on the way back to my car.

'ZORBACH!!!' I heard Stoya yell from behind me, this time not down the phone.

I ran. 'Let's meet in half an hour. Bring your fiancé, plans, tools and a torch,' I said, speeding up.

'Where?'

'What do you think?'

*Je meurs là. U10. M85.*

*I'm dying there: U10 line. Where the M85 stops.*

'Innsbrucker Platz!'

# 51

## EMILIA

'I'm terribly disappointed in you. Both of you.'

A grey hair, which had come loose from Dr Lieberstett's tight bun, fell untidily over her ear.

Emilia interpreted the red blotches on her cheeks as a sign that the Ambrosia's director was struggling to retain her composure.

Like a stork, Lieberstett paced up and down the treatment room Emilia had set out from to look for the mobile, past her and Tabea, standing next to each other by the patient trolley, their heads bowed like schoolchildren.

'We let you keep the "watch" and the earphones, Tabea, because we thought the music would help with your therapy. But all of a sudden we have the police knocking at the door because you failed to tell us that the device belongs to a kidnapped girl. And you, Emilia…'

*It's rude to point* was what shot through Emilia's head when Lieberstett pierced the air between them with her bony forefinger.

'You didn't tell us that you're the mother of this kidnapped child. What sort of a game are the two of you playing? You wangle your way in here, abuse our hospitality and instead of letting us in on it you show everyone a photo at the morning group session. We have absolutely nothing to do with this matter, and yet now they're trying to get a warrant to search our premises. Do you know what the two of you are wrecking here?'

The angry blotches on Lieberstett's face grew to the size of beermats. She looked deep into Emilia's eyes. 'I understand that as the mother of an abducted child you resort to extreme measures. So do we. But what's happened doesn't justify such selfish behaviour which is putting the welfare of our entire organisation at risk. Our patients have suffered traumatic experiences. We may well be the last chance they have to get better. At the very least we're an important sanctuary, which you've jeopardised with your behaviour. Now we're going to have to give up our site here far earlier than we'd planned, even though our new premises are nowhere near ready!'

She stood facing them for a while longer, her lower lip quivering, then she held up the mobile Emilia had found in the plumbing and hissed, 'This will of course remain confiscated.'

Lieberstett pursed her lips as if straining hard to avoid saying something she shouldn't before she left. But she did finally lose her composure: 'I wish you hadn't forced me to do what I have to. Jakob will take care of you now.' Lieberstett did an almost military about-turn, slamming the door behind her when she left the toom.

Emilia heard the jangling of a bunch of keys, then the door was emphatically locked. She waited until Lieberstett's stomping faded into the distance, then Emilia turned angrily to Tabea, who'd begun scratching her forearms again. 'How the hell did your boyfriend get hold of my husband's mobile phone?'

Tabea's ruined eyes looked into nothingness as she felt once more for the cigarettes in her coat. But Emilia snatched the packet from her hand.

'Hey!'

'Talk to me.'

No reaction. Not a word, no singing. Not even any humming.

Emilia felt such a rage brewing inside her that she needed an outlet, and fast. She felt like destroying something in this room and it took all her self-control not to smash Tabea's face in.

In a state, she turned to the window, beyond which she detected movement. A flock of birds flew low across the lake in an easterly direction. They'd been startled at the shore by Jakob coming out of one of the boathouses beside the lake. He was carrying in both hands what from a distance looked like a box of washing powder. A packet with a handle.

Emilia was just about to turn back to Tabea when she saw the surface of the package gleam metallically.

*'I wish you hadn't forced me to do what I have to.'*

As Lieberstett's assistant walked across the lawn past the main building and headed straight for the building they were in, Emilia realised the mortal danger she was now in.

Trapped with a blind madwoman in a hut whose exterior walls were basically made of wood.

*'Jakob will take care of you now.'*

The petrol canister he was holding left no room for doubt as to what that meant.

# 52

## ALINA

'Just so I get this right, Alina...' Nils spoke faster with every word, '... you barely slept because yesterday you lurched from one crime scene to the next and from corpse to corpse, all this with your ex who you'd successfully banished from your life for several years to avoid getting into such nightmarish situations as last night – and now, at the behest of this same Alexander Zorbach, I'm driving you to a ghost station where Germany's most brutal serial killer is keeping a young girl captive?'

*Hopefully. Hopefully she's still alive.*

Alina pressed her forehead against the cool passenger window and said nothing. Seeing as she was never shy of coming forth in an argument, Nils would definitely take this as a tacit sign of her agreement.

He was tense behind the wheel of his SUV – she could feel this as acutely as the vibrations of the powerful engine beneath her.

'Have you got everything?' she asked him.

*The laptop with the plans? Torch? A well-equipped*

*toolbox? Preferably something that can be used as a weapon...*

'I've even got a skeleton key that fits many construction site doors in German stations,' Nils snarled. 'What I'm completely lacking is any understanding.'

'But I told you,' Alina said, launching into another explanation of why she felt partly guilty that Feline hadn't yet been found. 'She had my MP3 player and—'

'I understand that. But what I don't get is what this so-called Eye Collector has suddenly got to do with it.'

They stopped, presumably at traffic lights. As Alina was hiding her eyes behind the opaque glasses again, she could orient herself only by sound. She heard the clicking of the indicator, the roar of the heating and Nils's tense voice.

'What happened again? The Eye Collector played some sort of game?'

'He carried out a test,' she replied. 'Or at least this was his primary motive years ago. Scholle called it "the love test". We know it from a letter he sent to a tabloid editor.'

'Whose love was he testing?'

'At the time, the fathers' love towards their children. If Scholle thought a child was being neglected by its parents – for example, if they paid more attention to their work than their offspring – he would kill the mother, kidnap the child and give the father forty-five hours and seven minutes in which to find it.'

'Why such an odd amount of time?'

They pulled away again and turned left. There seemed to be little traffic on the roads; the acceleration dragged Alina back into her seat. 'In his sick psycho-killer world, Scholle recreated a dreadful accident that had happened to

Zorbach's trainee, Frank Lahmann. Frank and his brother are the actual inventors of the love test, if you like. They were teenagers, and after their mother's death felt neglected by their father. To test how much he loved them, they hid themselves. They hoped their dad would be sick with worry and go looking for them. Stupidly they chose as their hiding place an old chest freezer, which some bastard had dumped in the woods. Once inside it they were trapped, because it could only be opened from the outside.'

'But didn't the father come to free them?'

Alina shook her bald head. 'A forester found the two boys by chance. After forty-five hours and seven minutes. Frank's brother had suffocated to death.'

Nils groaned – he must have understood the significance of Scholle's 'rules' or remembered them. Alina had never discussed the subject directly with him, but at the time the media were full of the most gruesome details, such as the fact that the Eye Collector would drown his victims if they hadn't been freed before the forty-five-hour-and-seven-minute ultimatum was up. After they died he'd remove their left eye, because the victim of the original love test, Frank's brother, only had one functioning eye, the right one. This had earned the psychopath his serial-killer moniker in the press.

*The Eye Collector.*

Alina shuddered when she recalled that her first encounter with this monster had taken place in her practice at home in Prenzlauer Berg, when Mike 'Scholle' Scholokowsky had booked a shiatsu massage with her under a false name.

'And you think he's playing this perverse game again with Feline?'

'If so then he must have changed his methods considerably.

Feline has been kept captive far too long. And the mother is still alive. The hiding place, on the other hand…' Alina pursed her lips thoughtfully. 'Scholle loved claustrophobic places. Shipping containers, lift shafts. That's where he took his victims.'

'A ghost station would fit the bill, then,' Nils said.

She felt his eyes on her face, which was pointing stiffly at a road she couldn't see.

'Is there anything there that's like a tank? One that's big enough for two people to be in? And which is close enough to the U4 line?'

Before they left Nils had told Alina that Innsbrucker Platz didn't just have a ghost station and motorway tunnelled beneath it, it was also the last station on the U4 line that started at Nollendorfplatz. Unlike the U10, the U4 was operational.

'A tank.'

'That's what Feline's mum said on the phone earlier.'

He cleared his throat. 'Well, the proximity to the U4 is logical. The two lines were going to be connected. They pointlessly sank one hundred and thirty million marks into the project, which also included the construction of a pedestrian tunnel.'

'So do you think it's possible that when a U4 train pulls into the station you can feel it through the concrete walls if you're standing on the unused U10 track?'

*And you've got Wi-Fi…*

'I presume so. But a tank?' Because Nils didn't say any more Alina assumed he was shrugging.

She reached for her mobile. 'How do you get into the U10 officially these days?'

'There's an orange door in the underpass, which every day thousands of Berliners walk past without noticing on their way to the U4. But it's been sealed for a while. And it's hardly likely the abductor will have opened it.'

Alina nodded. Too many witnesses.

'When we were taking measurements at the time we discovered some graffiti. I remember the building supervisors complaining about an unsecured air shaft very close to the city motorway exit, which young people would keep getting into.'

'That must be it.'

'Unlikely. We sealed it up. Nobody could get in there now. But there might be something else the police ought to take a look at.'

*The police.*

Alina bit her lip. She wondered why she hadn't at any point thought about notifying Stoya at least. And, even more astonishingly, why she had no intention of doing so now. Maybe she wanted to make sure her suspicion was correct. But she knew she'd be lying if she tried to use that as an excuse. The truth was, not only did she feel responsible for Feline, she was desperate to exact revenge on Scholle personally. And she was sure that Zorbach shared this need.

'Why was he never caught?' Nils asked. 'I mean, you know his name, there are photos, detailed descriptions of him...'

'... and plastic surgeons and millions of hiding places in Berlin alone. We're about to go to one nobody would ever find you in.'

They had indeed arrived. Alina felt Nils switch off the engine. It became noticeably chillier inside the car at once.

'Besides, Scholle was a policeman. An ex-colleague of Zorbach and Stoya. He was described to me as a boorish hulk, a big baby whose evil nature nobody saw because he decked himself out in the insignia of the good guys. But his badge of office was just a disguise.'

'I see. Do you think he's still got contacts at the police?'

'It might explain why he's managed to stay in hiding till now.'

'Because an insider has prevented a serious search for him from taking place?'

Alina nodded. It was just a theory, and one on very shaky ground, but it couldn't hurt to be careful.

'You lied to me, then.'

Alina blinked nervously behind her glasses. Her cheeks burned hotly, as if the criticism had hit her like a slap.

'You never intended to call the police.'

'No,' she said, feeling ashamed. 'But…'

She heard Nils open the door. A mixture of exhaust fumes and frosty air came streaming into the car, accompanied by the roar of traffic that surrounded Innsbrucker Platz every hour of the day and night.

'I think you're making a big mistake,' Nils said, getting out.

*I think so too. But there are mistakes you have to make if you want to live the rest of your life with a clear conscience.*

'Where are we?' She had to speak louder for him to hear her standing beside the road.

'In a bog-standard car park on the main road. Tell Zorbach we'll meet him outside number 45.'

He slammed the door. Angrily and energetically.

At least he had got out rather than driven back. The chances of him helping them weren't zero.

'Wait for me!'

Alina undid her belt then opened the door and the messaging service on her mobile at the same time. Before she could send Zorbach a voice message, however, Siri played her a WhatsApp message she'd tapped by accident.

'*Hello, Frau Gregoriev. Have you changed your mind about continuing your therapy with me? If not, I could recommend one of my colleagues. Please call me back. I hope you're well. Dr Samuel Rej.*'

Alina gripped the passenger door tightly for a while before closing it.

'Did you hear that? What does he mean "changed your mind"? Didn't you say *I* wasn't to contact him any more?' she asked Nils, who was a few paces ahead of her on the pavement. She removed the glasses to be able to see any obstacles that might be in the way as she followed her fiancé.

The shadows and patches of light were still confusing, but if the dark plane moving away from her was Nils's back then he wasn't so far in front that he wouldn't be able to hear her.

And yet he didn't answer her; he didn't even turn around.

*Probably because we've got more important things to discuss right now than my problems with getting therapy appointments*, Alina thought as she followed him uncertainly.

# 53

## ZORBACH

'I've no idea why I'm helping you,' was how Nils greeted me. He sounded considerably less friendly than at our last meeting, which was hardly surprising. He looked tired, was badly shaven and his college jacket was far too thin for the icy wind blasting across the pavement. We were standing outside a dark row of shops, almost all out of business now, their windows papered up. The only reminder of their former activity were the dirty outlines of neon signs that had been removed.

'I expect you're helping us because you love Alina,' I said, looking at the line of tail lights speeding past on the main road. A colony of people who had no inkling of the tragedy that might be playing out directly beneath the road, if our assumptions were correct.

'Where do we get in?'

'Over there,' Nils said, pointing at the one shop that was lit up, a building to our left.

'Through the Chinese shop?'

With a sign above the entrance bearing the fancy name

'royal asia market', this place turned out to be a rather exotic convenience store once you'd got past the bead curtain. Dense shelves stretched up to the ceiling, filled with ready meals, crisps, sweets, alcohol and soft drinks. Here and there the usual offerings were interrupted by Chinese spices, glass noodles, colourful, shrink-wrapped plastic novelties and a pyramid of sweet-and-sour soups. Oddly it didn't smell of incense sticks, but of an artificial room scent sprayed by a dispenser above the door each time someone came in.

We went over to the counter, Nils first, holding Alina's hand, and me as the back marker of our strange polonaise. 'We're interested in the special offer,' Nils said to the man at the till. The black-haired young man with alert eyes was wearing a handwritten name badge proclaiming him to be 'Kin – sales manager'.

'Three Fs, please.'

Kin eyed us suspiciously, then looked up at the round mirror in the corner of the shop, presumably to check that we didn't have anyone in tow.

Then he opened the till and Nils took out his wallet.

'Nobody's asked for F in months,' Kin said.

'Sixty euros?' Nils asked.

'One hundred,' Kin replied, grinning. 'Everything's more expensive since Covid.'

Kin took the banknote Nils offered him, placed it in the till, closed the drawer with a loud ping and made his way around the counter to us.

'F?' I whispered to Nils. 'What's that?'

*A special tool, a saw to open the padlock on a side entrance?*

Wasn't Nils going to bring a toolbox with him?

'Wait!' Nils said, putting his hand around Alina's waist a little too possessively for my liking, then pushing her down the aisle with toiletries, following Kin.

The sales manager led us through another bead curtain and into the back rooms. With a grunt he heaved aside some pallets of drinks piled in the kitchenette, revealing a metal grate in the floor. It turned out to be an entrance into the cellar. A narrow spiral staircase led down a dark hole, from where dusty odours rose.

'Twenty minutes,' Kin said, and went back to the shop.

I raised my eyebrows at Nils, who explained, 'Kin is what rail obsessives call a "mole". All over Germany there is a network of these moles who secretly sell tours, maps of tunnels and tracks or who – as in Kin's case – can open a secret entrance to the platform of line F, as the phantom section of underground was originally called.'

'Wait, are you saying there's an entrance to the U10 directly beneath a Chinese shop?' I asked.

'Exactly. Through Kin's cellar.'

# 54

When Nils put a foot on the top step of the spiral staircase he triggered a motion detector. A cold halogen light flooded the space below us, turning the dark hole into an empty room with bare brick walls. Above the clayey floor, less than two metres beneath us, I saw something like a washing line running diagonally across the cellar. From it hung construction hats and dark raincoats.

Full of curiosity I went down the slatted steps of the spiral staircase while Nils spoke to Alina. 'I suggest you wait for us up here. Alexander and I will take a look around and we'll be back in ten minutes at most.'

'Forget it!' Alina snorted. 'If there's anywhere I can find my way around, it's in the dark.'

'We've got light,' I called up, grabbing a construction lamp that was on a wooden shelf along with several others. The third one I tried worked. Kin was probably telling the truth when he said that nobody had plumped for his 'special offer' in months.

While Nils helped Alina down the steps, following a

short, unsuccessful attempt to get her to stay, I looked for the way in to the U10. But I couldn't find it in this low-ceilinged room.

The only door belonged to a narrow but solid metal cupboard, which Nils opened for us. And behind it was another dark hole from which dustier and substantially colder air blew in our direction.

'Through there?' I asked, pointing the lamp in that direction.

Nils nodded. 'They were going to put a special entrance here for maintenance, to be accessed via a claims recovery office – its premises are now the Chinese shop. They never walled up the opening and then it was forgotten about.'

'How did you come across it?' Alina said.

'Pure chance. I found out about it because my employees always used to have their lunch break here. One day Kin revealed the secret to my construction manager, who showed me.'

Again Nils let me go ahead so he could look after Alina, who couldn't be left to fend for herself in these unfamiliar surroundings. Especially as the narrow passageway I had to squeeze myself through sideways led to a platform that swayed precariously. I felt giddy, also because of the muffled whooshing that at first I thought was water flowing through a faulty pipe. Only later did I realise it was the traffic streaming through the motorway tunnel beside us.

'You have to go down the steps,' said Nils, who'd also taken a lamp.

I felt my way along the handrail of some crude wooden steps that acted as a makeshift access to one of the most astonishing places I'd ever seen.

*Plundered*, was the first word that came to mind. The underground station that stood before me looked as if over the years it had been raided by thieves who'd carried off anything of value: the tracks, benches, kiosks, station signs, displays – none of these existed any more. Although that wasn't right; they'd never been there in the first place.

My footsteps echoed off the bare concrete walls of the ghost station, which were covered in unintelligible graffiti. I came across the odd item of litter: fast-food packaging, disposable face masks, empty tins of spray paint, and condoms.

'What's that back there?' I asked.

'What do you mean?' said Alina, who of course couldn't see the object I was pointing at. It had appeared on the track bed, right at the end of the beam of light from the construction lamp.

'Looks like an egg. Or a fruit,' Nils said, thinking aloud. He seemed to be as surprised as I was.

'A huge, outsize pineapple,' I said, describing the object to Alina. 'As wide as a caravan and as tall as a lorry.'

'What's it supposed to be?'

'A work of art.' With his lamp Nils lit up a board on the wall that had once been earmarked for timetables and other information.

'What?' Alina and I said, almost in unison. We'd been down here long enough now that my nose had got used to the musty storeroom smell, but I felt the cold creeping into my bones. And I heard something that didn't tally with the motorway noise. A deep, rich hum.

'Here's a notice that says: "The DM51 installation draws attention to the explosion in Berlin property prices, which at some point will drive the city's residents underground, the only space left for them to live in." This was put in five years ago, after my time on the construction site,' Nils explained. 'Before Covid, this shell of a place was occasionally used for events, but now it doesn't meet any safety criteria.'

'What's a pineapple got to do with the housing shortage?' Alina asked.

'It's not a pineapple. Or an egg.'

Nils kept reading: '"This installation by the art group 'Engzeit' is based on the design of the German army DM51 hand grenade."'

'A hand grenade?' I interjected, baffled. But the closer I got to it, the clearer it became: the honeycombed casing, the lever on the side, even the pin at the top.

The humming got louder. Both inside my head and right in front of me.

'Are you thinking what I'm thinking?' Alina asked, who hadn't moved another millimetre and was now standing on this ghost platform in almost total darkness because both Nils and I were lighting up the strange artwork. I was standing slightly further away than Nils from the huge grenade that almost reached the ceiling, because he'd now climbed down onto the track bed to approach the installation from below.

'It's as the notice describes,' he called out excitedly. 'There's a ladder here. It was built for visitors as a room you could go into. Apparently it's set out like a flat inside. For a while you could even stay the night there like in a hotel.'

'I'll say it again,' Alina shouted. 'Are you thinking what I'm thinking?'

*A shell you can go inside, space for at least two people, close to the U4 tunnel wall.*

'This is the tank Emilia was talking about!' Alina said.

'We should call the police,' Nils urged, and then he made the fatal error of taking another step closer to the object we suspected Feline was inside.

*Hoped.*

The noise of splintering bones, followed by a baleful, drawn-out scream echoed through the tunnel and mixed with the horrific panicky noises of distress coming from Alina.

Pointing the lamp at the track bed, I saw Nils writhing in pain. Unable to believe what had happened and desperately yelling for help, he tried to prise open the jaws.

When I glimpsed the metal trap Alina's fiancé had stepped into, that was the definitive proof.

*We've found it.*

The Eye Collector's hiding place.

Who must be very keen we didn't get too close, which was why he'd set a hunting trap for uninvited visitors. Its serrated jaws had just chomped into Nils's ankle.

# 55

I couldn't open it.

Not without a crowbar or something similar. Not without a specialist tool. The bear trap was shut so tightly; it wouldn't release Nils's ankle until the foot had rotted off. The trap also had a chain that was anchored into the concrete floor, on which Nils was squatting in agony.

'Don't move!' I called out to Alina.

I carefully lit up the surrounding area in search of more traps.

When I didn't find any I turned to her.

'I'm going to get help,' I promised. Nils's excruciating cries had changed into a gurgled howling that resounded off the bare walls as an echo of the horror down here.

'What can I do?' Alina asked.

Her best bet would have been to follow me, for if we had found the Eye Collector's lair, then a bear trap might turn out to be the most harmless of all the dangers we could stumble into. Sensing, however, that no power in the world would be able to force her to leave Nils alone, I said, 'Stay here and talk to him. Give him heart. I'll let Kin know and I'll be back in a minute.'

She nodded, pursing her lips tightly. Then I left her, hurrying back exactly the way we'd come, running up the wobbly wooden steps.

And cried out in dismay.

*No!*

No, no, no!

No light, no draught, no change of smell.

I wondered briefly if I'd gone wrong, but there wasn't another way. And the cupboard we'd squeezed through was still there.

But now it was locked shut.

I hammered both my fists on the metal wall in front of me, then charged my shoulder into it.

But this was as futile as my attempt to get a signal with my mobile phone down here.

*Scholle!* I thought, on the verge of despair.

Nils had been the first to fall into his trap.

But now we were all in it.

# 56

'What was that noise?' Alina asked, alarmed, when I came back. She must have heard me hammering on the door. Down here in the bare tunnel, every noise was amplified.

'Were you in the shop? Is he getting help?'

Ignoring my advice, she'd moved to the edge of the platform and was sitting directly above Nils, who was now whimpering continually.

'Yes.' What point was there in telling the truth? At this moment it seemed right to reassure both Nils and Alina with a compassionate lie. 'The door to get out was stuck. But it's all sorted.' When I jumped onto the track bed my legs thanked me with a cramp-like tugging beneath the kneecaps. At least I'd used the lamp to check beforehand that I wouldn't fall into another trap.

'Help me, please!' I took the hand Alina held out so she could slide down too and sit right beside Nils. He was hunched on the ground in the foetal position, both hands pressed on the jaws of the trap. Alina felt gingerly for his brow and stroked his head.

'What are you doing?' she called out after me. I was already on the ladder Nils had found. It led up between the tunnel wall and the militaristic work of art.

'I'm making use of the time before help arrives,' I said, continuing with my half-truth. If Feline had been dragged into this structure then I wanted her to know that we'd found her, even if her saviours were totally helpless at the moment. And maybe there was something inside the grenade that could help us set ourselves free from here.

'Be careful!' I heard Alina shout.

The rungs of the ladder vibrated beneath my feet. I recalled how during a swimming lesson as a young boy I'd aborted my climb to the five-metre diving board, earning scoffs from my classmates. Now too, the desire to turn around grew with every step I took up. My hands went clammy and, as I needed my fingers to hold on, I could only grip the construction lamp with my thumb and forefinger; I was worried I'd lose it.

Once I was at the top, my lungs were pumping so hard, it was as if I was breathing at altitude, rather than having climbed up a mere two and a half metres.

I glanced down at Alina. She sat beside Nils in the yellowish-red glow of the other lamp, which gave a completely wrong impression of campfire cosiness.

'There's a platform up here,' I told her. 'With a metal ring about as big as a steering wheel in a lorry. It's right on top. I think it's a valve.'

'Can you move it?' Alina asked.

I put the lamp down on the edge of the platform, right beside a rope that was fastened to a hook on the platform.

When I pulled it, nothing happened. Then I grabbed the wheel with both hands. 'Yes.'

The valve turned with great ease and silently, as if it had been freshly oiled.

*Or used only recently.*

In the end there was some slight resistance, then I heard a *clack* and saw a crack of an opening. My heart pounding wildly, I pushed the wheel up with both hands and opened the top of the 'grenade' like the lid of a tin can.

*Or like the lid of a tank!*

'Nils has passed out,' Alina called out from below. Her voice sounded closer now.

To open the round lid completely I had to push it all the way, being careful my hands didn't slip and send me toppling off the grenade. There was also the risk of falling into the hole that was now there.

*What the hell is that?*

I stared down in disbelief at the brightly lit, semi-circular interior of the 'grenade', which was indeed furnished as a flat, with a bunk bed, a kitchenette and an armchair. Everything was so tiny it made me think of a room in a doll's house. I was so distracted that I knocked over the construction lamp, which fell onto the track bed, shattering beside the installation.

'Everything okay?' Alina called out from right below me.

'Yes,' I said, lying again, and staring into the illuminated grenade. Now I also realised where the humming was coming from. Somewhere, probably under the 'grenade', there must be a functioning generator connected to the power of the Berlin underground network. Right now it was supplying energy to a chain of lights inside the grenade.

'What can you see?'

A simple question. But I was unable to provide an answer. It would have been too horrific.

'I'm not sure,' I said, happy that Alina couldn't see what I could inside this doll's house, between the bunk bed and kitchenette: a folding table. On it, a person, hands and feet bound, mouth stuck with grey insulating tape, lit up by the spotlight of a camera on a tripod, the lens pointing slightly downwards.

As if Scholle had been keen to capture the best camera angle of the bloodbath.

# 57

I used the rope for my descent into the grenade. Presumably that's what it was there for.

The moment my boots made a squelching sound on the blood-soaked carpet I felt a huge sense of relief. The blood, which had turned the once cream-coloured carpet brown, wasn't Feline's. Nor the blood that had drenched the sheet beneath the bound, motionless body on the table.

Not a child. Not a girl.

But a grown man.

*Who's been tortured so bestially here?*

I was sure I knew this poor, tormented creature. I'd probably first thought it was Feline because I'd stumbled across something familiar in this unreal setting.

I bent over the table. And indeed the eyes beneath the dark hair that stuck to the victim's forehead like seaweed looked similar to Feline's, although I'd only seen them in photographs.

'Thomas!' I said to her father, in the forlorn hope that he

was still alive, and held his right hand. Now I could see why he'd lost so much blood.

His extremities were fixed to the table with brackets. Metal rings of the sort used to secure pipes. Scholle – assuming he was responsible for this – had made them so tight that their sharp edges cut into the flesh of the prisoner at the slightest movement. Thomas Jagow had obviously tried to free himself, cutting his wrists in his panic.

I bent further down and immediately recoiled. Thomas was still alive! He'd torn open his eyes so suddenly that his terrified look had hit me like a blow to the chest.

It was if he'd been connected to the generator too. He shook his head and groaned something unintelligible at me.

I grabbed a corner of the tape covering his mouth.

Jagow groaned even more loudly and shook his head more vigorously, as if he were now going to suffocate after losing all that blood.

'Hold on, just a sec...'

I ripped the tape from his lips in one go.

Then I finally heard what Thomas had been saying so urgently beneath his gag.

'No, no, don't take it off!'

'Why not?' I asked, baffled. On the inside of the tape in my hand there was a small bit of plastic. Like a remote control shrunken to the size of a thimble, which started flashing wildly.

'The transmitter!' Thomas moaned. 'You've activated it!'

'What?' I asked. And at that very moment I saw it.

Beside me in the kitchenette a light had come on and I could hear a buzzing.

The microwave!

As if switched on by a ghostly hand the plate inside began to turn. The digital clock on the microwave was running backwards.

I'd launched a countdown!

# 58

*4 minutes, 7 seconds.*

'What's in there?'

I went over to the microwave. An everyday black object without a brand name. A ceramic bowl spun in bronze-coloured light on the glass plate. In the bowl was a white block, around the size of a pack of butter.

'Ammonium nitrate,' Thomas gasped. He was a physics and geography teacher, so even before the disaster at the Port of Beirut he must have known how deadly this fertiliser can be.

'Deep-frozen. Once it's thawed...'

*... it'll blow up in our faces and produce a crater all the way up to Innsbrucker Platz,* I thought. A simple bomb, its ingredients available in any DIY store.

'How can I turn it off?' I asked, frantically pressing the buttons on the microwave. None of them seemed to work. The door wouldn't open either; it was welded shut. The device as a whole was built into the wall, which was why I couldn't find a plug to pull out anywhere.

'The letter,' I heard Thomas pant.

'What letter?'

I turned to Feline's father and saw him wiggle the little finger on his right hand. He was pointing to below the table, where I caught sight of a piece of paper, smeared with blood.

I picked it up, smoothed it flat and once I'd read the first few sentences knew that our chances of getting out here were virtually zero.

*Thomas, you know I always give players a choice. This is how I differ from the sadistic criminals I used to hunt down and bring to justice when I was a policeman.*

*You decided to be a bad father. Now you're the reaping the consequences, but you have the chance to change your destiny.*

*Just as your shameful behaviour was a puzzle for your wife, I'm setting you a musical puzzle which can get you back on the right track.*

*The puzzle is:*

*What does Ana weigh in the twinkling month?*

*A clue: The answer can be found in the song title as well as in Africa's longest river!*

*With the correct solution, dear Thomas, you can defuse the microwave as soon as someone finds you here and frees you from your shackles. On the front of the device you'll find ten buttons for the different programmes. The top left-hand button is 0, the bottom right-hand one is 9. Start and finish inputting the correct solution with the On/Off button. But beware: you've got only one chance!*

# 59

'What is this?' I yelled at Thomas. 'Is it supposed to be a joke?'

'No,' he said, shaking his head. His lips were blue, his entire body appeared to be empty of blood, and perhaps it was. It was a miracle he could still speak. The flow of blood from his wrist seemed to have clotted; maybe the clip had pressed tightly against the wound, but I doubted the loss he'd suffered would be without consequences. It was far more likely, I thought, that I was going to witness his final struggle. Maybe Thomas would even die before me. Before the bomb blew us all to bits, in...

*3 minutes, 35 seconds.*

'He's mad. But he's deadly serious.'

'Who is he? The Eye Collector? Scholokowsky?'

The puzzle bore his hallmark, that was for sure. A game. Supposedly fair rules. A countdown to death.

Thomas didn't respond. I was tempted to slap him, but was worried I'd knock him unconscious again.

Threads of saliva ran down his chin and throat.

'What's the solution?' I asked.

He closed his eyes. 'I... I don't know.'

I heard knocking sounds coming from somewhere outside the grenade, but that was in a different world. Mine here was restricted to the dying father, the microwave countdown and the riddle.

*What does Ana weigh in the twinkling month?*

'Help me!' Thomas moaned. And in fact that was the last thing he said. His eyelids fluttered once more as if still connected to the electrics. Then nothing. He didn't utter another word.

I did, however, hear a voice above my head. 'Everything alright down there? What have you found?'

I looked up at Alina, whose head had appeared in the hatch. Somehow she'd managed to climb the ladder.

'What the hell! Is she bleeding?'

She must have smelled the iron Thomas had lost along with his blood.

'It isn't Feline,' I shouted over the buzzing of the microwave.

*3 minutes, 22 seconds.*

'It's her dad.'

'Thomas? Is he still alive?'

'No idea. But the more important question is: are *we* going to survive this?'

I summarised the situation for Alina as quickly as I could without making her think I'd completely lost it.

'How long have we got left?' was her first question. She sounded calm and composed, not at all shocked. This was simultaneously the manifestation of her greatest strength and most serious weakness. She was able to suppress emotions altogether if she wanted to. Maybe that had helped her keep her distance from me all this time, assuming she'd still felt an attraction of some sort between us, as I imagined hopefully. Right now her cool head might be our chance to solve the puzzle and escape with our lives.

'Just under three minutes.'

'Then let's proceed logically,' she called out from above.

I put my head back, but from my place in the doll's house between the microwave and table couldn't see more than a movement of her head.

'Where to begin?' I asked in exasperation.

'Focus!' she rebuked me. And this was the only right approach. I was on the verge of losing my head even before it was torn off by the detonation.

'What's the first thing that strikes you when you read the question?'

'I don't know. The twinkling month. The longest river in Africa.'

'Which must be the Nile,' Alina said. 'What else?'

'Ana's written with only one N.'

'Good. What do we know?'

'What do we know? Nothing, or... wait.' I looked at the first words on the paper. 'It says here it's a musical puzzle!'

'Do you think the playlist can help us?'

I groaned. 'Even if it might, there's not enough time to go through all the lyrics for twinkling months or the Nile.'

'But maybe the titles.'

'Not one of them mentions these. But...'

We both had the brainwave at the same time.

'What twinkles?'

'Silver,' Alina said.

'And another word for month?'
'Moon.'
Silver Moon – Silbermond!

# 60

By now I knew the playlist by heart, having stared so often at the fifteen song titles, listened over and over again to the verses and choruses and looked for clues as to Feline's hiding place in the titles, lyrics and melodies.

'Okay, the track by Silbermond on the playlist is called "Million Tweets". Do you think the answer is a million? Is that what Ana weighs in grams?'

Should I press 1 followed by six zeros?

According to the Eye Collector's instructions this meant I'd have to press the On/Off button, then the second button once, the first button six times, followed by the On/Off button again to confirm my selection.

'Maybe,' Alina said, but she sounded as unconvinced as I did. 'But... what has a million got to do with Ana and the Nile?'

*2 minutes, 25 seconds.*

The noise of the microwave surged in my ears to become like the rushing of a waterfall.

'Go through the puzzle again,' Alina said, sounding ever hoarser.

'A musical puzzle. We know it's about Silbermond, Ana and the Nile.'

'Who's Ana? The singer's called Stephanie, isn't she?'

'And why's the answer in the Nile?' I said.

Alina sighed. 'When's the help you called for coming?'

'It's not,' I said, deciding to come out with the truth at what was possibly the worst moment. 'The way back was closed up.'

Under a volley of curses that Alina aimed at me I went back to the microwave. The lump on the glass plate that a few minutes ago had looked like a pat of butter, now appeared to have melted completely.

'What should I do, Alina? I've only got one go at the combination.'

'Let's keep concentrating on the unusual things,' she said. 'Like, who weighs someone in grams rather than in kilos?'

'Maybe because it isn't referring to a person's weight,' I said, and had an idea. It hovered in my mind like a small, transparent bubble. I was so nervous that I had difficultly not bursting it before I'd thought it through to its conclusion.

'The question isn't *how much*, but *what*,' I muttered to myself.

Thomas Jagow groaned on the folding table. His eyelids fluttered. He seemed to be coming round.

'What did you say?' Alina asked from the hatch.

'What does Ana weigh? Ana weighs gram!'

'Huh?' Now Alina was losing her patience.

'Anagram,' I explained. 'It's an anagram!'

A word puzzle, in which you rearrange the letters to make other words. *Like grenade – angered – grandee.*

If this was the work of the Eye Collector, he'd set us a puzzle within a puzzle.

'What if you jumble the letters of "Silbermond"?'

I bent down beneath the bunk where there was a child's desk, and on it a pad and pencil. I felt a hot flush when I saw it was a Depeche Mode pad.

Feline's favourite band.

I wrote SILBERMOND in capital letters.

'The Nile's in there,' I said. 'But the rest of it doesn't make any sense.'

The rest of the letters in alphabetical order were: BDORMS.

*MB rods, DM bros, BDSM or…*

No matter how I arranged the letters there was no clue to a number. My head throbbed as if it were itself being heated in the microwave. Then Alina said, 'How long was the countdown that Scholle set?'

'Four minutes and seven seconds.'

'Is that the length of the Silbermond song?'

'No idea, could be. Why?'

'Because Nile is also in "Million Tweets".'

'True.'

I scribbled on the pad.

'If you take out "NILE", that leaves the letters: M L I O T W E T S.'

'The number TWO is in there, isn't it?' Alina asked.

'Yes, it is! And TIMES. Times two. But that leaves us with an L.'

I looked up at the shadow in the hatch.

'Alina,' I said.

'What?'

'We've only got fifty-seven seconds left. I want to use them to say I wish I'd had a little more time with you.'

'Oh, cut the crap!' she cried, sobbing. I tried to think if I'd ever heard her cry before. 'Just tell me what "Nile times two L" means.'

'It must have something to do with the length of the river. Scholle wouldn't have specifically mentioned it otherwise. And L – could that mean the Roman fifty? So two L is one hundred – the length of the Nile times one hundred!'

'HOW LONG IS THAT FUCKING RIVER?' she screamed.

I was yelling in despair too, because I didn't have the slightest idea, and the clock was at 31 seconds when I saw Thomas Jagow open his eyes.

# 61

## EMILIA

The fire was a glutton, devouring everything that came the way of its glowing-red jaws. The flames that blazed as high as a building consumed the boxes, files and computer printouts, along with clipboards, some of which still had paper attached.

'You're covering your tracks.' Emilia had laughed out loud with relief when she realised Jakob wasn't going to use the petrol canister to set fire to the building over their heads.

Lieberstett's assistants, especially Jakob and the guard in the porter's lodge, had hurriedly taken box after box from the main building, and tipped out the contents to make a huge bonfire in the park. The patients from the morning sessions also helped destroy the evidence.

The flames shot high into the sky. Reaching higher than the crowns of the oaks in the park, they towered effortlessly above the main building, making the advancing evening as light as day again. The crackling of the fire was so loud that Emilia didn't hear the door to the treatment room open behind her.

'Let's go!' Lieberstett commanded.

While Tabea remained sitting silently and motionless on the edge of the patient trolley, Emilia turned to the 'director', who'd tidied her bun. She was wearing heavy winter boots and a thick woollen coat, as if about to embark on a long walk in the cold. The blotches on her face had disappeared and she no longer looked on edge, but determined. Full of drive.

'Forward, march!' she barked.

'Where to?' Emilia asked.

'You'll find out when we're on the coach.'

'What coach?'

'The one we've all got to take because you've turned this place into somewhere that's no longer secure.' She pointed to the fire through the window, as if both her prisoners had started it themselves.

Emilia shook her head. 'I'm not coming.'

A venomous smile darted on Lieberstett's narrow lips.

'Did I mention you had a choice? I can't leave you behind here.'

'Because you don't want a witness who might shop you?'

'Because I don't want my charges being put at risk any more by people like you. It's bad enough that you've made us move to a makeshift home prematurely. But I'm not going to permit you to spread your lies about us in the press and on social media.'

Emilia returned the scornful grin. 'Well, then, you're going to have to kill me, whether you like it or not. There's no other way you're going to stop me telling the truth about Ambrosia at some point.'

'Maybe that's not such a bad idea,' Lieberstett said. She clicked her fingers; Jakob came in. He must have been waiting at the door.

Emilia coughed. It was as if he'd squeezed the last gulp of fresh air out of the room, replacing it with acrid petrol fumes. His trouser legs were black, his hands oily. In the heat of the moment he must have spilled some of the petrol down himself. His eyes were marked by both exhaustion and excitement. His hands were calm, but he was breathing heavily. The way Jakob was acting made Emilia feel as if she'd come face to face with a serial killer.

*And the way he smelled.*

A single spark would be all it took for him to turn into a living torch, set the room ablaze and kill everyone inside it.

But Lieberstett's right-hand man didn't need to resort to such self-destructive measures. It would be much simpler for Jakob to kill them using the pistol in his hand, which he raised and pointed at her head.

'Stay where you are!' he roared at Tabea, who for some reason had got down from the stretcher and was moving towards him. Shuffling, with empty, dead eyes, she looked like a zombie, even though the moronic grin didn't fit. Nor did the fact that she was quietly singing a song from Feline's playlist, which Emilia recognised as 'Evermore' by Namika. One of the few which had stood out because she really liked the singer. Now, however, she found the melody gruesome, as the lyrics seemed to uncannily anticipate her fate.

*… canister of kerosine. Flick a lighted match…*

'I said, stay where you are!' Jakob repeated, aiming his gun at Tabea, who was holding the lighter Emilia had lit her cigarette with earlier.

It was more of a shriek when she sang: '… *and Rome will burn faster than ever!…*'

One second later the inferno began.

# 62

## ALINA

'Is this becoming some sort of habit? Wherever you appear the bodies seem to pile up.'

They were five hundred metres away from the Chinese shop and thus out of the danger zone the experts had cordoned off around Innsbrucker Platz. Alina was sitting, eyes closed, on the step in the sliding door of a police van.

Chief Inspector Stoya had stood over her and raged, 'You're lucky the brother of the murder victim turned up an hour earlier for his shift. Otherwise you'd still be lying among the ruins.'

'How did Kin die?' she asked Stoya, whose breath smelled of too much office black coffee.

So far all they'd told her was that it couldn't have been a pretty sight when his brother found him by the secret passage to the U10 in the cellar.

'Stabbed from behind,' the policeman said, reluctantly disclosing the information.

Frozen, Alina wrapped her arms around her body. Her

throat ached from all the shouting in the concrete ruins; she bet she had a cold too. Sitting partly in the wind out here certainly didn't make it any better, but she wanted to feel the weather on her face for the simple reason that an hour ago she didn't think she'd ever feel anything again apart from one final pain that shredded everything.

'Is he going to make it?' she asked Stoya, who was lighting a cigarette. She wondered if he'd always smoked. Perhaps he only did on certain occasions. Such as when he had to visit a bloody crime scene with one corpse and two critically injured.

After two drags he answered her question. 'If you mean your fiancé, Nils Sandbeck, then yes. We won't know if he'll ever be able to walk again until after the operation.'

Alina nodded. They hadn't let her go along in the ambulance. Shit, she didn't even know which hospital they'd taken him to because Stoya had insisted she make a statement first.

'As far as Thomas Jagow is concerned,' Stoya said, clicking his tongue pessimistically, 'things look considerably worse. Huge loss of blood, at least that's what the paramedic said. We'll see.'

The cigarette must have gone out because Alina heard the lighter click again.

'You've got to re-open the Eye Collector case. Scholle's back. It's him behind the madness,' she said, repeating the core of her statement. She'd given it twenty minutes ago in the police van, door closed, at a fold-out table with Stoya and an assistant. Stoya didn't let her go afterwards, however; he insisted she wait for the initial forensic findings in case there were any further questions. And Forensics couldn't get going until the ammonium nitrate in the microwave had been made totally safe and removed from the scene.

'He vanished for two years. Why should the Eye Collector reappear now?'

'I've no idea, but everything fits. Look at the piece of paper with the puzzle we found down there.'

*Which we actually managed to solve!*

'He writes about a test he's subjecting Jagow to because he's a bad father. That's classic Scholle.'

'Hmm,' Stoya grunted.

Neither had to speak at volume to make themselves understood because the cacophony of the traffic had been silenced. The main roads and side streets around Innsbrucker Platz had been closed, the railway and underground suspended. Thousands of Berliners and commuters were going to get home very late tonight.

Some of them wouldn't get home at all. Like Kin.

*Or Nils?*

*Feline's father?*

'If Thomas Jagow survives, he'll confirm it,' Alina swore to Stoya. 'Scholle dragged him here. He must have taken Feline to a different hiding place beforehand.'

'We don't know if she was ever there in the first place.'

'For God's sake, go down there and check. Zorbach told me there was a Depeche Mode notepad. Her favourite band.'

'We'll take a look,' he grumbled.

'Good. Can I go now, then?'

'No.' The smoke he'd blown into her face was irritating her nostrils. 'Not until you've answered my final question. Where the hell is Zorbach?'

# 63

## ZORBACH

*0 minutes, 11 seconds.*

This was the point at which the countdown on the microwave timer stopped.

Right after I'd inputted the solution to the deadly puzzle. When not only the clock stood still, but time itself, until the fast-forward button was pressed and events followed in rapid succession.

It was unbelievable that I was now sitting here. *In safety.* In a place that ought not to exist any more in Berlin.

*Unimaginable.*

I'd been expecting a searing explosion. Instead I heard a wild screaming coming from the entrance to the tunnel. After checking Jagow's barely detectable pulse again, I stuffed Feline's notepad in my waistband and climbed back up the rope. Exhausted by the debilitating ascent, I had to take a breather on the platform.

Alina had already gone back down the ladder and was trying to comfort a Chinese-looking man, who was marching up and down the platform, his mouth wide open and waving his arms around frantically. He was shouting in a language I couldn't understand and sounded as distressed and shocked as anyone I'd ever heard.

I soon learned the reason for his anguish. He was grieving for Kin. The man, perhaps a relative, must have found him dead by the passage to the U10. He probably knew about the secret attraction too and had opened the metal door, which I was able to slip back through before the police arrived.

'Look after Nils,' I'd shouted to Alina, before going back up the wooden steps, past Kin lying lifelessly in a pool of blood, up the spiral staircase, through the shop and onto the road.

From there I kept going, aimlessly and without a plan. Just one of many crazed Berliners who no longer stick out if they jog in work boots and a thick jumper in the drizzle, without stopping, not even at a red light nor when their lungs feel as if they're burning.

I ran and ran until my race with the invisible shadow of death had driven me here to this dismal relic of Berlin. A refuge from another age and which the free-market world ought to have seen off.

*Kurt's Cosy Corner!*

Endless stylish cafés, well-stocked bars and chic restaurants, whose owners had spent years ensuring the interior design created an atmosphere in which their guests felt relaxed, had been driven to ruin by an insolvency catalyst called Covid.

Kurt's Cosy Corner, on the other hand, an old Berlin pub which wasn't even on a corner and was about as far removed from cosiness as I was from inner peace, had somehow survived the wave of bankruptcy. Without adequate lighting, without comfortable furniture and without a friendly hello from the landlord, who must be going on eighty, as I sat at the bar.

From the expression on Kurt's wrinkled face, it looked as if he were intent on making sure I didn't stay here any longer than was absolutely necessary to drink the beer I'd ordered, even though I was the only customer.

6-6-5-0-0-0.

As I took my first sip I ran over again in my mind how this combination of numbers had allowed me to escape death by a whisker.

I looked for my notes in Feline's pad, my hands shaking. NILE TIMES TWO L.

If Jagow hadn't come to at the last second, when Alina yelled *'How long is that fucking river?'*, we'd never have found the solution. Maybe her screaming had wrenched him from his unconsciousness for a fleeting moment.

*'Six thousand six hundred and fifty,'* he'd said with the last ounce of his strength before passing out again. As a geography teacher he knew, of course, how long the Nile was. And I'd managed to multiply that figure by one hundred.

6-6-5-0-0-0.

*Scholle, you sick psychopath!*

My breathing slowly relaxed and I also managed to exert control over my trembling fingers as I leafed through Feline's notes in her pad. Some pages had already been torn out. The first one that was still intact listed the songs in the playlist that had led us to her prison in the ghost station.

UIO / M85.

A playlist that hadn't saved Feline's life, but may have spared her father's. Everything suggested that Thomas Jagow had been as much of a pawn of the madman as his daughter before him. In Scholle's eyes, a father who was fanatically possessive of his daughter was probably a parent who didn't give his child enough love. Maybe he'd worked too hard, spent too much time marking instead of being there for Feline. A mortal sin that justified the highest punishment in the Eye Collector's screwy worldview.

I picked up my mobile phone and opened the screenshot of the playlist.

1 Junkie
MAJAN

2 Evermore
Namika

3 Maze
LOTTE

4 Erlking
Kool Savas

5 Under
Justin Jesso

6 Rose
Rea Garvey

7 Silver Lining
Tom Walker

8 Live in Peace
JORIS

9 Alone in a Crowded Room
Charlotte Jane

10 Million Tweets
Silbermond

11 85 Minutes of Your Love
Alle Farben, Hanne Mjøen

12 Under the World
Johannes Oerding

13 I Need You
Beth Ditto

14 Open Eyes
Tim Bendzko

15 Para Paradise
VIZE, R4GE, Emie

The mobile began vibrating in my hand. I felt both cold and sick – the aftermath of shock from my near-death experience. The more I tried to repel the memories in my mind, the harder they came for me.

- Thomas Jagow on the table in a pool of blood
- Microwave countdown
- Nile Times Two L. The anagram

The image of the playlist blurred before my eyes, which were welling with tears, so I closed them. Now words flashed in my mind like neon signs.

- Playlist
- *Je meurs là*
- I'm dying there
- Anagram

*Fuck. We were so close and yet too late.*

- UIO = U$_{10}$

*Were we actually at the right place after all?*

- Million tweets
- Anagram
- *Je meurs là*

My head was spinning. I found myself thinking of the planet mnemonic in her bedroom, how Feline had adopted this method and sent an SOS using the initial letters of the playlist.

I wished Alina were with me now so I could order my thoughts and use her as a sparring partner. She was the one who really loved puzzles; with her ambigram tattoo she even had one on her skin.

Then – Kurt was just half-heartedly asking me if I'd like another drink – something occurred to me that was so obvious I wondered why I hadn't thought of it the moment I'd got out of the ghost station.

'Have you got a pen?'

Kurt stared at me as if I'd asked him when the UFO was coming to collect me. He reluctantly passed me a brewery's promotional biro.

'Thanks!'

I jotted down the initial letters of the first nine song titles in a column:

J

E

M

E

U

R

S

L

A

Without the pressure of a timer counting down, it took me far longer this time to solve the anagram. When I'd finally done it after about ten minutes, I could barely believe the clue that had assembled before my eyes.

# 64

## ALINA

When Stoya eventually released Alina, her mobile showed four missed calls.

She called a taxi, which set her down outside Virchow hospital, where she wanted to get to Nils in casualty as quickly as possible.

Alina paid with a card and went to the loo again near the lifts.

Only now did she listen to the message that Zorbach had left her.

Out loud, because earlier on she'd been in such a hurry to leave the flat and drive to Innsbrucker Platz with Nils, she'd forgotten her earphones.

'*I know where Feline is, Alina. JE MEURS LA is an anagram too. Like Million Tweets. If you rearrange the letters you get JERUSALEM. And if you google that together with "BERLIN" you come across a hotel in Mitte. It's been empty for the past six months but the sign is still there. I'm standing outside it now. Jerusalemer Strasse 85 M.*'

*Unbelievable.*

Alina was so churned up by Zorbach's discovery that she sat on the loo, squeezing her mobile like a sponge, as if trying to wring more information from it.

JEMEURSLA.

He was right. If you rearranged the letters you could also read it as: JERUSALEM.

*But, hold on a second...*

She put her phone away, pulled up her trousers and flushed.

*Were we wrong the whole time?*

After all, Feline's things were in the 'grenade'.

- *Je meurs là*
- I'm dying there
- Where the M85 bus crosses the U10

It fitted perfectly.

*So how can the anagram now lead us to a new place Scholle has supposedly taken Feline to?*

*How could the girl possibly know the address of her future hiding place in advance?*

*No, no, no...*

It only made sense if the kidnapper had access to Feline's playlist.

*And is using it for his own purposes...*

More than one shrill alarm bell went off in Alina's head, but the screeching warning sound faded to nothing just a few seconds later.

The moment she opened the door to the cubicle and was hit by the taser that shot fifty thousand volts through her body.

# 65

## STOYA

'Yes?' Stoya sounded grumpy as he answered his colleague. Even though it wasn't the policeman's fault he wasn't Zorbach, whose call Stoya was urgently waiting for, and why he was keen to keep the line free.

'There's been a fire at a hotel by Schwielowsee,' said the commanding officer from Brandenburg Police, coming straight to the point.

'The Ambrosia-Resort?'

Stoya put his foot down without realising it. The needle leaped to sixty-five, thus exceeding double the permitted speed limit on this road through Tegel forest.

'I knew it would interest you, Stoya. It's the very place you were after a search warrant for. Well, we seem to have got there before you. An anonymous caller reported a large amount of smoke, so we went along with the boys from the fire brigade and took a look around.'

Stoya's headlights caught a fox, which had second thoughts and darted back into the woods rather than crossing the road. On reflex he braked anyway and swerved slightly. Once back in control of the vehicle, Stoya said, 'Sorry, could you repeat that?'

'I said, apart from that, it looks like the vegan hunters' clubhouse,' the officer replied, clearly fancying himself as a bit of a joker.

'Nobody around?'

'Yup. Nor do we anticipate that those who started the fire will be back in a hurry. All the rooms are open and there are no suitcases or clothes to be seen. Even the safe in the office is empty. Apparently a coach full of people was seen turning out of the Ambrosia car park and heading for the motorway.'

Stoya's satnav announced that he'd reached his destination, which was wildly at odds with his impression that he'd never been further from the place he'd wanted to be. Not here in a car park at the end of a cul-de-sac that had led through a dark no man's land.

'And you're sure there's nobody there? We're looking for a young girl.'

'That's why I'm calling. The burned bodies aren't children.'

Stoya flinched behind the wheel. 'What burned bodies?'

'Weren't you listening? I was saying that the fire razed a cabin to the ground. Two adults died.'

*That must have been when I was trying to avoid the fox.*

Stoya switched off the engine and rubbed his eyes, which were aching from the strain.

*Sheer madness.*

A hotel, but no guests. A couple of corpses, but no child. Feline's prison camp, but no Feline.

Stoya feared that the rest of his life wouldn't be long enough to get answers to all these riddles.

'I see. I owe you one.'

He thanked the officer and hung up.

Then he opened the glove compartment and fished out a box of pills wedged in the leather wallet containing the instruction manual for his car. He carefully pressed two pills out of the foil, even though he didn't know why he was taking them.

So far Stoya had no evidence that they provided even the slightest relief for his pain. But he was worried that this pain would become unbearable if he did without them.

Stoya gritted his teeth, waited until the cramp-like twinges in his stomach subsided a little, then took advantage of the brief respite to get out of the car and start walking.

Deep down – as he realised in the twilight of his life – he was a conformist, a chicken. If a doctor told him he should take the drugs, he obeyed.

And if Zorbach sent him a WhatsApp, begging for one *last, crucial favour*, he damn well did it.

# 66

## ZORBACH

Very few people know that our system based on the rule of law is not geared towards individual justice. Most laws and regulations have been enacted to avoid us descending into chaos and anarchy. But not so that every aggrieved citizen gets redress. For example, there's nothing fair about a rapist being made responsible for his crime for seven thousand three hundred days, whereas the moment the seven thousand three hundred and first day dawns, he no longer has to go to prison.

Turning the page of a calendar doesn't mean that the victim is suddenly any less abused or harmed. And yet such unfair treatment as far as the individual is concerned is necessary so that the majority in our society can get justice. For if I were still able to bring a lawsuit one hundred years after the event, our courts would be even more overburdened than they already are, and the system would collapse.

This knowledge turns every law-abiding citizen in our country into a multiple personality. For example, I was an ex-policeman who scorned the death penalty because this punishment only targeted the individual, whereas if it ever transpired that the wrong person had been executed, our justice system would be irreparably damaged. As a father, on the other hand, I could understand anyone who personally wanted to torture their child's killer to death.

Burdened by this schizophrenic feeling – that objectively I was about to commit a wrong that no court could pardon, but subjectively I had every justification in doing – I broke into the M85 hotel through the delivery entrance, three quarters of an hour after leaving my voice message for Alina.

Because of course this was no longer just about freeing Feline. In all honesty, my hope for her had virtually evaporated. TomTom, who was kicked onto the tracks; Mathilda Jahn's slit throat; the gallows on Alina's mirror; the run-over courier; and not least the bomb in the microwave – all of these clearly bore the hallmark of the Eye Collector. Scholle loved puzzles; he loved to test people in extreme situations. He basked in his perversely inflated self-esteem of giving others a 'chance' to cheat the death he'd arranged for them. On my way through the dark corridor that used to connect the hotel's food store with the large kitchen, I was perfectly aware, therefore, that I'd placed myself onto the Eye Collector's chessboard.

*He lured me here.*

*And I'm about to take him on.*

In the hope that I'd be able decide this last game of death in my favour, I shone my phone torch at the area that used to be the reception. The desk stood partially dismantled on the filthy laminate floor. The contents of a 240-litre rubbish bag, perhaps torn open by rats, had been dragged out onto the uneven boards beneath my feet: yoghurt pots, beer cans, tissues, fast-food packaging.

My inner turmoil grew with every breath I took in that litter-strewn lobby. Part of me wished someone like Stoya would appear and obstruct my pursuit of revenge and retribution. The other part hoped I'd be left alone to continue to my destination in this abandoned hotel.

My law-abiding alter ego would give himself up to Stoya, whereas my vigilante self might not let him stop me and, in my thirst for revenge, put another innocent man's life in danger.

*Where are you, Scholle?*

An insect darted out of the light when I ran the beam from my phone torch over the empty pigeonholes for keys.

No pointers.

No smiley sticker in a particular pigeonhole. No note or letter sticking out of the shelves, offering additional clues or puzzles to ensure I'd fall slap bang into the trap that had been set for me.

*Nothing.*

I stared at an open toolbox that a careless tradesman or technician must have left here.

Pensively, I picked up the hammer sitting on top.

Did this make sense? Would Scholle actually provide me with a weapon? Was this part of his perverse game? It briefly crossed my mind that I might be in the wrong place. Had I, like a conspiracy theorist, cobbled together from fragments of information a twisted version of the facts that had nothing to do with reality?

I found the stairs beside the lifts and went up, hammer

in hand, from floor to floor. Long, narrow corridors, which must have looked bleak even in the hotel's heyday, led past the rooms – all of the doors had been broken open.

Here and there I came across the typical signs of an abandoned junkie's lair: needles, empty bottles, shit-smeared mattresses, spoons and plastic rubbish.

Nowhere in any of the eighteen rooms, however, did I find any indication that a girl had been kept prisoner here recently. Although the bunk beds in the larger shared bedrooms appeared to be the same make as the one I'd found in the 'grenade', that could be mere coincidence.

*Have I gone wrong again already?*

Like with Olaf Norweg, whose mother had only given us a clue by chance.

I reached the top floor. Unlike on the other floors, there wasn't a corridor here, nor any rooms; I was staring into a single empty space. The windows were covered in black plastic that blocked out the light. Broken spotlights with smashed bulbs hung from the suspended ceiling. The relics of what this floor used to house: a club.

Once upon a time hundreds of people would have partied here all night long; now the only thing dancing was the dust in the light of my phone torch.

'Good God, what sort of a place is this?' I wondered.

Out loud, even though I was whispering, for my whispers resonated through the bare room, intensifying like an echo in an empty church. I could have expected anything at this moment, apart from an answer.

It came – how else? – from the speakers of a sound system.

*Pa – Paradise…*

I clutched the hammer so tightly it vibrated in my hand. I touched my head, which all of a sudden was aching almost as badly as it had after Lieberstett's attack, and I was convinced I was losing my mind.

Track 15: VIZE, R4GE, Emie!

Was I actually hearing this, or was Emie just singing inside my head?

And getting louder – and louder?

My fear that I was no longer able to distinguish between hallucination and reality threatened to paralyse me completely when the room turned dark at a stroke.

It took a while to realise that it wasn't just the former club that had fallen into total darkness. But me too.

'Let's do a test,' was the last thing the invisible voice said in my head. Then this too disappeared as I, having been tasered, sank deeper and deeper into a sea of nothingness and darkness to the beat of a booming bass drum.

When I awoke, I was no longer in paradise.

But at the gates of hell.

# 67

At the gates of hell the ground was hard and covered with long metal struts that dug into my back.

'Dad? Dad, wake up!'

The insistent voice fighting its way into my slowly thawing consciousness wasn't Julian's, even though I'd come to beneath the sheet with the illusion of my son in my mind.

My brain was working like the engine on a car that slams on the brakes when at maximum load. I heard a tinnitus-like beeping inside my skull. My intellect was careening wildly from synapse to synapse.

*Je meurs là*
*Jerusalem*
*U10*
*Thomas Jagow*
*Scholle*
*Feline…*

'Dad, can you hear me?'

I instructed my right hand to free my face from the rough sheet covering my entire body.

The first thing I saw was the strip of light above me. Gentle rather than harsh, fortunately, but my eyes watered all the same.

When I lifted my head without having to vomit, I still was unsure of where the Eye Collector had taken me.

My first thought was a shipping container, which would explain the corrugated floor, but gradually I realised the true purpose of my prison. Sightly curved walls, towing ropes and guy ropes on the sides and a ceiling that was slightly curved too.

Double doors. A box-shaped space. Packing stickers and bits of cardboard.

I was in a delivery van.

*Wrong.*

Not I. But *we*.

'You're not my dad,' the girl to my right said. She was lying where the back wall of the driver's cab must be. Through the veil before my eyes I could only discern outlines. Her voice was filled with such profound sadness; no actor in the world could come close to imitating such a heart-breaking tone.

'No, no, I'm not,' I said, swaying as I got to my feet. At my first attempt I toppled backwards and ended up cross-legged, which would have been quite a funny sight if my situation hadn't been so bloody hopeless.

*Wrong. Not my situation. Our.*

'Feline?' I said, because this was the only logical explanation, even if the circumstances of our first encounter were utterly bizarre.

'Yes. Who are you?' asked the teenager we'd been looking for all this time and who, now I'd finally found her, still seemed light years away.

From where I was in the vehicle, she was sitting in the left-hand corner, on the driver's side, with one hand raised as if aping the Statue of Liberty. She was forced to do this by the handcuffs shackling her to a hook in the ceiling.

'My name is Alexander Zorbach,' I said, having to clear my throat several times until my voice was no longer too husky for even me to understand properly. 'A friend of Alina's. We want to help you.'

'Then free me, please!'

Feline shook her handcuffed hand. When I looked into her eyes I was horrified. Emptiness and despair.

*Rose, the wild Irish rose, had withered.*

Feline's expression had nothing in common with the photographs I'd seen of her. Gone was that fun-loving face, always ready to politely disagree, and which radiated a keen intelligence without being arrogant.

Her eyes looked as enfeebled and dull as her dark hair, parted in the middle and hanging flatly from her head. Her jeans had a tear in the thigh, through which a once white but now blood-soaked bandage stuck out.

'Okay, wait.' I looked around. 'Do you know where the key is?' I said, without much hope. At that moment a mobile phone rang.

It rang and flashed simultaneously like a children's toy possessed by the devil. And it mocked me too, for the ringtone was 'I Need You', the thirteenth track on Feline's playlist, which went like this:

*A little rough around the edges*
*Baby we've seen better days.*
*Honey we've been tested*
*And there was hell to pay.*

I stared, as if mesmerised, at the smartphone, which jiggled towards me from the right-hand corner of the van, vibrating to the soul singing of Beth Ditto.

'No, no, not again!' Feline groaned, then started crying in anguish.

*Again?*

I picked up the mobile, looked at the screen (*YOU'D BETTER ANSWER, ZORBACH!*) and knew instinctively what Feline must have meant by that.

'You've been in this vehicle before, haven't you? Your father climbed in here and was going to set you free. Then he got a call. Is that right?'

'Yes,' she sobbed. 'Please don't answer it. Please don't let me go back again.'

'I have to,' I said. 'Otherwise it'll never stop.'

And in the knowledge that I might be making the last mistake of my life, I took the Eye Collector's call.

# 68

'So, we speak again.' Scholle laughed ruthlessly, and my desire to devise an agonising death for him grew even further, which I'd have thought impossible.

'You've made a mistake,' I said. 'You ought not to have let me get close to Feline. I'm going to set her free, and her statement will finally lead us to you.'

'Like Frank Lahmann's you mean? Oh, please! You've never been a step ahead of me, Zorbach.'

'I'm going to hang up now and call for help.'

'I'd think twice about that.'

'Why?'

'Because that would be your decision in my love test.'

I bit my tongue in fury; the pain just spurred me on. 'What makes you think I'm going to play your sick game? You might have had a hold on Feline's father. Was it Mathilda? His pupil? Did he have to choose between Feline and the baby?'

'You're not as stupid as I thought you were.' Scholle

laughed. 'Either that, or the recent blow to the back of your head must have sharpened your intellect.'

Feline shook her shackles again.

'But let's not waste our time. If you think you ought to free the girl now, then be my guest. Hang up and call Stoya. You can even open the door and go. It's not locked.'

I warily set about verifying what Scholle had said. *Yes*. No lock, no resistance. The double doors opened outwards.

Damp, cold air hit my face like a wet towel. It didn't take me a second, not even a fraction of one. I knew where I was the moment I saw it.

'What happens if I hang up?' I asked. For the first time during this conversation, fear was the strongest of my emotions, anger and revenge having dominated up till then.

'What always happens in the love test. You make a choice and have to live the rest of your life with the consequences. Do you know why I like children so much, Zorbach?'

I couldn't believe I was hearing these words from the mouth of a serial killer who'd drowned a number of girls and boys, before cutting out one of their eyes. Even harder to believe was the fact that Scholle sounded as if he were being serious.

'Children are so much more honest than grown-ups. They happily rank things, quite openly. Like: who's your best friend? You must have done the same at primary school – a piece of paper with first, second and third position. No?'

I heard Feline groan and felt like screaming myself.

'Parents, on the other hand, lie to themselves when they claim to love all their children the same. That's rubbish. There's always a favourite. Always one they hug more tightly, want to stroke more and who they're readier to forgive than the others.'

'Maybe that's true in your sick world, where there's not enough love to go around,' I countered.

'No. My world is wholesome. Yours pretends that people can shed responsibility. You bring children into the world, only to hand them over to paid nannies, nurseries and au pairs while you go to work. You neglect your own flesh and blood in favour of your own personal fulfilment. You act as if there were enough time and love for everyone, not realising that to love is a decision you have to take. Day after day after day. And your decision is now.'

'What decision?' I barked down the line.

'No, please don't,' I heard Feline sob behind me. She must be experiencing a cruel déjà vu, for now I was certain that a similar scene had played out in this delivery van a few days earlier, when Feline watched her father climb out of the vehicle.

'You have to decide. Who do you love more? Yourself, or an innocent child? What is worth more to you, your life or theirs?'

'Do I have to shoot myself? Have you left a gun here like last time? Is that it? My life for Feline's? What's worth more to you?' I said, spitting with rage. 'Because if that's the case then you've forgotten something fundamental. Last time you subjected me to this test you had my son as a bargaining chip. I had to obey your orders. But now Feline's here with me.'

'I can't believe what I've just heard. Do you really think I'm so stupid that I'm not aware of that?'

'No,' I said, feeling hollow and impotent.

'Good. Now, why don't you see what's at stake if you call the police?'

Scholle hung up.

For a while I didn't move, exhausted by the phone call as if I'd just completed a forced march. Then I took the only option available to me: to discover what the assignment was. I moved over to the doors to find out what nightmarish chain reaction I would set off if I freed Feline.

'No, don't leave me alone. Please, not again, I won't be able to cope!' the girl begged.

'Don't worry,' I said, demanding the impossible from her, and promising to return.

Getting out of the van, I battled my way in the night-time darkness through waist-high growth, crossed the damp forest floor, then walked down the narrow, winding path straight to the natural harbour, hidden by trees and reeds, where my boat was moored.

# 69

This had once been my sanctuary, my refuge from a world I was increasingly keen to withdraw from because I no longer felt I had a place in it. It had taken Scholle just a few minutes to turn it into the most gruesome place on earth. For this was where he'd dragged the one person in this world who wasn't a blood relative of mine who still meant something to me.

Alina.

Of course she was here.

'Alex!' I heard her cry, even though that was impossible because her mouth was stuck with the same insulating tape that tied her hands behind her back and fastened her legs to the feet of the unlit wood burner. But I was sure it was my name she was trying to squeeze through the sticky coating on her lips.

'Hmmmmmm!!!'

A film of sweat glistened on her bald head. As she wasn't wearing the glasses I could see her wide-open eyes which must be causing her pain, because I'd switched on the overhead light.

'Wait, I'll help you.'

Although Alina must have known that her attempts to free herself were pointless, she jiggled her limbs like crazy the moment I entered the boat.

'Wait.'

Kneeling in front of her, I put out my hand and saw that she was injured too. Around her wrist was a blood-soaked bandage similar to the one I'd seen around Feline's thigh.

*What has he done to you?*

The phone Scholle had left for me in the van, and which I'd taken with me, rang again. Once more I read the order: *YOU'D BETTER ANSWER, ZORBACH!*

'I've made it slightly easier for you,' Scholle said, resuming our morbid conversation. 'Maybe you can see the bandage around Alina's wrist. It's a very tight tourniquet. You just have to remove it and she'll bleed to death in a trice.'

*Oh God…*

I stood back up, partly because I hoped it would allow me to think more clearly. And because I didn't want Alina to hear any of the conversation. 'Or you can go back and take off Feline's plaster, which is on her femoral artery.'

'I won't do either,' I said.

'Oh, yes you will. You see, I'm afraid you don't have a choice. Look.' Scholle actually seemed to be smiling as he spoke. 'I know you love her. You've never said so to Alina; you may not even have admitted it to yourself, but hey, that's what I'm here for. It's my honour to be able to open your eyes with the love test.'

'You're deranged.'

'And you have to decide. Alina or Feline? Who's going to survive? The woman you love? Or the girl who has the whole of her life ahead of her? Whose bandage will you remove?'

'Neither.'

Alina had stopped jiggling. How much could she have pieced together from my answers? Enough for the shock to have paralysed her?

'I think you'll go with Alina. Come on, admit it. You never really cared about Feline, did you? If you had, you wouldn't have fallen for my tricks. Of course I knew the girl was trying to send you messages via the playlist. I knew about the Wi-Fi connection in the underground and deliberately let her keep the "watch". Then I gave it to Tabea so you'd find it on her at Ambrosia. Although not without adding some of my favourite songs to lure you into my clutches.' He chuckled contentedly.

'I'd actually been intending to retire, which is why you haven't heard from me in so long. But then an opportunity opened up that couldn't have been a coincidence. It arose right after my last operation – you should know I've changed my appearance somewhat, after those really unflattering mug shots of me went into circulation. I've even gone into training to slim down and now I'm more of an athlete than a teddy bear. I know it's hard to believe but I've become obsessed by exercise. And well, when fate came knocking at the door after my most recent surgery, I seized the chance. And look, here we are again. Zorbach and Alina intimately reunited, busy doing what they do best: weighing up life and death. So, Zorbach, my old chum, what's your decision?'

'There's nothing to decide,' I hissed angrily. 'I'm going to free them both.'

I sensed Alina's head shoot in my direction. Like a child who thinks they won't be seen if they don't look, I turned away from her.

'Oh, do you really think I've got nothing to force a decision out of you?' Scholle sneered. 'Look at your mobile.'

I took it away from my ear and saw the image on the screen change. A text box appeared ('Please Wait') like in an online meeting when a participant shares their screen. Then a video clip played.

And once more it didn't take me even a fraction of a second to work out where the camera was positioned that was streaming me live images courtesy of Scholle.

*No, please, no!*

'You fucking arsehole,' I said, and now rage was again the principal force guiding my thoughts and actions. 'Get out of there. Piss off out of there right now, or I swear—'

'What? That you'll get really, really angry with me?' Scholle asked sarcastically.

At that moment the night-vision camera zoomed in even closer. Into the head on the pillow.

The head of my son, Julian, sleeping in his boarding school dormitory.

# 70

I ran outside. Back into the cold, the rain. As if that could change anything. As if it improved my chances.

My son was over thirty kilometres away. Even the quickest route between Wannsee and Tegeler See would take at least half an hour. And Scholle wasn't going to give me more than thirty seconds to decide.

'Right, you're going to remove one of the plasters. Feline's or Alina's. And you're going to film for me the one you've chosen bleeding to death. If not...'

On my mobile a pistol moved into view on the infrared camera.

I had no idea how Scholle had managed to do it, but right now he was standing in my son's room with a gun, the barrel of the pistol just a few centimetres from his head.

Feeling helpless, I swept my damp hair out of my face. A drop of rain had fallen down the back of my neck.

'If not, what?' I said, challenging him to utter the unthinkable.

'If not, I'll kill your son. It's your test. Your choice.'

I coughed and choked on the cold air filling my lungs. Smelled the woods. Tasted the dampness covering my lips and nostrils. And I immediately felt calmer. I touched the scar on my neck that I had Scholle to thank for. The day he'd forced me to kill myself to save my son's life. This time I wasn't going to play by his crazed rules.

As if the cold had cleared my senses and settled my voice, I replied firmly, 'I love freedom. Life. With all the people who are important to me. Only weaklings have to keep making comparisons. But there's no measure when it comes to love. You'll find this out, Scholle, the hard way. You're a pathetic, weak man. I'm not going to let you blackmail me any more. I'm not going to lay a hand on anyone. I'm not your puppet, you insane wanker. Not any more and never again.'

I was going to hang up there and then. But my fingers were too wet. From the drizzle collecting on the screen. And they were too shaky, for evidently I wasn't as calm as I'd felt prior to my brief speech.

That's the only reason we were still connected when Scholle said, 'Nice bluff. But I'm afraid your gamble hasn't paid off. Now watch your son die.'

'He won't.'

'Oh, really?'

I heard the trigger being pressed.

Click.

'No. Because I've changed the rules of the game, you cunt.'

Click. Click.

He managed to pull the trigger twice more, but no shot was fired. Instead I saw the screen go black. I heard shouting. Stoya and another policeman. But not my son. Then the line went dead.

# 71

On the way back to my houseboat I dialled Stoya's number and yelled, 'What's happening? What's going on there?'

Panting, rustling, footsteps and whining feedback filled my ears. But – and this drove me crazy with worry – no sign of life from my son.

'Julian? Julian, can you hear me?'

Silence. Someone coughed. The screen in my hand was still black. Then, finally, Stoya took the weight off my mind: 'Yes, yes, he can hear you. He's fine.'

*Thank God!*

Laughing hysterically I emptied my lungs in a single, protracted roar. So Stoya had done what I'd begged him to do just after my about-turn at the gates to Tegel prison. This was the text I'd sent him:

*Alina thinks the Eye Collector is Feline's abductor. If that's true then it's no coincidence that Alina and I are involved again. Which means Scholle will repeat his love test. For that he needs people closest to us. For me that means Julian. I'm terrified something might happen to him. Please look after him. For the next few hours at least. I don't know what Scholle's planning, but I'm counting on the worst. Please don't let anything happen to Julian. AZ.*

'Pass him to me, would you?'

I waited an eternity, during which I stood there in the rain as if paralysed until I finally heard the magic word: 'Dad?'

'Yes, yes, I'm here,' I said, fluffing even these few words.

'What's up? What's going on?'

Julian seemed confused, tired and fearful. And yet his voice had never sounded so beautiful.

I was gasping for breath. Pressing the mobile to my ear. There was so much I wanted to say all at once, but as I got back onto the boat I could only come out with clichés. 'Julian. I'm sorry, I'm so, so sorry. Are you okay?'

'Yes, but what are all these people doing here?'

'I'll explain everything later. The most important thing is that you're safe.'

I heard a voice in the background, then my son saying something I couldn't make out, and finally Stoya was back on the line.

'I've got to hang up now.'

'Wait. Where's Scholle?' I stumbled across the outer deck and opened a box I'd put by the rear entrance. This is where I kept my tools.

'I'm sorry,' Stoya said.

I felt as if the houseboat had been caught by a massive

wave, but it was Stoya's incomprehensible answer that made me stagger.

'What did you say?'

'He got away.'

'But…' I said, taking a bolt cutter from the box and clutching it like an axe, '… how is that possible?'

*How can Scholle have slipped through our fingers again?*

'He wasn't there!' Stoya said.

I looked around, at the shore, then the lake, as if I might spot him somewhere here on the water or in the woods. 'But I spoke to him and saw…'

*Of course.*

I felt like smashing something with the bolt cutters. Scholle wasn't so stupid as to put himself in danger by going there himself. He'd engaged someone to help him.

'Who did he get to do his dirty work?'

'A boy.'

'What?'

'His name is Ansgar. Scholle promised him money if he crept into Julian's room and put the willies up him.'

*Blood. Punches. Revenge.*

Ansgar!

The boy Julian had beaten up on the sports pitch.

I immediately thought of the man who'd watched us from the bench before vanishing into thin air.

*Scholle.*

'It seems as if Ansgar had a score to settle with your son. He was putty in Scholle's fingers. Ansgar thought he was going to terrify Julian from his sleep with a blank pistol, but Scholle gave him a real gun.'

I nodded.

So they'd swapped the pistols in advance. As an ex-cop I didn't have to ask why they hadn't apprehended Ansgar beforehand. By making Ansgar pull the trigger under false pretences, Scholle had made himself guilty of attempted murder as an indirect perpetrator. Another serious crime to add to the Eye Collector's long list. If they'd stopped Ansgar before he'd got to my son's room, Scholle might have escaped prosecution for this.

I held the phone away for a moment and shouted into the boat, 'Hold on, Alina, I'll be right there!'

Then I jumped back on land from the jetty and ran up the path through the woods.

'How was he controlling Ansgar?' I asked Stoya, the phone back to my ear and the bolt cutters in my other hand.

'Our technical guys are still trying to work that out. From what we know, Ansgar was going to film the supposed stunt on his mobile and somehow Scholle was going to forward the images to you.'

I was panting and had a stitch when I got to the top of the slope, but I kept running to the van.

'We've got Ansgar's mobile and we're trying to trace all calls from the last few hours, but...'

*... it's not going to tell us much.*

Scholle was a technical wizard and had been a policeman for too long to make a novice's error here.

'Are they there yet?'

'Who?' I asked, yanking open the rear door of the van.

My worst nightmare came true: Feline had disappeared. An empty load area blurred before my tear-filled eyes. Her open handcuff dangled from the pipe welded to the ceiling.

And on the floor of the van another mobile, this time with Majan's 'Junkie' as its ringtone. His song destroyed every last vestige of hope within me.

*... I've burned your dreams*
*and buried them outside...*

'The police and ambulance,' I heard Stoya say. 'We've located your mobile. They should be there any minute now.'

'No, there's no one here,' I panted, before hanging up and climbing into the van.

And with every centimetre I crawled further into this vehicle that reeked of fear and sweat, the nightmarish vision was dispelled. In real life, which I'd never loved so much as right now, the song faded away, the handcuff was closed again and the empty cargo area was filled first by a shadow, then by the body of a girl.

'You're back,' Feline sobbed, crying bitterly. Probably because she'd been less assured than me that I would come back and use the bolt cutters to free her.

Finally.

# 72

## ZORBACH

*Two days later*

The door to room 1310 was so thick that I couldn't be sure the person behind it had heard me knocking. I tentatively pushed it with my shoulder, holding the bunch of flowers I'd bought from a stand in Clayallee in one hand, and a book wrapped in red paper in the other.

'Can I come in?'

Feline sat up in her bed and looked at me with the circumspect politeness you show a stranger. It took her a second to recognise me as the man who'd cut open her handcuff in the van.

'Alex!' she said. Feline sounded surprised, but her tone was friendly. She was terribly pale, which was made more striking by the contrast with her dark hair and even darker eyes.

'I won't bother you for long,' I said, going over to her bed to give her the book: a biography of Depeche Mode. 'I've got something for you.'

She gave me a weary smile and thanked me. 'Thanks too for decoding my playlist and coming to my rescue.'

'That wasn't just me,' I said, thinking of Alina, who I'd also freed from her shackles and who'd avoided all contact with me since, refusing to take my calls.

'You're a remarkably clever young lady!' I was searching for the right words to express my admiration for her. 'In your situation I'd never have come up with the idea of sending out an SOS with fifteen songs. That was brilliant!'

She thanked me again and said, rather shyly, 'There were only five, actually.'

I nodded.

*'Million Tweets', '85 Minutes of Your Love', 'Under the World', 'I Need You' and 'Open Eyes'. The clue to the place where the U10 and M85 intersect.*

I'd thought as much. The Eye Collector had discovered that his far too intelligent hostage had found a way to communicate with the outside world. Then Scholle added songs to the playlist to give us the runaround. *And with 'Para Paradise' lead us directly to disaster.*

'I'm sorry we weren't able to solve the puzzle earlier and free you from Innsbrucker Platz,' I said. 'How on earth did you know that's where you'd been taken?'

'It was all because of Olaf,' Feline replied. Her gaze, now sadder, wandered to the window. 'Without him I'd be dead.' Her voice was cracking up. 'He taught me everything there is to know about the Berlin underground system.'

Including, no doubt, about a long-abandoned art installation in the ghost station of Innsbrucker Platz on the U10 line.

I gave her a while to push to the back of her mind the thoughts of her best friend's suicide and of those terrible hours and days in the 'tank', and waited for her to resume the conversation.

'Are the flowers for me too?' Feline asked, attempting a smile.

'No.'

I looked at the visitor sitting beside the bed.

She was also smiling, with even less confidence than Feline, which must be because she didn't know how she ought to respond. I could see that although she was eager to get up and hug me, she didn't want to let go of the hand of the person she'd been deathly afraid about for so long.

'The flowers are for your mother,' I said, handing the bouquet to Emilia Jagow.

# 73

'I don't know how I can ever thank you,' Emilia said in tears as soon as we'd left Feline to have a private chat in the day room. Situated at the end of the corridor, it was empty and hopefully would remain so for the duration of our brief conversation. 'You saved my daughter's life!'

'You played your part too. If you hadn't got into the resort, we'd wouldn't have realised so soon that we were dealing with the Eye Collector.'

'Still.' Emilia sat uncertainly on one of the uncomfortable-looking wooden chairs dotted around the room. 'Without you, my daughter wouldn't be alive today. Don't you want to take a seat too? Fancy a coffee?'

I thanked her, but said I couldn't stay long.

'Because of your prison sentence?' Feline's mother asked.

'No, fortunately I've still got a little time before that starts.' It was thanks to Stoya that there weren't any negative repercussions from not having appeared at the appointed time, and that the start of my sentence had been postponed by a few more days. He'd argued that I ought to be able to give my statement while still a free man. I got the feeling he'd turned soft with age, which might also be down to his poor health, although he wouldn't say exactly what was wrong with him. He probably wanted to give me another chance of a proper goodbye with my son. But – like Alina – Julian wanted to have nothing to do with me. *Understandable*. Whenever I turned up it wasn't long before either of them had to start fearing for their lives. You could set your watch by it.

'I've got another interrogation,' I told Emilia.

Feline was free, but the Eye Collector was still at large and the case was far from being solved.

'I fear I'm going to have to spend quite a bit of time at the station too,' Emilia said. She sounded exhausted, which was no surprise given all the commotion of the past forty-eight hours. The press hadn't just gone to town on Alina and me, feting us – wrongly, in my view – as heroes who'd succeeded in freeing a child from the clutches of an abductor. The media had also pounced on Emilia, who'd just escaped being burned to a cinder on the premises of an obscure hotel. The sensationalist reporting had gone into lurid detail about the Ambrosia, the cult-like place for victims of violent crime, which Emilia had infiltrated like an undercover agent because she suspected her daughter was there. And how her research had uncovered that the sect confronted the perpetrators with their victims, working on the principle of 'an eye for an eye'. Emilia's discoveries were the reason why the leaders of the sect had been forced to decamp and, before their hasty exit, had been keen to destroy not only incriminating material about their illicit activity, but the chief witness along with it.

'*Dr Lieberstett threatened to have her assistant shoot me if I refused to leave with them,*' one national newspaper quoted Emilia in its story.

'*But the assistant had spilled petrol all over himself and another patient saved me by threatening him with a lighter. There was a scuffle, in the course of which both of them went up in flames.*'

At which point Lieberstett and Emilia fled. Apparently the Ambrosia director had made it with her 'patients' over the Polish border, where they hadn't yet been located, despite intensive searches. Emilia, on the other hand, ran to the nearest house, from where she notified the fire brigade. They found nothing but an empty resort and two burned bodies: Jakob and Tabea.

'You know what, Alex? Of all the interrogations I've faced over the last few hours, the worst have been those from my daughter,' Emilia said, getting back up again. I tentatively took her trembling hand.

'*Daddy didn't free me,*' she said, citing Feline's words. '*Why not? Why did he leave me in the van?*'

I nodded.

This was one of the reasons I'd come. Because I knew the answer. Maybe even better than Stoya and Thomas Jagow, who wasn't certain to leave intensive care alive. Although there was a glimmer of hope that Feline's father would pull through, he was in a far worse state than Nils, who'd already been discharged yesterday following a successful operation. It seemed as if the fracture caused by the bear trap wasn't as complicated as first thought. Alina's fiancé didn't even need a crutch, only a splint.

'Your husband appears to have been the pawn of a

sadistic serial killer,' I said, revealing to Emilia a detail that the press hadn't yet published. Most of the journalists were certain that the father was behind the kidnapping. So far Stoya had kept all the information relating to Scholle secret for the purposes of the investigation.

Emilia nodded. 'I know. Alina only spoke about him as the Eye Collector. It was through her that I came across you, Herr Zorbach.'

I grimaced and shook my head sadly. 'It happened differently, I'm afraid. You didn't choose us; the kidnapper deftly manipulated you so that you'd come to me. Mike Scholokowsky, known as Scholle, has got unfinished business with Alina and me. I think that's why he deliberately picked your family, Frau Jagow.'

'Why? I don't understand.' She sobbed and I put an arm around her shoulder. I tried to explain as best I could.

'Somehow Scholle found out that your husband was having an affair with a pupil,' I said as gently as possible. 'Mathilda Jahn. He abducted Feline and made your husband choose between your daughter and the baby Mathilda had given birth to.'

'Are you saying that Thomas sacrificed Feline for the baby?' She freed herself from my arm.

'The test took place in the delivery van you saw him clamber out of,' I said, answering her question.

I outlined my theory that Scholle had taken pleasure in tormenting Thomas Jagow, putting him to the test time and again after this initial trial. The next choice he had to make was between Mathilda and the baby. Scholle abducted Mathilda and her child, taking them to below the motorway bridge in Albrechts Teerofen, and made Thomas decide.

Again he came down on the side of the infant. I presume he too just had to remove a plaster from Mathilda's neck, which made her bleed to death. The final round of the Eye Collector's game led him to the 'tank' in the U10, where Thomas Jagow was no longer the player, but the plaything that was now to put Alina and me to the test.

'I'm sorry. Time and again in the love test your husband chose the baby over your daughter.'

'But that doesn't make any sense,' said Feline, who was suddenly in the door of the day room.

We turned around to her like a pair of lovers caught in the act, whereas in fact we were ashamed she'd found out what she never ought to have heard so bluntly.

'It wasn't Dad's baby,' Feline protested vehemently, her right hand nervously clutching her hospital nightgown. 'Those were just stupid rumours at school. It can't be his.'

The colour drained from Emilia's face and she blinked as if something had flown into her eye. 'Are you sure, my darling?' she asked, taking a step towards Feline.

'Because Dad can't have children any more.'

'How do you know that?'

'What you should be asking is why *you* don't know,' Feline whispered, her head bowed. Then she looked at me, clearly finding it embarrassing to talk to her mother about this. 'Dad forgot to close his inbox. On the computer I'm allowed to use for school. I wouldn't have read it, but the doctor's message was still open. And because I didn't know what azoospermia was, I googled it. I was worried it was some terrible disease.'

'What is it?' I asked. Going by the expression on Emilia's face she was as clueless as me.

'It's when the semen doesn't contain any sperm.' Feline turned red. 'It was a check-up; he must have had the problem for years. In the email it said the problem wasn't going to go away and so Dad would remain infertile.'

'I... I had no idea,' Emilia said, her voice little more than a gasp.

I could see a storm brewing inside her head.

The fact that she looked numb on the outside was surely a sign of the mental overload this unexpected news – at once shocking and reassuring – must have caused. Because although her husband couldn't be the father of Mathilda Jahn's baby, he'd kept secret from her his medical problems, which basically meant he'd betrayed her trust.

'The thing about the affair was just a silly rumour at school, Mum. He looked after Mathilda in his role as pastoral counsellor, that's all. I know Dad loves you more than anything else.'

Emilia nodded, desperately trying to keep her composure, but she couldn't prevent a tear from welling in the corner of her eye.

'Well, the DNA test will give us certainty on this point,' I said. 'But if what Feline says is right, the Eye Collector must have made a mistake when he put Thomas to the test.'

I watched Emilia put an arm around her daughter and stroke her head. With every second that passed in silence, the more aware I became that I'd been very mistaken about Thomas Jagow's motives. And how far the Eye Collector still was from me and thus from his end.

'He made a mistake that throws up a much bigger question,' Emilia finally said flatly and so quietly that I could barely make it out. But I understood what she was getting at.

The key question.

*If Thomas Jagow wasn't the father, why did he choose the baby over Feline in the Eye Collector's love test?*

# 74

## NILS

'I don't think that's a good idea.'

They parked in Bleibtreustrasse itself, which was a miracle; in this area you were more likely to find a one-hundred-euro note on the street than a parking space right outside the door.

'How was driving? Okay?' Alina said, trying to sidetrack and pointing at Nils's splinted leg.

'Yes, it's only the left foot, thank goodness.' He tapped his thigh. 'I don't need it for an automatic. What about your arm?'

Alina felt the bandage on her wrist. Although the wound the Eye Collector had given her was no longer fatal if she untied the bandage, it still needed to be examined regularly by the doctor.

'I'm fine. I won't be long,' she said, feeling for the handle in the passenger door.

'You're making a mistake. It's too soon.'

'You've already said that. But if anyone needs a

psychiatrist after everything that's happened in the past few days, it's me.'

He leaned over to Alina and put a hand on the back of her neck to give it a gentle massage. 'Sometimes it's sensible to wait until some time after the traumatic experience before embarking on therapy.'

She took his hand off her neck, but didn't let go of it immediately. 'Look, darling, I want to come off my medicine. It's my final decision. I have to be one hundred per cent sure, because there's no going back afterwards. I'll be blind for the rest of my life.'

Playing inside her head was Tim Bendzko, the fourteenth song on Feline's playlist.

*Do you see the world as it is?*
*How can you bear*
*That its dark sides*
*Eclipse all that is fair?*

'I don't think I can bear to see the world as it presents itself to me.'

Nils turned her hand over and traced her lifeline with his forefinger. 'I love you with sight and without. I'm just not sure whether this Dr Rej is the right person to give you advice.'

She stroked his hair affectionately. 'I intend to sort that out too, Nils. I'm going to ask him straight out why he first fobbed me off through you, but then sent me a text telling me to get in touch.'

*Shit!*

Nils frantically thought of how he might get Alina to cancel this appointment with Dr Samuel Rej, which had been arranged at short notice. But nothing came to mind.

'I won't be long,' she said again, opening the passenger door. 'You could wait for me in a café? Just please don't go prowling around the area. I know how much you miss exercise, but you're not even supposed to be driving.'

She blew him a kiss, got out and shut the door. Just in time, before his mobile rang and Nils took a call from an irate individual who drilled him with questions.

# 75

## EMILIA

'Now you're answering? After all these weeks?' Emilia was in her car that was still in the hospital car park. On the top, open-air level, where apart from her there were four other vehicles, albeit several metres away on the other side of the concrete block.

'What do you want?'

'Did you know?'

'Know what?'

'Did you know that my husband wasn't having an affair? That it wasn't his child?'

There was a pause. Then she heard him laugh.

*Bastard.*

'Do you mean he concealed from you that he was only able to fire blanks in bed because he was worried you wouldn't think he was a real man? I found the doctor's report on his mobile. Of course I knew.'

'And still you carried out the love test?'

'Don't forget who was so desperate for it,' he clarified. '*You* came to see me at the Friedberg clinic. I wanted my peace and quiet and to be left alone. It was bad enough that the plastic surgery needed some touching up after that bungler in the Czech Republic. But then you came along playing the sensitive nurse. You were absolutely hooked on my story of the poor hero whose face was badly injured as he tried to pull his brother from the wreck of a burning car. My brother died years ago, for fuck's sake!'

'I thought we were kindred spirits.'

'Bollocks. You saw me as a victim like yourself. But it was about you rather than me. You used me as your agony aunt. Cried on my shoulder. Oh my God, all that whining about how worried you were Thomas was going to leave you. That he'd love the other woman's baby more than Feline. And all because you were taken in by a silly rumour doing the rounds at Thomas's school.'

'I found pictures and messages on his phone,' Emilia protested.

A photo of a little baby. In the arms of that young, gorgeous-looking schoolgirl.

Beneath it the following text: *Thanks! Without you this innocent little thing wouldn't be here today!*

'He was her pastoral counsellor, Emilia. He helped her after the rape.'

'Rape?'

'If you'd kept an eye on his mobile like I did, you'd have found this out yourself. It happened after a party. Mathilda wanted to have an abortion, but your husband gave her the support to keep it.'

*Without you this innocent little thing wouldn't be here today!*

'But...'

Emilia stared at her hands; her fingers had started to shake uncontrollably. 'But why did you suggest the love test to me? That was your idea!'

'Because it was the only way for you to find out what your husband really feels for you.'

Emilia looked through the windscreen covered in rain; the world beyond appeared blurred. Trees, clouds, a crane on a nearby construction site – everything looked crooked, wonky or bulgy. Like a distorted psychedelic picture that perfectly matched the ruined life she'd now have to live forever more.

'I was sick with worry,' she tried to explain to the madman. 'Depressive. You manipulated me like that boy you gave a pistol to.'

'No, no, no. *You* asked me to abduct Feline.'

'For show. You said you'd take her to a hotel for a few days. That she was in good hands with you. That your girlfriend would look after her.'

'And all that happened. Even the hotel room is true; it was just in a rather unusual location.'

Emilia closed her eyes helplessly, pressing the lids together so tightly she thought they'd be stuck fast when she tried to open them again. Which of course they weren't.

'Nothing happened,' she yelled, checking her rear-view mirror to see if anyone was approaching who might inadvertently catch their conversation. 'You didn't stick to any agreement. Feline was only supposed to be with you for a short while, but you waited weeks to do the test.'

'To intensify the emotional pressure on Thomas. Without that there can be no reliable findings from the love test.'

'Rubbish! You just enjoy seeing other people suffer.

That's why you kept playing your game even though you were supposed to bring Feline back to me immediately after the test.'

'Okay, I got a bit carried away.'

'Stop that revolting laughter,' she shouted. 'I was sick with worry and started looking for my daughter on my own. That was the intention, wasn't it? That was the plan all along. You wanted me to get Alina and Zorbach to investigate the case. From the moment you knew that Alina had worked in my hospital and treated Feline, you wanted to play your sick game with her.'

Emilia swallowed her own saliva and had to cough. Of course. All this had been planned from the outset. She ought to have suspected something was up when he asked her to give him her husband's mobile.

'*Nothing reveals more about a person's psyche than their smartphone,*' he'd told her. '*To test him I need to know how he ticks, who he's friends with, who he's regularly in contact with.*' All crap.

'You spied on Thomas to give you more blackmail material,' she said, more to herself than to him. 'To get Mathilda's number so you could terrorise and then kill her. And then, when you no longer needed the mobile, you hid it at the Ambrosia-Resort, presumably to work it into your sick game with Alina, who you wanted to cart off there.'

Emilia had to cough so hard again that her next sentence was barely intelligible. 'It was never about me or Feline, was it? Because there was no reason to do the test if you knew that THOMAS DIDN'T HAVE A CHILD WITH ANOTHER WOMAN!'

A torrent of rain pounded so loudly on the roof of the car

that Emilia could no longer hear the static that had been on the line when she paused.

*Has he hung up?*

No. She was almost relieved when she heard him giggle.

'Listen to yourself. You're cursing and screaming. Another sign of your mental disarray. You're forever trying to foist the blame onto others. Like when you tell everyone how anal Thomas is about being neat and tidy. But you're the one with OCD, who cleans the entire bungalow every day like a madwoman. You're obsessive in your views too. The moment you've got something in your head, it takes drastic measures to wean you off your delusions.'

'What are you trying to say?'

'You thought Thomas didn't love you any more. It drove you nuts. Because, hand on heart, what sort of mother has her daughter kidnapped for show?'

*A desperate, depressive one.* And yes, one who's sick in the head.

On this point Emilia had to admit he was right.

'Only my love test was strong enough to penetrate your crazed mental fog and give your mind the clarity it required.'

'It didn't bring any clarity. It ruined everything. My daughter is traumatised and Thomas might not survive. I don't even know why he decided not to choose Feline.'

'Well, that might be because I slightly altered the test question.'

*Altered?*

Emilia, who'd already put her seat belt on (something she felt compelled to do as soon as she got into a car, whether it was moving or parked), pulled it from her chest because she felt unable to breathe any more.

'What did you do?'

'You wanted him to choose between Feline and Mathilda's baby. But the result of that test was predictable because after a bit of research I knew the child couldn't be Thomas's. So I changed the options.'

Emilia's car had turned into an incubator; she was sweating and gasping for oxygen. She tried in vain to put a window down, but the engine wasn't on and the switch in the door refused to obey her.

'What did you ask Thomas?' she panted.

'When he was in the van and had the chance to free Feline, I told him that I had *you* in my telescopic sight and I'd kill you if he didn't let Feline drive away with me.'

'Me?'

*I was the stake?*

'He didn't choose the baby?'

'No, he chose you! His wife. That's right. It meant I didn't have to bring Feline back home, because Thomas had made quite clear who he loved more. You, Emilia. And that was all you wanted to know, wasn't it?'

Emilia stared at the ignition button beside the steering wheel.

*Thomas. Oh God. Darling Thomas.*

What had she done to him in her crazed fit of jealousy?

When she was the love of his life.

*What about me?*

He was only crazy for her, but she was crazy full stop.

'Probably he thought he could save you first, then Feline later. Thinking about it, I might have even promised to set your daughter free if he took part in more love tests.'

Emilia screamed. How she'd love to start the engine and

put her foot down. The car was only a few metres from the edge of the car park. Level seven. If she took off her seat belt she wouldn't survive the impact.

But she knew she wasn't brave enough. Jesus, she didn't even have the courage to hang up on the madman whose mental derangement probably wasn't much different from her own. Because that fucker was right. What sort of mother did that to her own child?

And so it was he, rather than she, who ended their phone call with a scornful smile in his voice when he said, 'But that's enough chit-chat. I have to go now, my dear, because I've got an appointment I'm relishing.'

# 76

## ALINA

*Strange*, Alina thought as she pressed the bell to Dr Rej's practice.

*What's up with Nils? Why does he behave so strangely whenever the conversation turns to my psychiatrist?*

She heard footsteps and felt a draught of air when the door opened.

*Is Nils worried Rej might find something out that could harm our relationship?*

Alina was about to say hello, but heard the doctor on the phone and didn't want to interrupt him. Dr Rej stood in the doorway and said, 'But that's enough chit-chat. I have to go now, my dear, because I've got an appointment I'm relishing.'

# 77

## NILS

His mobile rang for the second time in five minutes. And for the second time it was Zorbach on the line. Asking the same question as before: 'Once again, please would you tell me where Alina is?'

'Once again, why do you want to know?'

Compared to his first call, this time Zorbach was much more forthcoming. A few minutes ago he'd hemmed and hawed, but now he sounded harried, as if his life depended on what he was saying. 'Why do you think I'm not in prison yet? Why Stoya hasn't arrested me? Because I had to do something for him.'

'What?' Nils strained to peer through his windscreen at the building that housed the psychiatrist's practice.

'Less than fifteen minutes ago I hugged Feline's mother in the hospital. In the process, I managed to slip a tiny microphone into her coat pocket which allowed us to eavesdrop on her conversations and convict her as an accomplice. Right now she's being arrested by Stoya.'

'Okay, that's great. But what's it got to do with Alina?'

'Please, I haven't got the time to explain everything.'

'Then I'm not going to tell you where she is. She doesn't want to have anything to do with you ever again, and she's strictly forbidden me from giving you any information about her. For God's sake, she's even thinking of leaving the city because of you.'

A throbbing pain ran from the ankle of his splinted leg to the kneecap. The doctors had told him to avoid unnecessary movements. Obviously severe emotional stress too.

'She won't be able to go anywhere soon because she'll be dead,' Zorbach thundered.

Nils lowered his voice as someone was passing close to his car to cross Bleibtreustrasse.

'What do you mean?'

Zorbach groaned. 'After I bugged Emilia, Stoya was able to listen to her call the very man who tried to kill your fiancée only a couple of days ago. Michael Scholokowsky. The Eye Collector. He'll go by a different name now and will look different too. Even his voice is different, like he's wearing dentures. But it's possible he's meeting her right now. He sounded sadistic, referring to an appointment he was relishing. He could have meant Alina.'

*No!*

Nils felt as if the world around him had come to a standstill while inside he continued to spin around in circles.

'Shit. I knew it.'

'Knew what?' Zorbach said.

'That her psychiatrist isn't kosher.' Nils had had him checked out by the same agency that vetted top candidates before he employed them. And basically everything seemed in order. Rej's publications were first class and he had high ratings, even if they were all from abroad, most from Dubai, where he'd been practising until recently before moving to his brand-new premises in Berlin. He had just a handful patients, all of whom were women. None of them had wanted to speak about Dr Rej, and in its report the agency had wondered how a doctor with so few patients could afford such an expensive location. It had only been a quick, superficial check, but enough for Nils to conclude that there might be something slightly dodgy about Rej. If nothing else, Nils reckoned he wasn't the person Alina should confide in.

*Christ, if only I'd told her the truth.* He got out of the car as quickly as his splint would allow.

Nils hadn't dared admit to Alina that he'd broken her trust by going behind her back. Instead he'd come up with a white lie to try and stop her seeing Rej, but because of this she might now be trapped with him up there.

'WHERE IS SHE?' Zorbach yelled, finally tearing Nils from his gloomy thoughts.

'Dr Samuel Rej. Bleibtreustrasse 6, fifth floor,' he said.

Then Nils opened the front door to the building whose address he'd just given Zorbach.

# 78

## ALINA

'I don't understand. I never said anything to your fiancé about wanting to end your treatment. There must be some sort of misunderstanding.'

They were sitting, as usual, opposite one another in the consulting room, Alina on the sofa with a cushion behind her back, Rej in the armchair.

'May I?' Alina's nose was running, as it often did when she came inside from the cold.

'Help yourself,' Rej said, inviting her to take a tissue from the box he provided for patients.

'Okay, I'll have to clear that up with Nils,' she said, happy to be wearing her glasses again. She felt hurt that Nils had lied to her, and she was worried that Rej would see the tears that her fiancé's duplicity had brought to her eyes.

As her best friend John had once said, 'Only those we're close to can really hurt us. The more we love them, the worse it is.'

What a painful truth, although conversely perhaps it was

only when you were really hurt that you realised how much you loved the person who'd let you down so badly.

'At any rate, I'm very grateful you agreed to see me at such short notice, because I've got an important decision to make.' The wound the Eye Collector had cut into her wrist itched beneath the bandage. 'I want to stop taking the medicine that's preventing my body from rejecting the retina transplant.'

'Why? What's made you take such a momentous decision?'

'Heavens, where to begin?' Alina was about to wipe her nose then paused, the tissue right in front of her face.

*What the hell?*

It was just a hint. A minute essence, but it confounded her senses. First she froze, then began to tremble.

That scent!

*Cardamom, pepper and rosewood.*

Alina felt giddy with all the impressions exploding in her head.

The pungent aftershave she'd smelled in the underground and in her bathroom. And a few molecules of which must have become caught in the cellulose of the tissue.

'What's going on here?' she demanded. 'WHO ARE YOU?'

No sooner had she bellowed her question at Dr Samuel Rej, than it struck her:

JEMEURSLA

**JERUSALEM**

**SAMUELREJ**

# 79

'I see you've solved your last puzzle, my dear Alina.'

Scholle, whose voice suddenly sounded far less gentle (maybe because he'd been wearing false teeth and had removed them) clapped his hands. 'I'd hoped I'd taken a long enough shower, but some of the aftershave must have remained on my fingers. Do you like the scent? I think it's nice, but very overpriced, which is why I use it sparingly.'

Alina felt sick. She was tempted to take off her glasses and see the ugly face that belonged to the monster who was taunting her.

*Oh my God. I trusted this man. In all those sessions I served up my most intimate inner feelings on a plate. Like an open wound ready for him to poison.*

*But...*

'How's that possible? The senior consultant at the Hanover clinic where I had my operation recommended your practice to me.' There's no way he could have been in cahoots with the Eye Collector.

'Oh, really? Him personally, was it?' Scholle said. 'Or

did his assistant sound like this on the phone: "Hello, Frau Gregoriev,"' he warbled, disguising his voice again. '"Dr Clemens here, from the private eye clinic in Hanover. I'm calling on behalf of Professor Broder, the surgeon who operated on you. You may recall you talked about the importance of some psychotherapy afterwards. Well, he's asked me to recommend the following psychiatrist. Do you have anything to write with, Frau Gregoriev?"'

'You are one deranged psychopath.'

Scholle laughed. Something Dr Rej had never done because she would have realised who he really was. Alina might have a lousy memory for voices, but she'd never fail to recognise his sinister, diabolical laughter.

'Oh, come on, you're just pissed off that you fell for my tricks. I got your mobile number from Emilia, by the way. How wonderful that fate brought her and me together. In truth I never wanted to do another love test. Too much effort, too costly, too risky. But when Emilia invited me to kidnap her daughter, how could I say no?'

'Fuck off to hell!'

'Tsk, tsk, tsk. I'd have expected more respect from you. I mean, look what I've managed to achieve. My own private practice near Kurfürstendamm, without ever studying at all.'

Behind her glasses Alina screwed up her eyes so tightly that it hurt. 'Who did you kill to be able to afford all this?'

'Nobody. I seem to have a natural talent for getting total strangers to trust me.'

'Because you deceive and double-cross them.'

'Because people want to be deceived and double-crossed!' he said, raising his voice self-righteously. 'Even you, dear

Alina, allowed yourself to be taken in by my empathetic claptrap. I've no degree, no diploma, I didn't even pass my school exams, for God's sake, and yet I was able to help you find yourself.'

'Myself?'

'Who were you prepared to turn to, to discuss perhaps the most important decision in what remained of your life? Zorbach? Nils? No, me. Because I opened your eyes to the truth that this world is easier to deal with in the dark.'

*I can see you, even though it's pitch black…*

'I'm good at understanding other people and putting them on the right track,' she heard the madman say, ousting the recollection of the Silbermond song from her mind.

'Word gets around. I don't advertise because I want to keep well away from nosy enquiries, and yet I find my patients. Although Tabea gave me some help at the start.'

'Tabea?'

*From the Ambrosia? The woman the courier spoke about?*

'What have you got to do with her?'

'I met her on Tinder. She joined the site soon after losing her husband. And well, you know how it us when you have certain needs.' Scholle gave a filthy laugh and probably licked his lips like a lizard. 'Her husband beat the crap out of her. Twice she sought shelter in a women's refuge, and the second time one of the other women told her about Ambrosia. When her husband beat her up again Tabea called upon Dr Lieberstett. Well, that was the end of her husband and she was able to live comfortably off her inheritance.'

Through the windows Alina could hear the muffled

sound of a helicopter. Her heart was beating in time to the rhythm of the rotors.

'So you're behind those sick vigilantes too, are you?'

He clicked his tongue. 'Ambrosia isn't sick; it uses a method that's been tried and tested for centuries. I would say "an eye for an eye" if it weren't so inappropriate in your case.' He laughed. 'But no, I'm not behind Ambrosia. I just help Dr Lieberstett. As a therapist specialising in traumatised women, I have ready access to victims. I referred the really serious cases to Ambrosia and took my share when the abusive husbands were made to pay compensation.'

Alina stood up without knowing what she would do if her knees didn't buckle and she actually managed to stay on her feet, despite all those blows below the belt.

'Why all this hatred of me? What have I done to you?'

His answer came like a pistol shot: 'You ruined my most important love tests. Together with Zorbach you kept getting in the way. I wanted to pay you back for that. Wanted to tease all your secrets out of you before revealing my true identity just when you trusted me most.'

'You're a fucking nutcase,' Alina croaked, feeling as if the ground were opening up beneath her.

Scholle pretended to be offended. 'I don't deserve that. I've always given you a fair chance. And I warned you more than once about what would happen if you didn't keep yourself out of my love test with Thomas Jagow: TomTom in the underground, the gallows on your mirror. But you wouldn't listen. In spite of everything, you met the courier, thereby signing his death warrant.'

So it had been Scholle at the wheel of the car that brutally ran the poor guy over.

'Tell me one thing. Do you really believe all this shit you're spouting?' Alina hissed. She knew it didn't matter whether she stayed silent and cool-headed, or screamed the place down. Scholle's decision to end his game – and thus her life – here and now, had already been taken. Why otherwise would he be so willing to reveal the reasons behind his cruel deeds?

'Putting acid in Tabea's eyes – was that a warning too?'

'No. That was a punishment for Feline. I thought there wasn't any internet in the place I was hiding her. But she was crafty and she found a way to signal to the outside world with the songs. On the day I drove her home to carry out the love test with her father I checked her belongings and realised she must have discovered a network. There was no other explanation for why her playlist had changed – she was using it to call for help.'

Alina didn't have to ask how blinding Tabea was a punishment for Feline. In the Eye Collector's twisted, disturbed world, withdrawing affection was the worst possible punishment for a child. Taking away Feline's only human contact in the dungeon was for him more serious than blinding Tabea.

'You told Tabea I'd done it, and that's why the courier was sent to find me!' Alina concluded.

'Correct,' he said impassively. 'I realised it wouldn't be long before the truth came out, but I hoped you'd have at least a few stressful days in the Ambrosia that would make the game more exciting for you. I even left a mobile phone there to give you an opportunity to escape.' He clapped his hands again. 'I call that playing fair, what about you?' he said, most pleased with himself. 'You always had good chances in the game.'

*Playing fair.*

*A game.*

*Playlist.*

Alina unconsciously shook her head when she realised why Scholle had changed Feline's playlist when he found it, rather than deleting it.

'Feline had far fewer songs on her playlist, didn't she?'

M

85

U

I

O

Only the clue to where the ghost line U10 crossed the M85 bus route was crucial.

*Why didn't I grasp this?*

In retrospect, not only was this French phrase '*Je meurs là*' far too melodramatic and complicated, it was also no help in trying to find the girl. Unless Feline had known that her abductor was called *Dr Samuel Rej*.

*But she would have told the police this name when she was freed, and Scholle would have made a quick exit.*

'You expanded the playlist,' Alina concluded.

By way of acknowledgement Scholle gave a slow handclap.

*The first nine songs at the beginning. Then, at the end, 'Para Paradise', which must have been a sick gag for the showdown.*

She heard the creasing of leather.

'Right, that's enough chatting.' Scholle's voice sounded deeper; he must have stood up too. 'Let's finish this off, Alina. Wouldn't you like to remove your glasses for what's coming?'

Alina spat scornfully in Scholle's direction, but unfortunately seemed to miss him.

'Maybe you're right,' he said, undeterred. 'I mean, your operation wasn't such a success. Had it been, with the glasses off you'd now see I'm holding a 9mm.'

Before Alina could tell him to stick the gun in his mouth, the doorbell rang.

Not once.

Not twice.

But continually.

'Ah, finally. About time,' she heard Scholle say. 'I'll be right back.'

# 80

## NILS

Not once.

Not twice.

He kept his finger on the bell.

In the fervent hope that he was wrong and that he'd soon see Dr Rej's angry face and those cosmetically lifted eyes he knew only from the photo on the website that was short on detail.

Eyes that would stare at him indignantly while the psychiatrist demanded to know why on earth Nils was interrupting the session with Alina.

At the very least his ringing might prevent Rej from harming his fiancée.

He couldn't hear any screams, any cries for help. And the door opened.

A good sign.

'Hello, my name is Nils Sandbeck. Sorry to disturb you, but I urgently need to speak to my fiancée, Alina Gregoriev, please,' he greeted Dr Rej.

Politely. As was his manner. Unlike Alina, he wasn't used

to dealing with the evil you read about in the paper the next day, or on the internet just a few minutes afterwards.

His world was one of calculations, trains and propulsion systems.

He knew all about construction plans and integrated circuits, not the madness that made cold-blooded killers smile as they shot you in the right eye.

Which happened right now.

So quickly that Nils was already dead before the bullet came out of the back of his head.

# 81

## ALINA

'Noooooooo!'

Alina had heard Nils's voice. Then the shot. The muffled crack of a pistol with a silencer. Followed by the noise of a lifeless body collapsing into the arms of another and being dragged along the hallway before Scholle closed the door again.

'Nils!' she screamed, truly blind for the first time in ages. Blind with fury, with grief, with helplessness, with pain.

'What have you done?' she howled as she started running. Although she tripped over her own feet she kept sprinting down the corridor to the front door, stopped only by Scholle's fist, which hit her hard and unsparingly in the face.

Blood dripped from her nose. Stunned, she collapsed beside the body on the floor.

'I don't like witnesses.'

'Nils, oh God. No.' She screamed out her pain as she'd never done before. She knew, albeit not from first-hand experience, that some birth pains almost tore a woman apart. Right now she was experiencing the exact opposite. Death pains flowing from the outside inwards, sucking up all life around her and suffocating it.

'You fucking sadistic pervert!' she screamed at Scholle as she crawled around Nils's body, grabbing his hand, which was still warm, and stroking his damp hair.

'What are you waiting for?' she wailed. 'Finish it. Do what you like doing best, you psycho.' She was slurring with despair. 'Go on. Shoot me.'

The answer hit her almost as if Scholle had pulled the trigger.

'No,' he said.

*No?*

Alina had lost her glasses as she fell. When now she opened her eyes she saw Scholle's shadow moving towards her. But he didn't seem to be aiming his weapon. 'Killing isn't what I like doing best,' he said. 'I show people the consequences of setting the wrong priorities. Of being high-handed, selfishly thinking only of themselves and their own rewards instead of looking after their family. Like Zorbach, who abandoned his wife and child when he came looking for me. Or Thomas Jagow, who was more concerned about a raped schoolgirl than his own daughter, a loner at school because her technophobe father means she lives under a rock. And like you, Alina, whose world is all about yourself and your blindness, nobody else. Good God, in every session I had to listen to you blubber about how the operation was a mistake, about how afraid you are of the world you might not want to see after all. It was always *me, me, me*; you didn't listen to any messages, you totally blocked out what was around you and didn't realise that a young girl's life depended on a playlist that she was only able to put together thanks to your MP3 player.'

'You're twisting the truth to fit your sadistic vision of the world,' Alina hissed. 'You kill the innocent. There's no justification for it. You're not some kind of avenger; you're a cheap, nasty, deranged killer.'

'Not at all. And to prove it, I'm going to let you live.'

'What?' There was so much bile in Alina's mouth that she had to spit the word out.

'As I said, death is not my aim and killing not my passion. I punish ignorance and egotism. And given this, I think letting you live is a far harsher punishment.'

He clicked his tongue as if to endorse his reasoning to himself. 'Yes, I think that's worse than a quick, merciful death. Knowing you'll have to go through life all alone again. Without eyes that work, despite the operation. Without a husband, despite the proposal of marriage. Without Zorbach, who's already on his way to prison, while I'm about to leave Berlin and take a little holiday.'

Scholle climbed over them, as if she and Nils were nothing but bags of rubbish obstructing the hallway. 'You can tell Forensics they won't find anything in the car. I'll leave it in the garage all the same. I mean, you've got to start somewhere in your hunt for me.'

Opening the door, he said patronisingly, 'Farewell, my girl. It's been fun playing games with you.'

Then he locked the door from the outside.

# 82

Alina heard the lift hum as it got moving. Only then did she start to scream.

'I'm sorry, I'm so, so sorry,' she howled, her dead fiancé in her arms. She pulled him to her chest and felt a pain in her soul that ate away at her from the inside as if she'd swallowed acid.

'Please forgive me!' she stammered, grabbing Nils under the arms.

She dragged his dead weight down the hallway, leaving a trail of blood all the way through the consulting room to the balcony.

'Fresh air, my love. Fresh air will do us good,' she said, weeping silently.

*How normal everything is*, she thought, convinced she'd lost her mind.

She heard the traffic. Tuned in to the roar of the city, the noises produced by millions of people who had their own demons to battle and who couldn't have any inkling of the tragedy being played out here.

In the distance she could make out sirens, but she knew the police would be too late. She'd just heard the click of the electric strike that was activated whenever someone wanted to get into this new building. Or out of it, like now.

Although Alina had poor voice recall, she could identify sounds with the accuracy of a lynx, even at a great distance and height.

Did Scholle look up one last time before going?

Did he wave scornfully at Alina when he saw her on the balcony? She didn't know.

Nor did she know if she'd correctly estimated the acceleration, angle and the falling speed when, clutching Nils tightly, she threw herself over the balcony railings with him.

To bury Scholle with their bodies.

From five floors above.

*Our last journey, my darling.*

*It's just crazy*
*To fall from the world's highest peak*
*Overnight into emptiness*
*As deep as the Mariana Trench.*
*We were so close*
*The nothing between us became a goddamn ocean*
*It's just crazy*
*That after so long*
*It's all gone.*

**JORIS – 'Live in Peace'**

# 83

## ZORBACH

*Three days later*

In one of the final interviews I conducted as a journalist, a prison governor told me he could free ninety per cent of his lifers straight away.

'*Most of the killers in my establishment would never hurt a fly again,*' he said on the record. '*Their crimes were the result of an exceptional situation. A chain of tragic events that will never be repeated in the same way.*'

Whereas a vicious mugger on the underground certainly shouldn't be released after three years, because once out he would almost certainly have a relapse when the opportunity arose for him to practise the skills he'd cultivated in prison.

I wasn't sure if the governor was right. My crimes too were the result of extreme and improbable chains of events. But life had taught me that it was more often determined by chance than we'd like. And that lightning could definitely strike twice in the same place.

Sometimes even more frequently.

*Seen from this perspective, maybe society would be done a bigger favour if I were locked away for life rather than just a few years,* I thought, as for the second time in a few days I approached the iron-barred gate of Tegel prison. Again with my mobile to my ear. Again with Stoya on the line, who this time hadn't gone to the trouble of welcoming me in person.

'I've just spoken to your lawyer again,' he said.

'And?'

'I told Frau Höpfner that the public prosecutor is rather sceptical about your account and has asked us to continue the investigation.'

*No shit!* Only someone intellectually challenged, I imagine, would have swallowed my statement without suspicion. The investigator who'd spent half the night interrogating me summed it up like this:

'*You arrived at Bleibtreustrasse at the very moment when Alina Gregoriev fell from the fifth-floor balcony together with her murdered boyfriend?*'

'*Yes.*'

'*Before the police?*'

'*I'd given the address to Chief Inspector Stoya and in my car got there slightly quicker.*'

'*And you were so shocked that you mistook the accelerator for the brake?*'

'*Yes.*'

'*And ran over the suspect, Michael Scholokowsky?*'

'*Exactly.*'

'*In the gateway of the building where he was running a psychiatry practice under a false name?*'

'*Trying to avoid the falling bodies, he leaped right in front of my car.*'

'*And the next thing you did, while he was already under your car, was to put it in reverse?*'

'*I panicked. I couldn't think straight. Unfortunately I killed him as I was reversing.*'

'*Unintentionally?*'

'*Of course.*'

'Prepare yourself mentally for an extension to your sentence,' Stoya said. 'And pray to God that this Christine Höpfner woman isn't a shyster and she's got a good understanding of the law.'

'She does,' I said and probably made Stoya experience déjà vu. For just like the first time I was about to start my sentence, I cut him off, stopped only a few metres from the prison and took a call. From the same person who'd made me turn on my heels by the gates before.

# 84

'Thank you!' I said, for I knew how difficult it must have been for Alina to call my number.

The very fact that she'd physically managed to get from her hospital bed to her mobile was a miracle.

Yes, her fall had been broken by the awning covering the shops and boutiques on the ground floor, which bounced her into the evergreen hedge of a tiny front garden next door. But the impact had been so great that she was propelled from the hedge to the paving beside the entrance, where she'd lain motionless, her limbs at unnatural angles, still clutching her murdered boyfriend. At Scholle's feet, who as I arrived was kneeling beside her inquisitively, like a child examining a dying insect. And yes, when he got back up and stood in the way of my car, I mixed up the accelerator and the brake. 'I can't move my legs any more!' was Alina's greeting to me on the phone, and although that was dreadful, it was unbelievable that she was in a position to utter those words at all.

After I ran over the Eye Collector, I got out and one

glance at Alina told me that she couldn't have survived the fall. But unlike with Scholle, the paramedics detected some weak vital signs and took her immediately to the Charité.

They operated on Alina four times, and for a while it was uncertain whether she'd die from internal bleeding or the fracture of the breastbone that had punctured her lung. And now I had her on the phone.

'Just my right big toe. Nothing else.'

I could hear she was under the influence of painkillers, maybe sedatives too, but it wasn't medicine that made her voice sound so flat. This was the voice of someone who'd experienced so much suffering that her soul was broken along with the bones in her body.

'I'm really sorry,' I said – the most useless words ever. The first snowflake landed on the cobbles beside my feet. On the radio they'd said that winter had arrived and, putting my head back, I watched more heralds of the cold season fall from the dirty grey bank of cloud over Berlin.

'Will you…?' I asked.

'Ever be able to walk again?' She managed to squeak angrily. A laugh. Short, as if chopped off at the end by a hatchet. 'It's too early to tell at the moment. My spinal cord is very badly damaged, but not completely severed.'

'Well, that's good,' I said, the words just slipping out.

'Yes, couldn't be better,' she said, feigning euphoria. 'I'm an invalid, my fiancé's dead and, well, seeing as we're talking good news, I'm going to be blind again.'

So she'd stopped taking the medicine for good.

'By the time you're out of the nick I fear there won't be much left of me for you to destroy.'

I held my breath and said, 'I can understand that you hate me.'

She paused, then sniffed as if she had a cold. 'But that's the worst thing. I don't. I really want to. I'd love to blame you for everything, Alex. But I can't. No matter how hard I try. I mean, I'm a grown woman. I could have kept my distance from you. But I wasn't able to. And however sorry I am to say it, that wasn't down to you. It was down to my stupid sense of guilt and responsibility towards Feline.'

I wanted to contradict Alina, but she was quicker: 'The one thing I'll hold against you for the rest of my life was that you called Nils.'

'You think I sent him to his death?'

'Yes. And saved my life in the process.'

She sounded very much as if she'd rather it had been the other way around.

'What made you realise Emilia was tricking us?' she asked, just as I was trying to find a way to say goodbye sincerely, showing an appropriate level of grief, but without coming across as arrogant or like a sentimental idiot.

'The charger lead,' I said.

'How?'

'Feline's father knew nothing about the MP3 watch. Thomas would have immediately confiscated it from his daughter if he'd found her with it. Which makes it highly unlikely that Feline would take it from its hiding place in the box and take it to school on a normal day. She couldn't listen to it in peace there because he might catch her with it at any moment.' I checked my watch. Five more minutes, then I'd be late for my admission again. 'It was even more unlikely that she'd have taken the charger lead with her,' I continued.

'So her mother put it in her school rucksack,' Alina said. 'She lied when she told us she had no idea about the watch. And because she wanted her daughter to have her beloved music at least while she was captive, she packed her the MP3 player and the charger.'

'Yes.'

That had been my theory. Unfortunately correct, as it turned out.

'Emilia was giving us all the runaround.'

'Not completely,' I countered, changing the hand holding the bag with the things I was allowed to take to prison. 'She really didn't know where Scholle had hidden Feline and why he hadn't set her free after the love test. We were her only chance of finding the girl. I mean, Emilia could have hardly gone to the police.'

I started walking again. My last thirty paces of freedom.

'I hope they put her away for a long time for what she did,' Alina seethed. Her fury had found a vent.

'Far longer than her husband at any rate,' I said, wondering whether I might ever bump into Thomas Jagow, who seemed to be off the critical list, in the prison yard. If he survived, he'd be facing trial for the manslaughter of Mathilda Jahn at the very least. Even though being a pawn in the game of a psychopath had to be mitigating factor. He could see no other way to save his daughter's life than to rip the plaster from the gashed jugular of the young mother in Albrechts Teerofen. And let her bleed to death holding her baby.

*The love test. A child for a child.*

The infant, now in state care, no longer had any parents – like Feline, in practice. For even if Emilia and Thomas were still alive, no one in authority – no judge nor anyone at the child welfare office – would ever let those parents near their daughter again.

The mother had arranged her abduction. The father had failed to free her.

*My God, Feline, what's going to become of you?*

Twenty paces to go and the snow had got heavier. 'I've figured something out, by the way,' Alina said. 'I'm not the only person on earth who can't get away from you even though your presence always puts his life in danger. He's very nice. He's even brought me flowers. I'll pass him to you.'

# 85

My heart sank briefly before nearly bursting out of my chest when I heard Julian's voice.

'Hi, Dad.'

Good God.

I couldn't help it. My knees turned to jelly, tears shot to my eyes and I had to stop again. Even the fact that my son didn't sound as angry as when we'd last met, nor as distraught as during our last phone conversation, was a most precious gift.

'It's over, isn't it?' he asked. The most important question for someone whose young, innocent life had already hung by a thread more than once, threatened time and again by a madman who'd robbed him of his mother and alienated his father.

'Yes, it's over,' I confirmed, and couldn't help thinking of Alina's tattoo. *Luck or fate?* Was it a perverse whim of the universe or predetermination that Julian's situation was so similar to Feline's? Two teenagers whose childhoods had been destroyed by mistakes made by the very people they'd trusted more than anyone else in the world.

'That's good,' Julian said with a quiver in his voice. I closed my eyes and could see him very clearly before me. Those large eyes full of hope, the face still wary, marked by a fear that had entrenched itself in his expression. That's how Julian as a young boy used to look at me after a storm, when the aftermath still rattled the shutters but the thunder had past.

'It's really great you've gone to visit Alina in the hospital. Without her this nightmare wouldn't be over yet.'

A pause. Julian took a deep breath, then sighed. Partly relieved, and yet very sad.

'She paid a high price for that,' he said.

*How true.* 'Maybe the highest of any of us,' I said. Then I wondered whether I could put this onus on him, but Julian was old enough, so I said, 'Do you promise this won't be a one-off visit just to be polite?'

'What do you mean?'

'Alina's on her own now. I'd really like you to look after her.'

His reply stirred a feeling in my heart as if it had suddenly gone into reverse.

'Feline too?'

Without being aware of it I'd kept walking and was now at the prison gate that was opened for me from the inside.

'Have you met her?' I asked eagerly.

'Yes,' he said. I'd just been wondering what had happened to Feline and now Julian had the answer for me.

'We met this morning at breakfast in the dining hall. She arrived at Scharfwerder yesterday.'

*Good, very good.*

That made sense. If there was a traumatised child, betrayed by her parents, who needed the care of a boarding school specialising in psychologically vulnerable children, it was Feline Jagow.

*Besides Julian.*

I suspected that Stoya had had a hand in this too, and I resolved to thank him when I was in prison. After all, I'd soon have plenty of time to write him a letter.

'I've got to go now,' I said to Julian, biting my tongue. The pain helped me avoid howling out loud, although I wouldn't have felt ashamed to do so right now. Not in front of the prison officer and certainly not in front of my son.

'Look after Alina and Feline. But most of all look after yourself. I love you.'

Julian didn't say, 'I love you too.' Not even that he'd miss me, and I was grateful not to be fobbed off with some cliché.

Instead I heard him trying to suppress his own tears, so I wouldn't notice how difficult he found it to hang up without saying goodbye. His only parting words were, 'I promise.'

And as the gate rattled shut behind me I thought that was far more than I deserved.

## About This Book

I fancy that even those people who aren't trained in psychology find it easy to analyse me. I've said often enough in interviews that I originally wanted to be a musician. As a thirteen-year-old I dreamed of recording my songs in the studio, performing them live to a packed, hysterical audience at the Waldbühne, then getting straight onto the Nightliner tour bus with my band and heading for the next city. It's also no secret that this didn't work out, partly because with the drums I chose the wrong instrument. Wrong, at least, if you want to become famous, because nobody can see you behind your kit on the stage.

You don't need a degree in the human soul, therefore, to realise that my repeated attempts to slip into the music business via the back door are my way of dealing with these unfulfilled dreams of becoming a pop star. Like at my concert readings, where a soundtrack composed specially for the novel is played live while I read excerpts from the book – most recently in 2019 for *The Gift*. (On this tour, which took me to twenty cities, I was finally able to sniff the much longed-for air of the Nightliner tour bus. It took me less than ten seconds to realise that the phrase 'smells like a monkey house' is a serious insult to those beautiful primates.)

After the premiere of the last soundtrack show I sat down with my old friend Stephan Moritz, CEO of MOKOH Music, and asked him what he thought of making a single out of one of my short stories. I imagined someone with a better voice than me (out of seven billion people, this is an easy choice) belting out the chorus while I told an exciting story for the verse. Stephan was so keen on the idea that he talked me out of it at once. Although his version of events is that he'd in fact come up with a better suggestion: rather than setting a story to music, how about doing an entire album?

Anyone who's ever tried penning a short story knows that they don't write themselves. A short story needs everything that a good novel does, from an exciting beginning and interesting characters to a surprising plot twist. So I said to Stephan, 'I don't think I'll be able to think of fifteen short stories just like that. But what if I made fifteen songs the central element of a thriller?'

And thus the idea of *Playlist* was born. A psychological thriller where the music isn't a soundtrack, but an essential feature of the plot. A story in which fiction and reality merge in a completely new way, inventing what is verging on a new genre. A reality fiction thriller, so to speak.

Till now the protagonists in my novels have inhabited only the worlds I've created. In *Playlist*, however, the fiction comes alive in reality. For the fifteen songs that Feline's life depends on actually exist. They've been composed specially for the book, not commission pieces, but works of art independent of the novel. Inspired by the plot, they reflect the themes in the book. They deal with isolation, bullying, vigilantism and toxic relationships, as well as positive topics such as courage, hope and self-discovery. But the artistic exchange wasn't one-way. Fifteen of the best and most famous artists working today, some German, others international, inspired me with their music and in their lyrics dealt with topics that influenced the plot. The interplay between book and music has been ongoing, giving rise to what we believe is something completely new. Hopefully, a unique reading and listening experience.

By the way, I wasn't totally dissuaded from my idea of the single. There is, you see, a sixteenth song on the musical playlist. Performed by Batomae, it goes by the now confusing title of 'Playlist', and my voice can indeed be heard alongside their singing. But don't worry, I don't sing. Even as a thriller writer, I can't expect anyone to put up with that much horror.

Most people aren't particularly keen to recognise themselves in a psychological thriller, which is why I always avoid using real people as the basis for my characters. With the Höpfner family it's a different story, and intentionally so. During an RTL telethon, Daniel Höpfner bid in an auction for his wife, Christine, to have a character named after her, and showed he had a big heart for children. His understandable request was that the Christine Höpfner character wasn't a psychopathic killer and shouldn't suffer too gruesome a fate. Admittedly this narrowed down the choice somewhat, but I hope Christine is happy with her role as Alexander Zorbach's highly competent lawyer.

# Acknowledgements

I've recently had an increasing number of emails to fitzek@ sebastianfitzek.de, stating that many readers like it when I inject humour into my acknowledgements. Simply because it helps reconnect them with reality after a sombre thriller. So I'll oblige you all and make myself a laughing stock once more – this time, in keeping with the 'Playlist' theme, by trying to turn the 'credits' into song lyrics.

As you read the following lines, therefore, please picture me behind my turntables, in baseball cap and hoodie: DJ Fitzi Fitz, featuring 'The Never-Ending Script', aka WORD! Presenting:

## THX

*If you imagine an author like me*
*Manages all this on my own,*
*You must think Corona's a beer.*
*It's time the truth was known.*

*When writing a book*
*You're alone for day after day.*

*But after the last full stop*
*A cast of helpers enters the fray.*

*The team at Droemer Knaur*
*Toil away like oxen,*
*None working harder than the bosses:*
*Josef Röckl & Dr Doris Jahnsen*

*If I write rubbish*
*That nobody could publish*
*I'm saved by the editors.*
*They're like my creditors.*
*250 corrections might drive me mad,*
*But deep down I'm glad – look!*
*They've really improved the book.*
*So let's all applaud*
*Carolin Grahl and Regina Weisbrod.*

*I'd like to offer particular thanks*
*To Katharina Ilgen – what is her thing?*
*Communication and…*
*The very best marketing!*

*I endlessly fret about the title;*
*Luckily someone else has the knack.*
*It's none other than*
*The brilliant Steffen Haselbach.*

*What about the cover?*
*A book needs it like a child does its mother.*
*We start with Stolli's design,*

*Which is then made even more fine*
*By two women I seriously admire:*
*Carola Bambach and Daniela Mayer*

*Antje Buhl in sales:*
*The queen of details.*
*Moni Neudeck in PR:*
*The best by far.*
*Nicole Müller and Ellen Heidenreich:*
*Both geniuses of production alike.*

*Then, of course, there's this man,*
*Whose first name is Stephan.*
*His surname is Moritz,*
*Though he only answers to 'Playlist'.*
*He brought together the acts,*
*Produced all the tracks,*
*Did the deals,*
*Ignored the squeals*
*Of those who couldn't help smirk*
*As they said, 'It won't work!'*
*But oh, what fun!*
*The CD is done*
*And the playlist is ready to stream.*
*Thanks also to Maria Moritz, integral to the team.*
*When put to the test*
*MOKOH showed it's the best.*

*Thanks to Stephan, Sony is in,*
*Which we all see as a big win–win.*
*Don't think we could make it any higher.*

*Thanks to Julia Nolte, Clemens Fiedler, Dariusch*
*Bozorgzadeh and Philipp Meyer.*

*Someone hoping he won't be mentioned*
*In these rhymes surely*
*Is that brilliant composer*
*And lyricist: Sera Finale.*

*In a musical dream team with Joe Walter*
*Both of them making it look easy,*
*Joe and Sera have written more hits*
*Than there are fish in the sea.*

*Oh dear, I've overslept*
*And missed an appointment.*
*I'm the one to blame,*
*Not Raschke-Entertain-Mega-*
*Management.*
*Named after Manuela,*
*Call her Manu or Ela.*
*Friend, confidante,*
*The best artist trainer,*
*An eye always on everything,*
*A financial juggler.*
*Without her I am nothing,*
*To her I owe my name.*
*First she makes the rules,*
*And then she makes the game!*

*Her daughter, Sally Raschke,*
*Is a social media ace.*

*She deserves Moët and Chandon*
*Deliveries by the case.*

*Kalle Raschke also merits a greeting,*
*For without him I'd have to stop eating.*
*He tames my bloodlust in his gym;*
*I curse and curse, but owe so much to him.*

*Is that everyone in the Raschke team?*
*No, far from it.*
*For let's not forget*
*Angela Schmidt.*
*Thanks also to Franz Xaver Riebel,*
*My first reader – smart and able.*
*Barbara Herrmann and Achim Behrendt:*
*Both of you are heaven-sent.*
*Then we have Micha and Ela Jahn too,*
*What would the Fitzek shop do without you?*
*And Jörn 'Stolli' Stollmann,*
*The very best illustrator,*
*Whirlwind creative*
*And cartoon creator.*

*If I forgot my agent*
*It would be a bit of a shocker,*
*So all hail to the wonderful*
*Roman Hocke!*
*When he gets dealing*
*There's only one guarantee:*
*Roman Hocke will go all the way*
*While others will go down on one knee.*

*If you want to make sure*
*The papers never show your face*
*Don't dial her number*
*Just in case.*
*I'm talking about the PR queen*
*None other than Sabrina Rabow.*
*In the evening she gets you on the telly*
*And in the morning on the radio.*

*I'm so grateful to you, Christian Meyer!*
*Friend and member of my merry band.*
*You go with me from reading to reading,*
*Up, down and across the land.*

*For medical advice*
*I know on whom to draw:*
*Clemens and Sabine*
*Big brother and best sister-in-law.*

*Then Torsten Surberg – sensational.*
*Responsible for all of Audible.*

*Regina Ziegler, Markus Olpp and Barbara Thielen too,*
*Many, many thanks to all three of you*
*For the films, all those you've done.*
*Let's hope there are more to come!*

*Oh, Thomas, I'm sorry,*
*I did it again.*
*For Alexander*

*I used your Zorbach name.*
*But I don't really think*
*Against this you will clamour,*
*Unless, like in the book,*
*You're heading for the slammer.*

*At this point I must offer*
*My eternal thanks to fate,*
*For giving me Linda:*
*You make me happy and you motivate.*
*You always put me back on my feet*
*And when you read my writing*
*You ask the right questions*
*Without bootlicking.*
*I couldn't lift my happiness*
*If it had a weight,*
*For something so incredibly heavy*
*Just holding it would be great.*

I think you all now realise why a volume of Fitzek poetry is the least likely of any future projects I've got up my sleeve. Let's finish with the untalented doggerel, not least because I don't dare spoof the following in verse. Jan Uwe Leisse (Grethler Rechtsanwälte) is far too good a lawyer for that. I believe he's negotiated so many contracts for this project that you'd need an aircraft hangar to accommodate them all, and that's only the covering pages!

Johanna and Sven Schwarze, Günther Sollfrank, Sahre Wippig and Tarik Sarzep gave me an insight into the not-quite-so-dark world of blind and visually impaired people.

Here I am indebted to Jennifer Gruhlke, who once again arranged the contacts.

Markus Christmann deserves a Fitzek T-shirt with the inscription: 'Because I'm a friendly person I was talked into trawling through the 400-page manuscript to check for major errors relating to the portrayal of police work – and all I got was my name in these lousy acknowledgements.'

Representing all those many people at Sony supporting this project, I'd like to thank Patrick Mushatsi-Kareba, the CEO of Sony Music GSA at Sony Music Entertainment GmbH. Which pretty much means: boss of all labels. And very many of those have supported this unique project.

In this regard, many, many thanks are also due to all artist managements, composers, authors, music publishers and agencies, especially Ralf Heuel (GF Kreation/Partner – Grabarz & Partner), Manuel Wenzel (Executive Creative Director – TBWA Switzerland) and Nils Haseborg (Creative Director & Trainer BRIDGEHOUSE).

If you listen to the playlist, at some point you'll be bound to come across Zoran Bihać's fantastic videos. His unbelievable talent for putting his foot in it is as great as mine. But that's another story...

Finally, as ever, I mustn't forget the people without whom my books wouldn't make it into your hands or ears: the librarians and booksellers. I'm delighted to see it's been officially acknowledged that all of you provide an essential service.

Best regards

Sebastian Fitzek

Berlin, 14 June 2021

Twenty-six degrees in the shade, incidence rate 15.4 – both much lower than the volume of my car stereo, through which I'm just about to listen to Feline's 'Playlist'.

## About the Author

SEBASTIAN FITZEK is one of Europe's most successful authors of psychological thrillers. His books have sold thirteen million copies, been translated into more than thirty-six languages and are the basis for international cinema and theatre adaptations. Sebastian Fitzek was the first German author to be awarded the European Prize for Criminal Literature. He lives with his family in Berlin.

Follow Sebastian at www.sebastianfitzek.com and @sebastianfitzek on Instagram.

## About the Translator

JAMIE BULLOCH has translated over fifty titles from German including works by Timur Vermes, Birgit Vanderbecke, Romy Hausmann, Robert Menasse and Arno Geiger. He is twice winner of the Schlegel-Tieck prize and lives with his family in London.